Under the blazing Colorado sun, a miracle happened. Soulless Jake Malone began to care about Alexandra Merritt, an indomitable, heaven-sent beauty, and the small, squalling life she'd helped bring into this world. But could she help Jake forgive himself his past so that they could have a future?

"Just what the hell do you think is going to happen between us? You think I'm just going to stop with a kiss?"

"Yes. I know you, Jake."

He shook his head, as if she'd said she could fly. His boots scraped at the ground as if he wanted to run but couldn't. Something wild rose up in Alex. Her deepest instincts told her that this man needed to be touched—gently, deeply, often.

She'd put up with too much today. "Listen to me! You're not nearly as bad—"

He snatched her hand and held it tight. "I'm warning you, Alex. Stay away from me."

* * *

Of Men and Angels
Harlequin Historical #664—July 2003

**Harlequin Historicals is proud to introduce
debut author VICTORIA BYLIN**

Of Men and Angels

Victoria Bylin

TORONTO • NEW YORK • LONDON
AMSTERDAM • PARIS • SYDNEY • HAMBURG
STOCKHOLM • ATHENS • TOKYO • MILAN • MADRID
PRAGUE • WARSAW • BUDAPEST • AUCKLAND

ISBN 0-373-29264-3

OF MEN AND ANGELS

Copyright © 2003 by Vicki Scheibel

**Available from Harlequin Historicals and
VICTORIA BYLIN**

Of Men and Angels #664

Dedicated to my father,
Jack K. Bylin

This one's for you, Dad,
for the encouragement,
the coffee,
everything.

ACKNOWLEDGMENTS

I'd also like to thank my husband and sons
for their love and support, my mother
for just being herself, and my community
of friends for sharing this journey with me.

Chapter One

Western Colorado Plateau
June 1885

The rain hit without warning.

The mules balked as a flash of lightning cut through the sky, and the driver spurred them with a crack of his whip. ''Haul your sorry butts outta here, or you're gonna be swimming in that goddamn river!''

That wasn't what Alexandra Merritt wanted to hear.

After a week on a crowded train from Philadelphia and another three weeks in a dirty Leadville hotel, she was almost home. She had given up waiting for repairs to the Denver Rio Grande train tracks and booked passage to Grand Junction on the worn-out stagecoach being used to deliver the U.S. mail.

Waiting another month had been unthinkable. Like a clock that needed winding, her father's heart could stop without warning. She couldn't stand the thought of never seeing him again. With the letters they had exchanged over the past ten years, a bridge had been built. William Merritt knew her better than she knew herself. She hadn't thought twice about leaving her post as president of the Philadelphia Children's League, or postponing her marriage to Thomas Hunnicutt. She had to get home.

Thunder boomed across the plain, and the stage-coach lurched like a staggering beast. Sitting across from her on the lumpy seat, Charlotte Smith stirred from an exhausted sleep. "What's happening?"

Alex pulled back the leather flap covering the window. Cool air and the heavy scent of mud rolled into the coach. Charlotte had been as eager as she to get to her destination, and her reason was just as urgent. Alex's fellow passenger was close to nine months pregnant and eager to reach her sister before the baby came.

"It's raining," Alex answered, raising her voice over a staccato burst of hail. "I think the driver's worried about the road."

"The road!"

Below them, a streambed writhed with the muddy runoff. Alex could see the water rising, slashing at the sides of the gorge. A shriveled juniper tore loose in the flood, and a man-size boulder tumbled after it.

"Hold up, you beasts!" the driver shouted. The coach skidded but didn't stop. Gravity flung Alex against the seat just as the driver pounded on the roof.

"Mrs. Smith! Miss Merritt! Hang on!"

The stage lurched as if it had been tipped by an unseen hand. Charlotte screamed. Alex pulled the woman into her arms, but she couldn't keep her grip. They were bouncing like stones, and the next thing she knew she was weightless, floating in the air like a bird, until the coach hit rushing water with a splash, throwing her against the door with a bone-crunching lurch.

Pain shot through her shoulder. Thunder ricocheted

like a rifle shot, and the wheels spun with the rushing water. The mules screamed and kicked in a worthless effort to wrench themselves free. Water seeped through the wooden seams of the coach. It soaked her shoes and pooled at her ankles. Her white blouse was torn at the elbow, and the cool air stung the strawberry scrape on her arm.

Charlotte grabbed her stomach with both hands.

"Help us!" Alex screamed, pushing at the door over her head. "Smitty! Hank!" There was no answer, so she climbed through the opening and sat with her feet in the door well, hanging on to the frame for balance as waves of brown water pounded the brittle wood.

By a stroke of luck, the coach was wedged against a huge rock and a slab of mud. The torrent whipped through the wheels and raced down the gorge, ripping at boulders and exposing tree roots, taking what it wanted. The mud wall melted like chocolate in the sun, and the coach scraped along the bottom of the stream-bed, moving in inches that threatened to become feet.

"Charlotte, we've got to get out of here. We've got to hurry."

Bracing her feet against the door frame, she grabbed Charlotte's arm and pulled. The coach lurched and slid a foot closer to the wall of the ravine. A juniper branch scratched her face with prickly green needles and Alex grabbed it, pulling to test it with her weight. The trunk was just a foot away. The makeshift rope would have to do.

"Charlotte, grab that branch. *Now!*"

Sheer terror yanked Charlotte out the door and into the vee of the trunk. Alex hoisted her skirts and fol-lowed. It was like climbing a tree as a child except the water had been doing its work, and the coach had slipped farther downstream.

Grabbing the branch with both hands, she clamped it between her knees and shimmied toward the relative safety of the trunk. Rough bark scraped her thighs and soft palms. The weight of her sopping skirt pulled her down, but she kept a firm grip on the bark, sliding to the trunk in inches until she reached Charlotte.

The water was ebbing, and the coach was twenty feet away. By some miracle, Charlotte was still wearing a coy red hat with a bobbing feather. From her perch Alex looked for the drivers, but she didn't see either of the gray-bearded men. Two of the mules were still screaming with pain. The other two had drowned.

Turning to see how well the tree was rooted, Alex saw what had happened. A slab of mud had wiped out the road, and the hillside had collapsed into the watery torrents. It was a stupid place for a road, she thought. A stupid place to be.

"How are you doing?" she said, reaching for Charlotte's blue-veined hand. The pregnant woman looked like a very fat sparrow. Until a few days ago, they had been strangers, but the boredom of travel had made them acquaintances if not friends.

Charlotte moaned and clutched Alex's fingers as she doubled over, squeezing back her tears.

Alex rubbed her shoulders. "It's going to be all right. You've just had a scare."

"I hurt."

"Where?"

"My middle. The baby's kicking."

Dear God, no. Not now. Not yet.

Alex knew about orphans and babies, but she had

only witnessed one birth in her life. It hadn't been easy, and her cousin had nearly died.

"Maybe it will stop," she said. "We've both had a shock."

The rain lessened to a drizzle, and the water ebbed as quickly as it had risen. Where had the storm come from? It had been so sudden, uncontrollable and devouring. Dampness chilled the air. The women had goose bumps, and night was coming fast.

The third mule had died, and the fourth was on its side, heaving with exhaustion. The stream had thinned to a ribbon, leaving puddles that looked like dirty mirrors.

"Charlotte, I'm going down to look around."

"No, stay with me!"

"I'll only be a minute." Alex squeezed her hand and slid out of the tree. Mud oozed over her high-buttoned shoes as she sloshed to the coach. As if nothing had happened, their trunks were still lashed to the baggage rack, and she thought about the silly shoes she had packed. She needed sturdy boots and walking clothes. She needed help. Maybe even a miracle, but she'd settle for what she could find.

Standing on a rock, she peered through the window and saw the ruined contents of her food basket floating in a foot of water. Holding back an ache of worry, she walked to the driver's boot and opened the small door. Water gushed down her skirt, but she found a wad of men's clothing, a knife, a pistol and a box of bullets. Could she possibly hunt for food? The thought was laughable, but she took everything, and in a second compartment she found two canteens of water and a sack of apples. They would have to last until help came.

Help...but when would that be? Surely someone would come looking for them when the stage didn't make it to Grand Junction, yet delays were common.

"Alex! I need you *now*." Charlotte's voice cut through her thoughts, and she turned back to the tree just in time to see the woman's face go white with pain.

Setting the meager supplies on a rock, Alex stretched her arms upward as if to catch the woman if she fell. "Let me help you down," she said gently.

Charlotte's belly was huge. Her eyes widened with fright and, choking back a sob, she said the one thing Alexandra Merritt was afraid to hear.

"My water just broke."

The last thing Jackson Jacob Malone wanted to hear was singing, especially a woman singing in a high, sweet voice that reminded him of angels he didn't believe in. The words drifted to him from the bottom of a rocky gorge, and he wondered if he was still drunk. The singing was bad enough, but as the trail dipped and curled, he recognized the words. She was singing a hymn, and for a moment he thought he'd died and gone to hell.

Two seconds later a scream burst out of the ravine, and Jake heard the devil himself in that cry. It tore through his head like a bullet burning flesh. A bead of sweat broke across his brow and he wiped it away.

"Hang on, Charlotte! Hang on for the baby!"

The angel's voice reminded him of sleigh bells on a winter morning. Hopeful and bright, they defied the cold even as it settled into a man's bones, and he wondered if the angel had ever shivered in the dark. Somehow he doubted it, and he was sure when she started singing again, even louder than before.

"Oh, come, let us worship and bow down,
   Let us kneel before the Lord, our God, our maker…"

The noonday sun stung his skin and cast shadows through the sage. His jaw throbbed just below his ear, as if the pain in his bruised eyes had leaked down the side of his face. He clenched his teeth against the misery of it. He didn't want reminders of his brother's fist slamming into him, the mess he'd left in Flat Rock, and especially not the melancholy hope of a woman singing in the desert.

"Oh, no! It's starting again!"

"Breathe easy, Charlotte. Easy…"

"I can't!"

A moan rose from the gorge and snaked around him.

"Try to pant," the angel crooned. "Like this… hhhhh…hhhhh…hhhhh…"

It was the sound of sex, of life being formed, of need and desperation, and he recalled the pleasured cry of the last woman he'd bedded. He didn't know her name, but he remembered her breasts, the taste of her, and he felt himself going soft inside. He had to get away from Charlotte and the angel before he did something stupid. Grimacing, he nudged his horse into a faster walk.

The trail twisted around a boulder rimmed with goldenrod, then cut straight across a hard slope. A dry mud slide blocked the way, as if a huge hand had pushed the trail into the mountainside. Tugging his hat low, he nudged the bay with his knees. The horse shimmied nervously, sending ripples of apprehension through Jake's thighs and up his spine.

The heat of the day pressed against him, and the stench of bad meat was unmistakable. His stomach nearly heaved, and he squinted into the gorge where pale green sage made a fence along the streambed. His gaze followed the trickle of water down the ravine to the graceful curve of a red stagecoach. The front wheel spun as if set in motion by an invisible hand, and someone had draped women's clothing over the rocks and bushes.

The bay splayed his forelegs and balked.

"Whoa, boy," Jake said softly.

He'd just won the horse in a card game, and the animal's distrust was mutual. The bay was likely to buck, but Jake took a chance and nudged him forward until he had a wider view of the gorge. The women were nowhere in sight, but he saw three dead mules tangled in the harness. The fourth was lying on its side, braying like a forgotten pet. Sensing the presence of the bay, it raised its head and snorted before falling back against the sand.

"For He is our God,
And we are the people of his pasture,
And the shee-eeee-eeep of his hand…"

The singing was closer now, as resonant as a howling wind, and his stomach clenched. He wanted a drink. He wanted to block out the rotting mules, the women, the god-awful singing. Suffocated by dust and sweet sage, he dug his heels into the bay, bracing himself as the animal coiled and lurched over the slick of dry mud.

The crust collapsed beneath its hooves, and Jake fought for balance as the horse jerked its head and pedaled backward.

"Breathe, Charlotte! Don't squish up your face. Breathe like me…hhhh…hhhh…hhhh…"

The voice was clearer now, and as the sagebrush thinned to a veil of green lace, Jake saw the angel. She was less than ten yards from him, on her knees in front of the other woman's sprawled legs, splattered with blood and birth water. Her hair was the color of Arbuckle's coffee, and it fell over her shoulders in a tangle. Her blouse was torn at the shoulder, and he could see a hot pink crescent where the sun had burned her skin.

Trails of sweat streaked her dusty face. The high collar of her blouse was loose and gaping, and he saw the curve of her breasts as she laid her hand on the birthing woman's belly, leaned down and peered between her legs.

Pushing back the woman's dark blue skirt, she said, "Don't push, Charlotte."

"I've got to!"

"It's too soon. You'll tear."

Jake cringed. The woman moaned, and the mix of grunting and agony turned into a wail. Her pain was terrible to hear. The bearing down of her hips and the writhing of her belly was the most horrible thing he had ever seen.

"Breathe, Charlotte!"

But the birthing woman was beyond understanding. Instead of listening to the angel, she curled her spine, grabbed her knees and screamed. A bullet to the head would have been an act of kindness, and yet he couldn't look away.

There was no singing now, only the blue skirt and streaks of bright red blood on the petticoat spread beneath her hips. His gaze traveled from her thighs to her belly, and then to her ashen face. He had never seen a baby being born but he'd seen a few men die, and Charlotte plainly needed more help than any man or woman could give.

Her face registered shock and stark fear. "My baby! Oh God, my baby!"

For a man who didn't give a damn about anyone or anything, he was dangerously close to tears. He prodded the bay with his heels, but the animal refused to budge, giving an angry chuff that carried through the gorge.

The angel raised her face toward the blistering blue sky. Her eyes locked on him, and for one painful second she stared at him with fierce brown eyes.

"Go away! Go away, you son of a—" Her lips locked together, as if she had never spoken a curse word in her life. He nearly laughed at the stupidity of it. She needed help. If not now, then later when she had to get to a town.

Jake wasn't enough of a gentleman to feel honorbound to stay, but he was enough of a rebel to pick a fight. He held the bay at the top of the trail. At this point he wasn't going anywhere.

"Alex! Help me—" Charlotte grabbed her bare knees and grunted like a crazed animal.

"It's coming! The baby's coming!" The angel touched Charlotte's belly as a low cry poured from the woman's throat. Weeping and laughing, she said, "I see the head. Push, Charlotte! Push."

Jake held his breath.

"Charlotte! You can do it! *Push!*"

The torture went on for a small eternity, until the baby squirted out of the womb and landed in the angel's hands. Covered with blood and a waxy white cream, it seemed small and gray in the vastness of the plateau, and far too quiet to be alive. The angel reached into the baby's rosebud mouth and cleared away the mucus. She held it upside down and slapped its bottom, and still there was no sound.

He saw panic in her eyes, but she choked it back and blew oh-so-gently into the baby's mouth. He heard a cough, then mewling, and then a healthy wail. Tears spilled down her cheeks, and he blinked away his own.

"Alex…" The mother's voice was weak.

"It's a boy, Charlotte. He's little but he's perfect." The angel set the baby on the mother's belly. "We've got to get the afterbirth."

From his vantage point on the trail, Jake saw the angel cut the cord with a knife. The afterbirth followed the baby, and fresh blood gushed from Charlotte's womb. The angel's eyes burned with fear. She reached for a cloth to stanch the bleeding, and in a minute it was soaked.

A cloud shifted. A dark shadow fell over the three of them. He saw Charlotte's face relax. Her fingers stilled and her chest sank emptily against the sand. The only sign of life was the baby stirring on her belly, its mouth opening and closing like a blooming flower.

The angel pressed her hands to her cheeks and wept.

There wasn't a thing Jake could have done to keep the woman alive, but he could dig her grave. Silently he climbed off the bay and led the horse into the ravine. The woman named Alex looked up at him.

"If you tend to the baby, I'll see to the mother," he said.

"Who are you?" Her voice was hoarse, and he could see every minute of the past twenty-four hours in her face. Something stirred in his gut, and an uncharacteristic urge to be kind softened his eyes.

"My friends call me Jake."

"I thought you were…" She shook her head. "I thought I imagined you."

She looked as if she could still hear Charlotte's moans, and he wondered if she would ever sing that hymn again. He looked at her eyes, red rimmed and inflamed with the dust and the sun, and somehow he knew she would sing it again this very day, just to make a point.

Brushing off her hands, she rose and smoothed her skirt. Jake tethered the bay to the stagecoach and inspected the mule writhing in the harness. If the animal could walk, perhaps the woman and baby could ride it.

"Whoa, boy," he said, but the beast didn't want anything to do with him. A broken foreleg told Jake all he had to know. He pulled his Colt .45 from its holster, cocked the hammer and put the animal out of its misery.

The angel gasped at the sudden blast. He expected her to be hysterical or sentimental about the animal, but she didn't say a word and he had to admire her. She had been a fool to travel the Colorado Plateau alone, but she wasn't softhearted about life.

Jake holstered the Colt and opened the driver's boot. The mail was ruined, but the tools were in place and he took out the shovel. He wondered about the driver and man on shotgun, but the watermarks in the gorge made the facts plain. The two men had drowned in the flood.

Jabbing the shovel into the ground, Jake took a pair of leather gloves from his saddlebag and looked for a suitable grave site. He wasn't about to bury Charlotte where a flash flood could steal the body, so with his black duster billowing behind him, he climbed over the cascade of rocks on the far side of the gorge.

The iron-rich plains stretched for a million miles, but just a few feet away he saw a sprig of desert paintbrush. It was the best he could do, and he started to dig. When the hole was deep, he collected rocks from the stream-bed and piled them nearby.

Two hours had passed when he wiped his hands on his pants and looked at the sky. The sun was lower now, as bright as orange fire, and above it, flat-bottomed clouds boiled into steamy gray peaks. Another storm was coming, he could smell it in the air.

He jabbed the shovel into the earth and strode down the rocky slope. The angel was holding the baby, crooning to it in that sweet voice of hers. It was bundled in something clean and white, and she had managed to dress the mother in a fashionable traveling suit.

Without a word, he brushed by the angel and scooped Charlotte into his arms, rocked back on his heels and rose to his full height.

He felt the angel's gaze as he walked past her, and rocks skittered as she followed him. As gently as he could, he laid the dead woman to rest, picked up the shovel and replaced the dirt. He half expected the woman named Alex to pray or say a few words, but she settled for a mournful humming that made him think of birds in autumn and the wail of the wind.

Down in the valley, the valley so low,
Hang your head over, hear the wind blow.

One by one he piled jagged rocks on the loose earth. Alex didn't flinch. The child mewled now and then, but her humming soothed him. It should have soothed Jake, too, but it didn't. His head had started to pound, his back hurt, and his stomach was raw with bad whiskey.

A few hours ago he had been on his way to California, or maybe south to Mexico. He was alone by choice, and now he was stuck with a woman and a child. His life had taken a strange turn indeed.

He set the last rock on the grave with a thud and took off his gloves. Studying the angel's profile, he said, "I'm done."

She turned to him, and in her eyes he saw the haunted look of a person seeing time stop.

"I suppose you should say a few words," she said.

His mouth twisted into a sneer, and he stared at her until she understood he had nothing to say. Bowing her head, she uttered a prayer that told him Charlotte was a stranger to her, this child an orphan, and the angel herself a woman who had more faith than common sense.

A determined amen came from her lips. The baby squirmed and, cocking her head as if the world had tilted on its axis, she looked at his face.

"You're hurt," she said.

He shrugged. Bruises were common in his life, like hangnails and stubbed toes. Bending down on one knee, he straightened a rock on the grave. "She had a bad time."

The angel's skirt swished near his face. He stood up and she sighed. "I've never seen someone die before."

"I have."

She gaped at him, and he felt like Clay Allison and Jesse James rolled into one. The corners of his mouth curled upward. He wasn't in the same class as the James Brothers, but with his black duster, two black eyes and a three-day beard, any sensible woman would have crossed the street at the sight of him. He could have scared her even more with the truth. He'd shot a man, and depending on Henry Abbott's stubbornness, Jake was either a free man or wanted for murder.

"Death isn't a pretty sight," he finally said.

She went pale. "My father is ill. I have to get to Grand Junction. Could you take us there?"

If he didn't take her, the baby would die. Was there even a choice here?

There's always a choice, Jake, and you're making the wrong one. Lettie Abbott's angry face rose up from the hot earth, shimmering with accusations, and he didn't answer.

The angel was close to begging. "I have to get home as soon as I can. I know it's out of your way, but I could pay you."

He considered taking her up on the offer, but the stash in his saddlebags gave him a rare opportunity to be charitable.

"There's no need," he replied. "Can you ride?"

She shook her head. "I haven't sat on a horse in ten years, Mr....?"

"Call me Jake."

"I don't know you well enough to use your given name."

"You will soon enough." With four dead mules and one horse, they'd be sharing a saddle and he'd be pressed up against her shapely backside for hours. With a lazy grin, he added, "Lady, you and I are going to be intimately acquainted before nightfall."

Her eyes went wide, and beneath her thick lashes he saw dark circles of exhaustion, sheer terror and rage. Her loose hair caught the sun, and her eyes hardened into agate. "I doubt very seriously that's going to happen."

"Are you afraid of horses?"

She answered him with a glare and Jake eyed the bay, wondering how the animal would feel about the extra weight. From the corner of his eye, he saw her shift the baby and reach into her pocket, probably for a handkerchief to wipe away the day's sweat. He pushed back his hat and blew out a hot breath as he turned to look at the angel.

"Do you think you can—"

A muddy Colt Peacemaker was aimed at his chest. Hell, she had hidden it in her pocket and he hadn't noticed.

"Get out of here, or I swear I'll shoot," she said.

"Go right ahead. It'll be a short trip to hell at this range."

Her eyes flickered, and he knew she couldn't possibly send a man to his death, let alone eternal damnation.

"Leave! Now!"

"I don't want to." The angel's challenge pulled him in like a moth to a flame. "Lady, it's just plain stupid to stay here. You might make it for a week or two, but Charlie there won't."

The baby was pressed to her breast, his head nestled at her throat. She looked up at Jake with frightened brown eyes and his common sense kicked in.

Lady, you and I are going to be intimately acquainted before nightfall.

His eyes settled on the angel's face, and he wondered why on earth he had said something so stupid to a woman stranded in the desert.

The baby's lips went crazy against her neck, and he knew why. The angel was beautiful. She radiated goodness, a kind of light that made his heart ache. He adjusted his hat so that she could see his face.

"I won't hurt you, miss. You can call me Jake, or Jacob, or Jackson or even Mr. Malone if it makes you feel better."

"Jacob…" Her voice went to a whisper, and she lowered the gun. "I've always hated that name."

He felt insulted, but if the truth be told, he hated his name, too. Jake the rake, Jake the snake, Jake the fake. She seemed to like formalities, so he tipped his hat. "Jake Malone at your service. And you are?"

"Alexandra Merritt. Alex for short."

A man's name. It didn't fit the dark-haired angel staring at him with those sweet brown eyes.

"Well, Miss Merritt, I don't like your name, either."

Chapter Two

"How long have you been out here?" the stranger asked.

"Almost two days. A storm washed out the road. I don't know what happened to the drivers."

"They're dead."

Coming from the man Alex had taken for the Angel of Death, it was a statement of fact. When she looked up from between Charlotte's legs, she had seen a black ghost sent to take a life, a messenger from the darkness that came with the raging waters that had sent Charlotte into labor.

On the first day, the pains had lasted from dusk to dawn, but then they'd stopped as suddenly as they had started, except for a mushy ache that made Charlotte moan in a fitful sleep. Last night, the baby changed his mind again and decided to come into world. Charlotte woke up screaming, clutching her belly and begging God for mercy.

Alex had stayed calm until she'd seen this man silhouetted against the sky, a crow in black, with wings that billowed as he climbed off the bay and walked in her direction. Only when she saw his face, with two black eyes and a purple lump on his jaw, had she realized he was a man and not a hallucination brought on by heat and fatigue.

Even now he didn't seem quite real, but she could see he was tall and lanky, loose jointed in a way that suggested he was quick on his feet, perhaps because he had to be. She was tall herself, and her eyes just reached his shoulder. His nose was straight in spite of the puffiness across his cheeks. His lips had a masculine thinness, and black stubble covered his jaw. Wisps of soft dark hair grazed his frayed collar. He needed a haircut, badly.

He was staring back at her. "Have you eaten anything?"

Alex shook her head. "Our food baskets got soaked in the flood. We lost everything except a few apples."

"Then you need to eat." The outlaw strode to his horse and came back with jerky and a canteen. "Take this," he said, opening the jug and handing it to her.

She reached for it with one hand, but the weight was too much and he didn't let go as she guided it to her lips. The brackish water trickled down her throat like melted snow. She tilted her head and guzzled.

"Don't overdo it. You'll get sick." His eyebrows knotted as he closed the canteen and handed her a strip of jerky.

"Chew it slow. It'll do you more good."

The dried meat tasted wonderful, rich and brown like her mother's gravy. She sighed with pleasure.

Satisfied that she wasn't going to faint, the man looked from her face to the top of the baby's head. It was still caked with blood and birth fluids, and a gamy smell rose from his skin.

"Is he okay?" he asked.

"I think so. He's pink and angry. That's a good sign."

The outlaw handed her the canteen. "You need more water."

The jug was lighter now, but she had short fingers and she couldn't hold it steady with just one hand.

"Here, let me help you."

He tilted it to her lips, and she drank until she couldn't hold another drop. Thanking him with a smile, she said, "I feel better."

"That's good, because we've got to get going. There's going to be another storm this afternoon."

Alex glanced at the western sky. A wall of clouds towered in the distance. "I need to get a few things for the baby."

"I'll do it." He left her standing with the canteen and began gathering the clothing spread on the rocks. The fine silks and lacy unmentionables belonged to Charlotte. The cotton drawers and everyday skirts were hers.

"Which stuff is yours?" he asked, picking up a red silk petticoat and holding it up for inspection.

Irritated, Alex shook her head. "Just take cotton things for the baby."

As he picked up her plain drawers, a night rail, and a white petticoat, his lips quirked upward.

No man in the world had seen her underthings until now, and her skin prickled. "You seem fascinated by my wardrobe, Mr. Malone. I take it you've never seen a lady's undergarments before."

"Actually I have. Quite a few as a matter of fact." He brushed right by her and stuffed the clothing into his saddlebags. "I'm not bothered if you're not."

She shrugged. "I don't suppose it matters at this point. Some compromises in life are necessary."

"That's true," he said, tightening the buckle with a jerk. "We can be in Grand Junction tomorrow if we start out now. Of course that's assuming you don't mind sitting in my lap for a long ride."

"I don't have a choice, do I? Of course we'll both ride your horse," she answered steadily.

"Fine, but you can't wear that skirt. The bay's too skittish."

"Is that so?"

"God's truth. I won him in a poker game last week. He's not fond of me, and I don't want to find out what he thinks of your skirt chasing after him."

Alex didn't like it, but glancing at the bay, she suspected he was telling the truth. He went back to the clothing on the bushes and selected a pair of striped britches that looked far too wide in the waist for her.

"Those belonged to the driver," she said.

"They're yours now. You can change behind the coach." Stifling a smile, he added, "I won't peek, miss. I promise."

His words said one thing, but his eyes another, and Alex forced herself not to care about something as small as modesty. "Can you hold the baby while I change?"

His eyes twitched, and he shook his head. "I'll pack up, but you're on your own with Charlie."

He'd named the baby after its mother, and tears pressed behind her eyes as she walked to the stage-coach, knelt behind it and set the baby down in the shade. His tiny face puckered, and an angry squall cut through the air as she stepped out of her skirt and pulled on the baggy pants. The length was tolerable, but the driver had been as round as Charlotte, and the waist was a foot too wide.

Pulling the drawstring as tight as she could, she tied a sturdy knot. Then she tucked in her blouse and knelt down to pick up the baby.

She would be holding him for hours, and so she took one of Smitty's huge shirts off the impromptu clothesline. Laying the baby in the folds, she fashioned it into a sling. It wasn't ideal, but the baby would be secure against her chest.

"I'm ready, Mr. Malone."

He was waiting by the horse. "I'll lift you up."

She had no idea that horses were so tall. "He's big, isn't he?"

"Just average. Now take the horn with your left hand, hold the baby with your right, and put your foot in the stirrup." His face knotted as he whispered to the horse. The bay was every bit as skittish as he had said.

"Here we go," he said. "One—two—three."

He flung her right leg over the horse's rump, and she landed in the saddle with a thump. A second later he was behind her with the reins loose in his hands.

She felt like jelly spilling out of a jar as she clutched the baby with one hand and the saddle horn with the other. The animal seemed ready to take flight, like Pegasus shooting through the sky.

"We've got to get out of this gully," Jake said. They were headed west into the sun where dark clouds were billowing near them.

"It's going to rain, isn't it?"

"Probably."

Alex nestled the baby closer. How would she keep him dry? Her heart lurched. She'd shield him with her body as best as she could, but soon he'd lose the resources God gave a newborn, and he'd need milk to survive. At the mercy of the elements and Jake Malone's good graces, she could only pray they'd reach Grand Junction in time.

The baby whimpered, and the heat of his pink skin soaked through her blouse.

"Can't you make him shut up?"

"I'll try."

Alex hummed until the baby settled against her chest, soaking the last bit of strength from her bones. She had gone without sleep for two days, and the bay swayed like a rocking chair. She couldn't keep her eyes open, and she slumped against the outlaw.

Jake Malone squeezed her waist and she jerked awake.

"I won't bite, miss. Just lean back."

"I'll be fine."

Even as she spoke, Alex knew it was wishful thinking. Sheer exhaustion had robbed her of the ability to sit up. She was a little girl again, a sleepy child being carried to bed by strong arms, and she curled against Jake Malone's chest.

His forearm rested on her hip, and she could feel his fingers just below her breast. With the slightest pressure, he held her in the saddle. She felt every inch of him pressing against her back, every twitch in his arm, and the strength in his thighs as he nudged the horse into a faster walk.

It was the closest she had ever been to a man. She had kissed Thomas on the lips, but they had never been hip to hip, knee to knee. She had no idea if Thomas's muscles were hard or soft, if his back was straight or slightly curved, if his waist was thick or narrow.

But she knew all these things about Jake Malone.

There wasn't a spare inch of flesh around his middle, his thighs were long and lean, and his forearms were all muscle. She could also smell his breath, a sour whiskey odor she remembered from a bad time in her childhood, and she knew he could change as quickly as the weather. Safe one minute, dangerous the next.

Alex stiffened. She wanted to push his hand away from her waist and sit up straight, but she was exhausted beyond the strength of her will. She sagged against him, and with his arm holding her steady, she closed her eyes to the orange sun and faded into a dream.

She heard Charlotte's cries, the baby's wail, the roar of thunder, the rush of flooding water. A whimper rose in her throat as a raindrop jarred her awake. They were out of the gully, on a plain dotted with boulders, and a silvery curtain of water was racing toward them. She clutched the baby against her chest.

The outlaw pulled the horse up short. The bay almost bucked, but he settled the animal with his voice.

"I've got a slicker." He reached behind the saddle and untied the rawhide laces holding a black oilcloth. She scooted forward to give him room to maneuver, but it was a mistake. The bay sidestepped.

"Stay still, dammit."

She didn't know if he was talking to her or the horse. She had seen what angry men did to their wives and children, and she remembered the night she learned that monsters sometimes wore familiar faces.

With a grunt, he unfurled the slicker, draped it over her legs and held up the center. "Put your head here," he said.

Rain was already beading on the oilcloth. Eager to cover the baby, she shoved her head through the opening and spread the garment as best she could over herself, the baby and the outlaw's knees.

"You're going to get wet," she said.

"It won't be the first time."

Lightning slashed the sky, thunder shook the air, and a burst of rain drenched her hair. The baby howled with misery. She wanted to feed him mother's milk and wrap him in a clean diaper. She would have given a year of her life for shelter for them all, even Jake Malone.

She had prayed for an angel to rescue them, but God had sent her a flesh-and-blood man instead, a man who was dark, worn-out and dangerous. Hours had passed since they had buried Charlotte, but she could still smell liquor on him. He wore a revolver on his hip and carried a rifle in a leather scabbard. And then there had been that remark about seeing men die.

He hadn't intended to stop, either. Jackson Jacob Malone wasn't a hero, and probably not much of a gentleman. But an unseen force had compelled him to watch as Charlotte gave birth, and another force, something sad and human and decent, made him put down the mule and dig the grave.

Alex could feel the rise and fall of his chest against her back. She believed him when he said he wouldn't hurt her, but she could hear her fiancé's words, too.

You're far too trusting, Alexandra.

Thomas may have been right, but her faith had always been rewarded. She sowed seeds of trust with her orphans, her friends, everyone she met, and not once had she been lied to or betrayed. It was her gift, this special kind of encouragement, and Jake Malone was no different from any other needy soul.

Except she was sitting in his lap, and he was a grown

man and not a child. Except he owned two guns, had
two black eyes and smelled like whiskey. Except his
hand was too close to her breast, and the dampness of
his shirt had soaked through to her own skin.

The rain gave him a strong musky scent. She could
smell the baby's dirty diaper, and she hoped the slicker
would keep the odor away from the outlaw's nose. His
patience seemed thin to start with, and the tension in
his body told her it was getting thinner by the minute.

As suddenly as it started, the rain stopped and the
clouds blew apart. The sun turned the earth and sky
into orange glass, a hot sea of glistening light.

"Oh my," she whispered, squinting in the fiery
glare. Perspiration poured from her skin, and the baby
wailed.

"Can we stop?" she asked.

"If you'd like."

He maneuvered the horse toward a boulder and
climbed down from the bay. She pulled the oilcloth
over her head and handed it to him. The cool air felt
like a damp cloth, and her skin tingled.

"Hand me the baby," Jake said. "Your legs might
not hold you."

As he lifted the tiny thing with his hands, she saw
shock in his eyes, then something dark and clear as he
cradled the baby against his chest. Holding him with
one hand, he spread the slicker and a petticoat by the
boulder, put the baby on its stomach and came to help
her.

"Swing your leg back like I did."

She tried, but her knee wouldn't move. The bay
shifted its weight. She could have sworn it growled,
but she knew that was impossible. A second later she
felt Jake's hands around her waist, lifting her, pulling

her close as he dragged her away from the skittish horse.

He set her on her feet, but her legs buckled and she fell against him. Her knees wouldn't straighten, and she wondered if he would have to carry her. She was facing him, and she couldn't take her eyes off his wet shirt sticking to his chest and dark hairs curling at his throat.

She looked into his liquid blue eyes and froze at what she saw. It was the same hard light she saw every day in the eyes of hungry children, the need for something so basic she couldn't put it into words, a need she had never known because she had always been loved and cared for, safe and fed.

The darkness in his eyes made her shiver. She didn't believe in lost souls, loneliness or pain that couldn't be chased away by love as easily as dust disappeared with a broom. The darkness of night always turned into dawn. It was the unfailing truth of her life.

Until now. Until the baby's needy wail clawed at her insides and she had no way to feed him. Until her own hunger blurred her vision and made her shake. Until her wet clothes chafed her skin and she could barely stand. Until she thought of her father and his failing heart and of Charlotte buried in the desert by strangers. Until the terrible truth that she was wet and hungry and lost took possession of her.

Tears welled in her eyes and her lips trembled. She pressed her dirty hands against her cheeks to hold back the flood, but it was too late. The pressure built to a throbbing ache that exploded in a throat-tearing sob.

Wrapping his arms around her, the stranger pulled her close. His breath echoed in her ear, and she smelled the rain and whiskey on his skin. She struggled to hold her breath, but she couldn't hold back the tears.

When her knees buckled, Jake Malone did what no man had ever done for Alexandra Merritt. He held her while she cried.

Jake needed a drink.

The angel was crying her eyes out, the baby was bawling along with her, and between the noise, the dark spots floating in his eyes, a headache, and the misery in his groin that came from rubbing up against her, he was in a sorry state.

He knew how to comfort most women. You let them cry, then you kissed him and said you had to leave because you weren't good enough for them.

Most women bought that line without a fight, and he suspected they were relieved to see him go. He was sure that deep down, Lettie was glad to see him leave even if she said otherwise, even if her brother had other ideas.

But the situation with Alexandra Merritt was entirely different. She expected comfort from him, and he wanted to comfort her, simply because he could. For all of her courage and confidence, she was a garden rose in the desert. She needed him, at least for a while, and it felt good in a deep, silent way.

She was sobbing like a train, all force and steam against his chest. Her fingers were digging into his arms but her legs had yet to take her weight. Holding her close, he learned that she had a man's name and woman's body. She was as soft as any woman he had ever held, and judging by the way her breath touched his bare throat, she was far too innocent to be held by someone like himself.

Jake wasn't a patient man, but he didn't move a muscle until her sobs turned into steady breaths. She shifted in his arms, but he didn't let her go. Instead he reached into his back pocket for his bandanna and wiped her face.

God, she was a mess. Her cheeks were sunburned and dirty, and the tears had left streaks that glistened in the light. Her nose was running, too. She wasn't the kind of woman who cried pretty, meaningless tears, and Jake wasn't at all surprised when she straightened her back and stepped away from him.

She reached into her pocket and pulled out her own filthy handkerchief. She was shaking, and he kept his hand on her shoulder as she blew her nose, loudly and without apology. "I don't usually fall apart," she said simply.

"You're safe now. That's usually when the shakes hit." She looked pained, and he felt a strange urge to make her smile. "There's no need to apologize. I've made lots of women cry."

She gave him a serious look that told him she wasn't used to flirting, then she nodded, as if making women cry was a confession she heard every day. Her loose hair grazed his knuckles. It was far softer than it looked, even dirty, wet and unbrushed.

"Can you stand now?" he asked. "I think Charlie needs some cleaning up. I can handle gunshot wounds and dead bodies, but the diapers are up to you."

Blood must have rushed to her feet, because she managed to stumble to the baby. "Can you get something clean from the saddlebag?"

Jake pulled out a white petticoat and tossed it to her. "We'll camp here tonight. My horse needs rest."

"All right," she answered, deftly wrapping the baby in the cotton and cradling him in her arms. She held him close to her chest, sharing her body heat.

Jake made a fire, cooked coffee and opened his last can of beans. He hadn't been prepared to leave Flat Rock. His stash had included some jerky, a few canned goods and a flask of whiskey, most of which was gone.

As soon as the can was warm, he handed it to her with his only spoon and poured coffee into his only cup.

"You go first." He was about to say *Save me some,* but the ravenous look in her eyes made him bite his tongue. She barely got out a polite thank-you before she nestled Charlie in her lap and reached for the can.

"Careful, it's hot."

Their fingers touched as he maneuvered the hot pad into her palm. Even before he could stand up straight, she was shoveling beans into her mouth. She closed her eyes as if she were dining on pheasant, moaned with pleasure, swallowed and licked her lips.

All over a can of beans.

There wasn't a doubt in Jake's mind he'd go hungry tonight, and if it meant listening to the angel sigh with pleasure, he'd do it gladly. Night fell as he unsaddled the bay, set his gear near the fire and slouched against the saddle with his hat pulled low. He heard the spoon scrape against the tin can, then it stopped with a rattle.

Alex cleared her throat. "I've saved half for you."

"I'm not hungry." But his wayward stomach chose that moment to growl.

She must have heard his hunger pangs, because she was holding back a smile. "If you're not hungry, I'll put the rest out for the birds."

"Finish it," he said. "You haven't eaten for two days."

She shook her head. "You're a lousy cook. I don't want it."

She was dangling the can in front of him like bait, and she looked as if she'd die if he didn't eat something. His stomach rumbled even more loudly, and she smiled. "Please, Jake. I really can't eat any more."

His name rolled gently from her lips, and he liked it.

"All right then." He reached across the fire and took the can in his bare hand. The metal was cool now, but still warm where her fingers had been. As the angel picked up the baby, he polished off the meal in four bites and poured coffee.

Charlie was squeaking like a kitten, and Jake washed down an unfamiliar lump of worry with the dregs from the pot. "Is he all right?"

"Just hungry. Can you hand me the canteen?"

He picked up the flask, stretched his arm as far as it would go and he handed it to her. She took it in both hands, tore off a piece of the petticoat, twisted it into a teat, and soaked it with water. Tickling the baby's chin, she slipped the cotton into his mouth.

"With a little luck, he'll figure this out," she said.

The baby's lips moved in that birdlike way, and he started to suck. Jake breathed a sigh of relief.

As Charlie's jaws worked the makeshift nipple, Alex rocked him. "He's fairly big for a newborn."

Jake looked doubtful. He'd seen plucked chickens with more meat on their bones. Curiosity loosened his tongue and he sat higher against the saddle.

"Isn't it kind of crazy for a woman to be traveling when she's so far along?"

"It is, but she didn't have much choice. She was stuck in Leadville for weeks because of the bridge being out over the gorge. If the train had been running, we would have reached Grand Junction a month ago."

"Do you know anything about her?"

"Only that her last name was Smith and that she was a widow from Chicago. She mentioned starting a restaurant with her sister in California, but we talked mostly about the weather and the miserable ride. She seemed like a very private person.

"Being a widow named Smith sounds pretty convenient to me," Jake said.

"I thought so, too."

Charlie started fussing, and Alex dipped the cotton in the canteen. The baby made tiny sucking sounds, and the angel started humming, a lullaby he recognized in some hidden depth of his soul. The sun was gone, and in the firelight he watched the baby fall asleep in her arms.

Her eyelids were drooping too, and he kicked himself for noticing the thick lashes that shadowed her eyes. With thoughts of warmth and sweetness nipping at him, Jake stood up and spread his bedroll near the fire. "You and Charlie can have the blanket."

"I'm not cold." She pulled the baby closer and scooted against a rock.

Jake dropped the blanket over her shoulders, but she shrugged it off. He glared at her. She was making things more difficult than they had to be. "You're either stupid or a liar. Which is it?"

"I'm too polite for my own good."

"Then you're both."

She grinned at him, and he saw both truth and humor in her eyes. "Actually, I'm neither, but you're still wet and I'm dry enough to be comfortable by the fire."

He left the blanket lying in the dirt. For a man who didn't have a considerate bone in his body, he was acting like a fool. He should have taken the blanket, gotten his whiskey from the saddlebag and concentrated on forgetting the past two days, but this woman made him irritable.

"You like to argue, don't you?" he finally said.

"It's a family trait." Her eyes darkened. "How soon before we get to Grand Junction?"

"A day or so."

"I'm already a month later than I wanted to be."

"What's waiting for you?"

"Family," she said. "My parents. I haven't seen them in five years."

The baby was quiet, and Alex was on the verge of sleep. In less than a minute her head rolled forward and her breathing blended into the deep rhythms of the night. He spread the slicker on the ground and urged her down so that she was on her side with Charlie cradled in her arms, then he covered them both with the blanket.

As for himself, he had other ways to keep warm. Crouching by his gear, he pulled the whiskey flask out of the saddlebag. It was half-empty, but it was enough to help him sleep.

Behind him, the angel rustled beneath the blanket. Smoke from the fire wafted to his nose. Lowering the flask, he turned to make sure she hadn't rolled too close to the coals. Still curled around the baby, she was staring at him as if he'd grown two heads. A nightmarish fear beamed in her eyes. No matter how thirsty he was, she looked like she needed it more.

"Do you want a swallow? It'll help you sleep."

"No, thank you." She closed her eyes and blew out a lungful of air. He could almost see her measuring her next breath, taking it in, and forcing the fear out with it, until she went back to sleep.

The flask dangled in his hand as he breathed in the night air and its peculiar mix of smoke and emptiness. The baby cooed at her side, and a familiar stone shifted in his gut. He would have given ten years of his life, hell, all twenty-five years, just for five minutes of that kind of peace.

The flask grew warm from the heat of his hands. He had never cared for the taste of stale whiskey, and the dregs had been cooking for two days now. He heard the angel sigh in her sleep, saw her feet twitch, imagined her dreams of a fiery red desert and a baby being born.

And then he had thoughts of his own, of the crimes he'd committed, of Lettie, and his brother Gabe, of the last night in Flat Rock. He had been close to vomiting for two days now, and he knew if he took even a swallow of the warm liquor his guts would spill at his feet. He'd shame himself in front of her, and she'd be on her feet in a heartbeat, holding his head while he puked up his guts.

He couldn't bear the thought of the angel hearing him vomit, so he put the whiskey back in his saddlebag and walked into the darkness. Stopping at a boulder silhouetted by the moon, he rolled a cigarette, slipped it between his lips and struck a match.

The tip glowed and faded, an orange flower blooming in the darkness, too bright to be real and too beautiful to last.

Chapter Three

She was dreaming of cicadas chanting on a summer night, but the rattle in her ears wasn't quite right. It stopped and started while cicadas made a noise that never ended. The crickets got louder as the night lengthened and they always sounded far away. This rattle was too close to be a dream, then she heard the click of a rifle, the baby's sudden wail and a man's low voice.

"Hold still, Alex, real still."

Something slithered over her feet. Her eyelids flew open and she saw Jake Malone's dirty boots planted three feet away from her face.

"Don't move, honey."

Dear God, how could she hold still with a rattler rippling over her feet? The baby was wailing now. Only the bundling kept him from thrashing and attracting the snake. His red face was next to hers, but she didn't dare move. The rattling stopped, and the silence was more frightening than the hiss of its tail.

"He might leave, so stay still. He's looking kind of bored right now."

Was that supposed to make her feel better?

"I can't shoot him from this angle so I'm going to move behind you. This fella is as good as dead. He'll make a nice band for the hat I'm going to buy for you."

Her legs were shaking, and her jaw throbbed. Tears squeezed out of her eyes, and she looked down without moving her head. The snake studied the baby with its slitted eyes. Its flat head swiveled, and she wondered if snakes could hear, and if the baby's wails would make it strike.

Fresh terror pulsed through her. She would die, the baby would die, or Jake Malone would save them both.

"He'll be tasty for breakfast once I nail him," the outlaw said.

The man was out of his mind.

"They taste like chicken."

Her stomach lurched. Hot tears streaked her face.

Sssss… Sssss… Sssss…

Jake's shadow touched the coils. "I'm going to shoot on three."

He raised the rifle and took a step. "One…"

The baby kicked inside the bunting.

"Two…"

The snake's fangs glistened in the sun.

"Three."

The rifle blasted hot metal. The snake lunged for its prey, and Alex flung herself in front of the baby. Razor-sharp fangs sliced through her arm. Blood and bits of the snake spattered her face and hands.

"Oh, God! Oh, God!"

Charlie's mouth was moving, but she couldn't hear him cry. Her sleeve was in shreds and covered with blood. She struggled to her knees. The snake was a bloody rope at her side, and Jake Malone was in front of her, pulling on her arm, ripping at the red cotton sticking to her skin.

He was talking, but she couldn't hear him. She wanted to tell him everything would all right, that the snake was dead, but she couldn't force the words out of her throat. She could barely breathe, and when he ripped the sleeve up to her elbow, she saw two red gashes where the rattler's fangs had ripped her skin.

"Alex? Can you hear me?"

He was shouting, but she could barely make out the words. Not trusting her voice, she nodded to him.

He had a knife in his hand. It was short, with the sharpest silver blade she had ever seen, and his eyes were glued to her forearm where the red streaks were oozing blood. The knife shifted in his fingers.

"No!"

She tried to pull her arm away, but he had a firm grip on her elbow. The blade sliced into her flesh just above the two gashes, and a second later he was sucking the blood. He spat one mouthful on the ground, then two more. With a jerk of his hand, he tore the rest of the sleeve, made a tourniquet and twisted it just above the bite.

Wiping her blood away from his mouth, he grabbed her elbow and squeezed. "Talk to me, Alex. Does your whole arm hurt or just where it's bleeding?"

"Just—just the bite."

"Does your arm tingle? Is it going numb?"

She was trembling with pain and terror, but she managed to shake her head.

"Here's the situation, honey. I don't think the snake shot you full of venom. Those were scratches, not puncture marks. I had to cut you, though. I had to be sure."

His eyes were as wide as hers. If the snake had shot its venom, she would die, and no amount of hope or letting of blood would stop the progress of the poison.

She blinked and saw her father's face. She tasted ripe peaches and her mother's homemade jam. Charlie's wail pierced the silence, and Jake's breath rasped as he pressed his fingers against her throat and felt her racing pulse.

A sob exploded from her chest. Regrets buzzed in her mind like insects with ugly black wings and she couldn't swat them away. Her body was a shadow, empty and gray, but her vision sharpened and she saw the bright beauty of the arid plateau. Her ears pounded with the vastness of the silent earth. There was so much of life she had missed, so much she hadn't tasted, touched, understood.

"I don't want to die," she said, choking on the dryness of her own mouth. A thunderous tremor traveled from her toes to her scalp. Her whole body shook with it, except for her injured arm being held steady in Jake's strong hands.

"Can you still feel your fingers?" His eyes were the brightest blue. She hadn't noticed that until now.

"My—my arm doesn't hurt—except for the bite."

"Are you sick? Can you breathe?"

She sucked in air and nodded. "I hear Charlie."

"He can wait a minute."

She saw the baby kicking on the blanket. As faint as his wail seemed to her ears, it was distinct, as welcome as the first strains of a symphony. Jake let go of her arm and went to the saddlebag. The buckle flashed in the sun, and he came back with the flask and one of his own shirts.

"Sit back," he said. "This is going to hurt."

She leaned against the boulder and stuck her arm out as if she were a child with a skinned elbow. Sweat beaded on her face, and she gritted her teeth against the speckled light spinning through her head. Closing her eyes, she clutched at Jake's sleeve to steady herself. He rested her bloody arm on top of his, cupping her elbow and trapping her fingers between his chest and biceps.

He splashed alcohol over the wound, and she shrieked. She thought of her mother blowing on her skinned knees, then she felt soft cotton on her torn flesh and the heat of his hand. The wound stung terribly, but she was breathing more easily.

"We'll wrap it up, and then we're gonna beat all hell for Grand Junction," Jake said. He sliced the shirt with his knife, wrapped her arm as tight as she could stand and tied the ends. "You stay still while I pack up."

His eyes were full of a glassy blue light, and Alex knew that hers were just as watery. He wrapped the baby in a fresh petticoat and tucked him in the crook of her good arm. Then he rolled up the blanket and the slicker, kicked sand in the ashes of the fire and vanished behind a boulder.

She figured it was nature calling, but then she heard a low moan, a single cuss word, and the sound of a man losing his breakfast and his pride. She wanted to go to him, but her legs were too weak. It struck her then that some things were private, and this was one of them.

When he came back, he took a swig of water and spat it on the ground. Taking Charlie in the crook of his arm, he pulled her up with his other hand. He didn't let go, and she didn't want him to.

"How are you feeling?" he asked.

"I'm just shaken up."

"Can you ride?"

The bay was tethered to a scraggly juniper on the other side of the campsite. It was a foot taller than she remembered and twice as skittish. She worried even more when it curled its lips and snorted at her.

"He's not as mean as he looks," Jake said, tugging on her good arm.

Her feet refused to budge. "He doesn't like me."

"It doesn't matter what he likes. I've got to get you to a doctor."

Something ornery and hysterical took root just below her ribs, and she shook her head. "I want to walk."

"You want to *what?*"

"I'm going to walk to Grand Junction."

"Okay," he drawled. "I'll take Charlie, and you can meet us in town. How's that sound?"

"That sounds good."

"I'll even wait around and buy you supper when you get there. That should be in about a week, that is if you don't fall in a ditch and break a leg, or die of thirst, or starvation. And don't forget bobcats and rats. You know about rattlers, but coyotes can get mean, too."

"I'll be careful."

"You've got outlaws and Indians to consider, and then there's sunstroke. You'll have to sleep during the day and walk at night. It gets pretty dark, but there should be a full moon in a few days."

"Anything else I should worry about?"

"Scorpions. Tarantulas are just big hairy spiders, but scorpions sting like hell. Now centipedes are downright cute."

Laughter bubbled in her throat. The entire situation

was beyond all reason, beyond anything she had ever imagined. She was sobbing and laughing at the same time, and Jake was grinning like a man who had wrestled a bear and won. His eyes glowed, and she saw that in spite of his toughness, he liked to laugh.

In her most formal voice, Alex said, "Considering the tarantulas, I suppose I'll take my chances with your horse, Mr. Malone."

"A wise decision, Miss Merritt."

With a bold-as-brass smile, he slipped his hand around her waist and pulled her to his side. His body was warm and strong against hers, and with a tiny smile, she said, "I feel better."

His fingers cupped her waist, and somehow she knew that everything would be all right.

But it wasn't all right. Pressure built deep in her chest, and something wild and insane took root low in her belly. The trembling came back with an energy of its own. Maybe the snake had left its mark. Maybe that was why her legs went weak and she couldn't breathe.

Maybe it was the snake, and not the shimmering light in Jake Malone's eyes, the sheltering wing of his arm and the parting of his lips. Slowly, like a drop of rain trailing down a leaf, he lowered his mouth an inch closer to hers. Closing her eyes, Alex faced the certainty she was about to be kissed and acknowledged the truth that she wanted him to do it.

Only she couldn't possibly want that. She was engaged to Thomas. Jake Malone and his shimmering eyes and soft lips had no place in her life, but he was already kissing her and she couldn't pull away.

Kissing him was unthinkable. A betrayal, a lie, and she couldn't do it. Except her lips had come alive, and she shivered as his tongue grazed them. The kiss was tender, searching, like Charlie's rosebud mouth looking for his mother's breast.

Her hand flew to his chest and she felt the beat of his heart. A soft hum rippled through him as he eased his tongue past her lips. She had never kissed a man like this before, never felt his need mixing with her own. The strange and glorious closeness of his soul made her tremble, and she liked it.

But it had to be a lie, an aberration borne of fright and danger. She loved Thomas. He needed her. She had no right to kiss an outlaw in the desert. She had no *interest* in kissing him, and yet a small squeak, a tender cry of need, escaped from her throat.

Jake pulled her closer, and she wanted to laugh and dance and touch the sun, to feel the hardness of his muscles and the coarseness of his beard. She wanted to pour herself into him, to fill the hidden corners of his soul, and so with the morning air on her face and the sun blazing across the plain, with her aching body daring her to do it, she filled the hot emptiness of his mouth with her breath.

The moment turned both tender and fierce. His free hand traveled down her spine, past her waist, down to the small of her back, and a notch lower. His fingertips drew a slow circle that deepened with each turn of his wrist.

When he touched her bottom, she gasped. He hesitated, but she couldn't force a single word past her lips and so he went on kissing her. His tongue dove deeper, his lips became hungrier. Everything about this man was confident now, and in a rush of hot, wet panic, she planted her hands on his chest and pushed.

"What the—"

He staggered backward, struggling to keep his balance with the baby cradled in one arm. Charlie shrieked, and Jake landed on his backside like a rodeo clown.

He glanced at the baby, tucked the cloth over its head, then rose to his full height and squinted at her. Rimmed with purple shadows, his eyes seemed wise and all-knowing, scarred by life's battles and experienced with its pleasures.

"Jeez, Alex, what did you think I was going to do? It was just a kiss." His voice softened. "It's just nature."

Shaking her head and close to tears, she held up her hands to stop him. "I'm not an idiot. I know exactly what *it* is. And *it* isn't an excuse for what I just did."

His blue gaze pinned her to the spot. "You wanted to kiss me. You want to prove you're alive and kick death in the teeth. Whorehouses always fill up after a gunfight."

What in the world was she supposed to say to that? That she had never needed to kick death in the teeth before now, that everything in her world was orderly and simple, because she worked very hard to keep it that way?

Or should she tell him that until now, she had never lost her mind while kissing a man; that her insides felt like warm milk and she could still taste the salt of him on her tongue? Alex bit her lip. She had to keep the moment in perspective.

"Frankly, Mr. Malone, I just made an embarrassing mistake. You see, I'm engaged to a man in Philadelphia, and well, I—uh—"

"You just got carried away."

"Yes, that's it."

"Whatever you say." He shrugged as he held out

the baby. "Here, you take him. I'll check on the horse."

For some reason, his opinion mattered, at least for today, and Alex followed him to the bay. "My fiancé's name is Thomas Hunnicutt. We work together. With children."

Jake fiddled with a stirrup. "Is that so?"

"He's kind and thoughtful. We've known each other for years, and when his wife died, it seemed right to get married. She was my best friend."

The desert air hurt her lungs, as if it were too thin to support a human life, and she took a deeper breath. He glanced at her, and a fleeting shadow passed over his face.

"Thomas Hunnicutt is a lucky man, Miss Merritt. I apologize for my earlier indiscretion." His manners were impeccable, his voice as sincere as a prayer, but something about the tilt of his head made Alex tremble all the more.

The horse fidgeted next to her, but she no longer cared. She would have climbed on a kicking mule to get away from this man. But what would she do with this terrible ache? This desire to touch his face? Even now her heart felt swollen with a need to taste more than the desert air, to feel more than the heat of the earth rising through the soles of her shoes.

There's more to life, Alex, so much more....

Her father's words came at her like a forgotten promise and a strange realization seized her heart. Not once had she been hungry or thirsty, in need of clean clothes, or desirous of a man's kiss. Until the stage crashed in that torrent of muddy water, she hadn't felt fear. Until the snake bite, she hadn't felt pain. And until Jake kissed her, she hadn't tasted desire.

Standing by the bay, with her arm wrapped in his shirt, with her sunburned skin stinging from the salt of her own perspiration, Alex felt her nerves rippling like grass in the wind. Did misery really sharpen a person's senses? Did sugar taste sweeter after a mouthful of sand? She had to hope so. What else could explain the trembling in her bones?

Jake Malone saw it all in her eyes, and she could only pray the heat pulsing in her veins was nothing more than shock, an illusion, something that wouldn't last, because her feelings for this man turned her well-planned future into a wasteland.

She belonged in Philadelphia. She belonged anywhere but here. And that meant she had to push back the glittering mirage of passion and see the true dryness of the desert.

Jake had heard of people going insane on the Colorado Plateau, and Alexandra Merritt had as much cause as the next person. It gave him a reason to be charitable, but temporary insanity was no excuse for bad manners. She hadn't said a word since he lifted her onto the saddle, and he didn't take kindly to being shoved on his butt.

Between the baby's hungry wail and the fact he hadn't had a drink for two days, Jake was brimming with indignation. They had a half day's ride ahead of them, and as long as Alex wasn't in desperate need of a doctor, he was grateful for the chance to sort through his thoughts.

At the very least she owed him an apology, but if the truth be told, he wanted a lot more than that. The angel made him hungry for things he'd never had, simple things like respect and a clean bed, and dangerous things like her body, and even her trust.

There wasn't much in his life that made Jake proud, but killing the snake with a perfect shot was one of them. Wishing the snake would slither back to its nest but knowing it wouldn't, he'd grabbed the Winchester and aimed. Instinct had forced the snake to strike, just as a piece of Jake's own nature, a piece he had either forgotten or wasn't sure he had, made protecting Alex and the baby as necessary as breathing.

An hour had passed since that moment, and they had all been amazingly lucky. Lancing the bite had been the most awful thing he had ever done. He would never forget the terror in her eyes or the taste of her blood.

Nor would the softness of her lips fade from his memory anytime soon. She had to be the luckiest person he had ever known, and the most pitiful at the same time. How could Thomas Hunnicutt look at himself in the mirror, when it was as plain as the desert sun that Alexandra Merritt didn't know the first thing about kissing a man?

Jake didn't understand men who treated women as if they were merely useful, like an extra right arm or a hot-water bottle for their beds. He knew from experience that something wondrous happened when the right man and the right woman got naked together.

He had been nineteen years old and not fully grown when a widow hired him to work her ranch for the summer. By July his muscles were hard and he was sharing her bed. She was close to thirty, but he would have married her if she hadn't sent him away.

Leaving her cut him to the bone. The widow liked having him in her bed, but she didn't want him in her life. A few months later, she'd pushed him away like a bum calf, and he remembered the taste of snow as he rode away.

And then there was Lettie Abbott. He'd broken all of the rules when he'd taken her to bed.

"You've got to pay for it or marry it," his brother Gabe used to say, but Jake had done neither with Lettie. It had been nothing more than meeting a man's need. Not once had he imagined she would conceive a child.

With spots drifting like flies in his field of vision, Jake had to admit there was more than one way to ruin a woman's life. He had nothing on Thomas Hunnicutt when it came to using a woman. He had spent one night with Lettie for the pleasure of it. It wasn't even worth remembering, except for the baby she'd conceived.

With the angel pressed against his thighs, the memory of Lettie's pregnant belly tweaked what was left of his conscience. Never mind that she had invited herself into his bed. He had taken less than she had to give, and Jake knew in his gut how it felt to be treated as less than the person he wanted to be. Gabe did it to him all the time.

You worthless piece of trash. What makes you think you belong in school? You'll never get it right, little brother. Smart kids read books. Dumb ones shovel shit."

For a while, he had read them anyway.

Ma would die if she saw you puking like that....

Yeah, but Ma was already dead.

Rolling his hips in the saddle, Jake shifted to give the angel more space. He knew how to skulk through life. He was hardened to his own misery, but what would happen to her if her husband made her feel worthless and weak?

His stomach clenched around its own emptiness. Alex deserved all the joy life could bring. Pure goodness radiated from her bones as she cuddled the baby. Warmth rolled off her back, and Jake couldn't stop himself from wrapping his arm around her waist.

She stiffened, but he didn't loosen his hold until she relaxed and leaned against his chest. His mind took off for places it had no business going, and his eyes followed suit. He gazed at the curve of her neck where her blouse gaped, and he could see a line where her white skin ended and a fiery sunburn began. She was on the verge of blistering, so he tugged her blouse higher on her neck. She tensed beneath his fingertips. "What are you doing?"

"You're starting to look like a tomato."

His fingers brushed her skin, not by accident, and she sat straighter, as if her backbone had grown back.

"I'll be glad to get home," she said.

"Must be nice to have a home to go to."

Her voice softened. "Where are you from?"

"Nowhere in particular."

"You must be coming from somewhere," she probed. "What do you do?"

It was the kind of thing a woman would ask at a dinner party. "You don't want to know."

"Yes, I do."

He grumbled at her. "Didn't anyone tell you it's rude to ask questions?"

She didn't answer, and he felt bad for scolding her. The woman made him prickly all over, and he gave in to a strange wave of pity. "I pretty much go where I want."

"Where were you headed when you found us?"

"California," he replied.

"Do you have family there?"

She was like a child rummaging through a box of puzzle pieces, looking for ones that fit, excited at the prospect of a pretty picture. Irritation leaked into his voice. "What I do isn't anyone's business but mine."

"Maybe not, but Charlie and I are alive because you stopped. I won't forget what I owe you."

"You don't owe me anything except an apology." Her cheeks flushed, and it charmed him enough to be kind. "It's not smart to kiss a man and then knock him on his butt."

"I guess I had a sudden urge to kick death in the teeth, or something like that," she said with dignity. "I am sorry, though. I behaved badly."

"No offense taken."

Alex turned in the saddle and looked at him with those rich brown eyes and sunburned face. With a sweet smile, she said, "You're a good man."

He wasn't anywhere close to being good. His eyes drifted to her pink lips. Lightning shot to his groin and ricocheted to his chest. Pure lust would have been easy to put in its place, but Jake knew his reaction wasn't that simple. Yes, he wanted to show Alex a thing or two about kissing a man, but he also wanted to keep her safe, to be someone she would want to know.

But he was on the run. He had no business lusting after an angel, even if he had kissed her and seen need in her eyes, curiosity, and the hunger that comes with a child's first taste of sugar. Even if she asked him for more, he had nothing to give except a glimpse of pleasure, and that wouldn't be enough. She deserved more from life, and so did the baby in her arms.

His jaw tightened as he thought back to Lettie and the baby she was carrying. He didn't love her, not even a little bit, and the child would be better off without having a son of a bitch like himself for a father.

Charlie was propped on Alex's shoulder. Patting his back, she crooned a vaguely familiar melody, and with a dim ache behind his eyes, Jake recognized the hymn she had been singing when he found her. The baby's face was red, and his wispy hair, the same dark brown as Jake's, was damp and matted. His eyes were blue slits, glassy with tears, and needy enough to make a grown man cry.

It was more than Jake could stand. He would take Alex to her family in Grand Junction, then he'd find a saloon, order a bottle of whiskey and drink himself senseless. He had plenty of money. He could drink all night if he wanted, and maybe even find a woman to share the pleasure.

The miles passed quickly once he had a plan. The trail dipped through a canyon full of sage and scraggly junipers until the ravine widened into a thrusting desert plain. Grand Junction rose in the distance, and Alex stretched to see the rows of buildings.

Charlie let out another wail, and Jake sighed. He could already feel the whiskey tickling his throat.

"We're here!"

Her joy flowed through him. He really had saved her life, and he wondered if saving an angel made up for the rest of the misery he'd caused through the years. He even let himself wonder what Gabe would have said about his little brother riding into town with a woman and a baby.

With the thought of Gabe, his good mood soured like old milk. His brother would have told him he was a fool. He would have called him a drunk and a cheat and told him to keep his dirty hands off of Miss Merritt's slender waist, to mind his manners, brush his teeth and get a job.

Jake was scowling when they reached the middle of town where Waltham's Emporium was doing a brisk business. A large man with silver hair walked down the steps toward a loaded buckboard.

"Papa! Papa!" Alex cried.

She squirmed like a kid at Christmas, and the old man froze in his tracks. Jake saw shock in his eyes, then a blossom of pure joy. He half expected the man to break into a run, but he couldn't seem to get his legs to work any faster.

The bay chuffed, and Jake reined him in at a hitching post. Sliding out of the saddle, he reached for Alex. She shoved Charlie into his arms and slid off the bay. Half staggering with her arms spread wide, she ran to the silver giant of a man.

"Oh, Papa! You won't believe what happened."

The old man hugged his daughter like there was no tomorrow, and Jake stood by the horse with Charlie squalling in his arms.

He needed that drink worse than ever.

Thank God. Thank God. Thank God.

William Merritt was a man of great emotion on even a quiet day, and having his daughter home at last was enough to make him shout with joy. It had been five years since he had seen her and more than ten since she had lived at home. It had been her mother's idea to send Alex to live with her aunt in Philadelphia. William had fought the idea, but Kath insisted on giving their daughter a taste a taste of Eastern sophistication, including the opportunity to meet educated young men and wear stylish dresses. As always, Kath had stood her ground, and he'd given in.

And so he and his daughter had written letters, and because of the strange intimacy of paper and pen, William knew his daughter better than she knew herself. He had an uncanny ability to read between the lines, and for the past six months, he'd been worried about her engagement to Thomas Hunnicutt.

But those worries could wait. He squeezed her shoulders and something between a laugh and a roar ripped from his throat. She leaned back, her hands still in his, and he saw a thousand questions in her eyes.

"I'm fine," he said. "Just slowing down a little."

But the dark circles under his eyes went beyond a man feeling his years, and if the truth be told, the pounding of his heart at the shock of seeing her scared him just a little.

More time…more time…more time…

Dear God, he'd be grateful for every minute.

"Papa, I've got so much to tell you." She stepped back and William took a long look at her. Her face was red and near blistering. Baggy trousers hung from her hips, and a sleeve had been torn from her white blouse. Dried blood caked the bandage on her arm.

He grabbed her shoulders. "My God! What happened?"

"The stage crashed in a thunderstorm. There's a lot to tell, but there are two people you have to meet first."

William's gaze roved to the man holding the baby. With his black eyes and black duster, he seemed more like a shadow than flesh and bone. Hard living, and only God knew what else, had etched deep lines in the young man's face, and he had a thirsty look in his eyes.

William knew the craving when he saw it, and he felt a stab of sympathy for the young man. With his stubbled jaw and bruised face, he looked like a rounder, but the baby turned him into something else. He looked like a father, too, and William dared to hope his daughter had found a diamond in the rough.

The cowboy stepped toward Alex and she reached for the baby. Holding the infant against her breast, she nodded at the stranger.

"Papa, this is Jackson Jacob Malone. He saved my life. Twice." Smiling, she held up the baby. "And this is Charlie."

"Who does he belong to?"

"No one right now."

William felt a twinge of disappointment that the cowboy wasn't the baby's father, and he cringed when he saw a light in his daughter's eyes that reminded him of his wife as a younger woman.

I want another baby, Will.

Any man who had fathered a child by choice knew that look, and most of the time a woman got her way. Peeling back the white cloth shielding the baby's head, he peered into his tiny face. "He looks brand-new."

"He is. His mother died giving birth."

"And his father?"

Alex shook her head. "She never said."

William watched as the cowboy took off his hat and wiped his forehead with his sleeve. The man was ready to hightail it out of town, but someone had hammered good manners into him, and he didn't even twitch while he waited for Alex to finish talking.

He had the air of a perfect gentleman, but William saw through him. He was polite because it had been beaten into him, and beneath his hooded gaze, William saw a man who cussed God and took comfort where he could find it.

He had known countless men like Jackson Jacob Malone over the years. He'd prayed with them and even buried a few of them when things went bad. He knew these men in his bone marrow because he had been one himself. Kindness would only make a man like Malone run, so William got tough and mean.

"This kid looks just like you, son. What lies are you telling?"

Anger rose from his black duster like smoke. "Let's see, old man. The last woman I bedded was a whore in Glenville, and that was a lot more recent than nine months ago when Charlie here got started. Let me think...." Jake rolled his eyes skyward and twisted his lips into an insolent grin.

William saw right through the ploy. The young man wanted to shock him.

"As I recall," Jake continued, "a sweet young thing spread her legs for me about then, but she was a blonde with big tits and the woman I just buried—"

"Stop it!" Alex glared at them both, then zeroed in on Jake. "How dare you speak like that about someone you—"

"Bedded?"

"I can ignore the language, but not the disrespect."

William wasn't surprised when his daughter turned on him next. "Papa, that question was out of line. You have no right to question Jake's integrity."

So it was already Jake and not Mr. Malone.

The young man didn't say a word, and William, who never kept his mouth closed and only rarely regretted opening it, wasn't at all sorry for riling him. He believed that "fight" and "flight" were God-given instincts, and Jake Malone was a fighter.

"My daughter's right, Mr. Malone. I have a rude streak a mile wide. I owe you far more than gratitude for saving her life. She's a treasure." He stuck out his hand and waited for the man to take it.

William guessed he still wanted to get drunk and throw a few punches, but at the mention of Alex, Jake Malone's eyes shimmered with a tender light. He took William's hand with a firm grasp.

"The privilege was mine, sir."

Alex smiled up at the cowboy, and William saw the precise moment when the fight in Jake Malone turned to flight. His eyes lingered a moment too long on her face. His mouth softened, and in his old bones William felt the young man's longing for something pure and good.

Glancing at Charlie, the cowboy almost smiled, but instead he tipped his hat to Alex. "Miss Merritt, I wish you all the best."

Turning on his heels, he walked way.

Alex shot after him and tugged on his sleeve. "Jake! Wait! You can't just leave. At least stay for supper."

Malone didn't stop walking, and William didn't know whether to respect him for wanting to protect Alex from the likes of himself, or if he despised the man for a lack of courage.

Either way, there was hope for Jake Malone, and once the cowboy found that out for himself he'd beat all hell out of Thomas Hunnicutt as a son-in-law. He knew where the young man was headed, and he wasn't going anywhere as long as William had anything to say about it.

"I've got a bottle of twenty-year-old whiskey with your name on it, son."

The cowboy stopped dead in his tracks. Dust billowed at Alexandra's feet, and William prayed he hadn't just made the biggest mistake of his life.

Chapter Four

Pivoting on his heels, Jake locked eyes with William Merritt. The old man's boots were planted a foot apart, and he'd crossed his arms over his chest. He felt the weight of Alex's grip on his sleeve and glowered at her. She let go as if he had started to smell bad.

Good. He didn't want her kindness. He wanted to get drunk and get laid, but he liked William Merritt for his rudeness, and, hell, he deserved a little consideration for saving the man's daughter. A bottle of whiskey seemed like the least the old man could do.

"That sounds like an offer I can't refuse," Jake said, smirking. A frown spread across Alex's face, and he got even more irritable. "Do you have a problem with that?"

"Of course not."

But she was glaring at him as if he'd just kicked a puppy. She had no right to judge him. A man had needs. Some men had holes in their guts that made them hard and mean.

He remembered holding her when she had cried, the recoil of the rifle as he shot the snake, the curiosity and fear on her lips when he had kissed her. And it made him realize she had gotten some very wrong ideas about the man who had found her on the Colorado Plateau.

But none of those things mattered now. The angel was about to meet the real Jake Malone. And he'd be damned if he'd apologize for saying "tits." He was about to tell her just that when Charlie let out a miserable wail and arched his back in frustration.

"He's hungry and I'm taking him to the doctor," Alex said, looking over her shoulder. "You can do any fool thing you want."

She marched down the street on wobbly legs, and Jake wondered what was holding her up. If she had asked him to stay nicely, he would have stomped off, but that sassy tone was a dare he couldn't resist.

William clapped him hard on back. "Come on, Jake. You can't argue with Alexandra when she gets like this."

"I know, sir. I landed on my butt once already."

The old man grinned at him. "Now that sounds like a story I've got to hear."

Pushing his hat lower on his brow, he said, "She pulled a gun on me, too."

Alex stopped in her tracks. "You had it coming."

"Both times?"

Her cheeks flamed. Aiming a pistol at a stranger was self-defense, but knocking him flat after the kiss had been something else altogether.

"My father doesn't need the details."

"Sure he does."

His silky voice teased her like a ribbon against her skin, and her eyes flickered as she weighed her options.

If she stopped him from talking, she'd have to explain things to her father herself and a simple kiss would seem like more than it was. On the other hand, she didn't know what he was going to say.

Holding his gaze, she blinked twice against the bright sun and took a chance. "Go ahead."

Her tangled hair swished as she turned her back, and the sight of her neck, pink and blistered by the sun, made Jake's mouth go dry. The woman had been through hell and a man had to respect that. Clearing his throat, he remembered her too-sweet lips and tasted the urge to be truthful, and even kind.

"Well, Mr. Merritt, it all started when I heard an angel singing in the desert, and I have to say your daughter is the bravest, most levelheaded woman I've ever met."

He relived finding the stagecoach, Charlotte's blood in the sand, and the muddy gun aimed at his chest. He told William about the rain and the rattlesnake, lancing the wound, and finally the last few miles of the ride to Grand Junction. He deliberately left out kissing her, but William didn't miss a thing.

"So how did you end up on your backside?" he asked.

Jake gave Alex a long, slow smile. Her lips came together in a frustrated line. "Let's just say she's not fond of my horse."

William huffed, but Jake saw a twinkle in his eyes. They both knew it would take more than a bucking bronco to rile Alex, and a soul-deep kiss from a good-looking man qualified. Hooking his thumbs in his belt, the old man studied Alex's straight back. His eyes narrowed to a hard squint, and Jake knew he'd have a helluva of time keeping secrets from this man.

Stopping in midstride, William wrapped his stubby fingers around Jake's arm and squeezed. His grip was strong enough to crack nuts, and Jake found himself pinned to the spot by a white-haired giant. The look on the old man's face chilled his bones and made him hot with anger, but he wouldn't answer the question lurking beneath the white arch of his eyebrows. What had happened in the desert was between himself and Alex. She could tell her father any damn thing she pleased.

The old man studied him as if he were a bug on a pane of glass. Letting go of Jake's arm, he grinned and scowled at the same time. "Well, son, for your sake I hope it was just a kiss."

"You'll have to ask your daughter."

"Don't worry. I will."

They started walking again, and William continued as if nothing else had been said. "I can't see any reason for you to rush off. I've got ten acres of peach trees, with plans to add more. There's work here if you want it."

Staying in Grand Junction with this crazy old man and his beautiful daughter was surefire trouble, but the bright sun was a torture to Jake's bruised eyes. His head was pounding. He needed rest and supplies before he headed further west. "I could use a place to stay for a few days, but I've got business in California."

"What takes you there?"

"Work." It was a lie, but no one would ever know.

"You can stay here as long as you like."

He had no intention of staying long enough to leave

more than a few footprints in the dust. Staring straight ahead, he said, "I'm much obliged, but I'll be moving on in a day or two."

With Alex in the lead, the three of them walked down Colorado Avenue. The smell of dust and paint filled the air, and the old man pointed to a building so new Jake could smell the freshly milled pine.

William raised his voice a notch so it would carry to Alex. "Dr. Winters's office is right there."

She was three steps ahead of the men, but with two strides, Jake caught up with her and held the door. She thanked him with a nod, as if she had expected him to be there, and led the way into the office.

Lacquered chairs lined the wall, and the scent of lemon verbena made his skin feel sticky. A man in his early thirties with short sandy hair, spectacles and squeaky shoes came out of the back room. He smiled with recognition at Alex and shook William's hand.

"Good morning, Mr. Merritt. It looks like you found your daughter."

"Yes, I did, Doc." William hooked his thumbs in his waistband." "Alex, this is Dr. Richard Winters. He came to Grand Junction about a years ago. And Doc, this is my daughter, Alexandra."

Winters flashed a smile. "It's a pleasure, Miss Merritt."

"We found a few others, too," William continued. "This is Mr. Jake Malone, the man who saved my daughter's life, and the little fellow is Charlie. The stage went down a day away from here. Check the baby first. Alex won't rest until we know he's okay."

After acknowledging Jake with a curt nod, the doctor

put on a toothy smile for Alex. Indicating the exam room, he said, "Miss Merritt? After you."

Jake watched as she hurried through the door, holding the baby tight against her breast. For propriety's sake, Winters left the door open, and Jake saw her bend slightly at the waist as she laid the baby on a high, narrow table.

Charlie whimpered like a kitten while the doctor washed his hands, but the wail turned to a howl as Winters poked and prodded. Jake was ready to jab the man in the ribs and ask how he liked being manhandled when Winters handed the baby to Alex.

"He's hungry, but he seems to be in good shape. I've got milk in the kitchen."

"I'm sure he's starving," Alex said, jiggling the baby to soothe him. She hummed to the child, and a few minutes later the doctor came back with a nursing bottle. Charlie must have smelled the milk, because his shriek got louder and he kicked Alex with all his might. His heel caught her bad arm and she winced.

Jake nearly shot out of his chair, but the doctor was already taking the baby from her.

"I've got him," Winters said.

Slipping the nipple into Charlie's mouth, he carried him to the waiting room. The silence was as welcome as rain in July.

"Now which of you gentlemen will take care of this little guy while I tend to Miss Merritt?" the doctor asked.

"Give him to the young fella," William said with a pained expression. "I don't think my heart can take it."

Jake knew he was being set up, but for once he didn't mind. "Fine by me," he answered.

As Winters handed him the baby, the nipple popped out of Charlie's mouth. Another shriek shook the room, but Jake slipped the tip back in place. The wailing stopped instantly as the baby's mouth overflowed with warm milk. It dripped over Jake's dirt-stained fingers, through the dark hairs on his wrist, and down to his pants where it made a wet circle on his thigh.

Propping his ankle on his knee, he nestled Charlie in his arms and settled in the chair. His shoulders relaxed inside the black duster. "This isn't so tough," he said.

Charlie looked at him as if he were heaven-sent. Jake clicked his tongue as the baby suckled, and with a stupid grin on his face, he looked up and saw Alex watching them from inside the exam room. A mother's love, and something more, filled the space between them.

"Your turn," said Winters, touching her arm. She looked away as the doctor guided her to a chair with a wide armrest.

The door stayed open, and the doctor's chitchat drifted into the waiting area as he numbed her arm with ice. "This incision is placed perfectly," he said casually. "Your young man did a fine job."

Her face knotted with confusion. "Oh, you mean Jake. He's not my young man."

For some reason, the truth hurt just a little.

Winters nodded, but it was as plain as day he'd found out what he wanted to know. Jake's stomach tightened. He didn't want to listen, but he heard every word that passed between them. The doctor was flirting shamelessly now, and Alex was too naive to know it.

The memory of being shoved on his butt was still fresh, and he figured she wouldn't know a man was interested unless he sent her a telegram.

Winters took a final stitch and snipped the thread with a pair of scissors. "That finishes it," he said.

Alex stood up and gave the doctor a deliberate smile. "Thank you. I'm sure I'll be as good as new in no time."

"I hope so, but perhaps I should visit you in a few days."

"That won't be necessary."

"Really, I don't mind."

"Thank you, but no," she said, just a little too sweetly.

Jake stifled a smile. She was giving Winters the royal brush-off and he didn't know it. Even Jake hadn't seen it coming.

"I really should check your arm," the doctor insisted. "I'm sure that knife wasn't sterile, and an infection could set in. That cut could be as dangerous as the bite."

Like hell it was. Jake didn't like being called stupid. He'd done what he had to do, and he couldn't let the slight pass. "Look, Doc—"

Alex cut him off. "Thank you for your concern, Doctor. But you weren't there. I have no doubt that Mr. Malone did right thing."

"Not medically."

"Nonetheless, he saved my life, and I'm grateful."

William's deep voice broke the tension. "The man thought fast and took action. That took guts."

An unfamiliar warmth filled Jake's belly, and in spite of the effort it took to balance the baby and the bottle,

he rose to his full height. He had a good six inches on
the doctor, and somehow it didn't seem the least bit
ridiculous to hold a baby and glare at the same time.

Winters stared back. "It looks like someone got the
better of you in a fight. Let me know if your eyes give
you any trouble."

Jake's jaw twitched. It would be a cold day in hell
before he'd ask this man for anything.

The doctor jammed his hands in the pockets of his
pressed trousers and smiled at Alex. "I'll be in touch."

She nodded politely, but Jake saw the frayed edges
of her smile. She lifted Charlie out of his arms without
a word, thanked the doctor again and opened the door
before anyone could do it for her.

The three of them left the office in a line, with William bringing up the rear as if he were herding sheep.
When the boardwalk widened, he went to his daughter's side, leaving Jake to follow a few paces behind
them.

It gave him a perfect view of father and daughter.
At first glance they looked nothing alike. In spite of
being a mess, Alex's hair had a healthy shine, while
the old man's white head made him look worn out.
They both jabbered like blue jays, but her chattering
never stopped, while William panted for breath now
and then.

Jake wondered about those differences, but he also
saw that their steps were perfectly paced and their
shoulders matched in posture if not size. There was no
doubt about it. Alex and her father were cut from the
same cloth.

Even with the baby to hold, Alex couldn't stop
touching the old man's arm. Jake knotted his fingers

into a fist and looked away. He envied them for reasons he didn't want to understand.

They were headed to the stagecoach office, and just about everyone they passed knew William. It seemed a bit strange to Jake. The man grew peaches for a living, and yet the town treated him like some sort of celebrity.

"See you on Sunday, Will."

"How's Katherine doing?"

"Welcome home, Miss Merritt. We think the world of your parents."

"Howdy, Reverend."

Reverend? Jake took a long look at the old man. He was tall and broad across the back, paunchy around the middle, and ruddy from hours in the sun. In worn dungarees held up by leather suspenders, a cotton shirt and boots, he was dressed for work, not a Sunday sermon.

He didn't look at all like a man of the cloth. Aside from his size and his rough hands, he wore his white hair in a ponytail. He looked more like a half-crazed mountain man than he did a preacher.

He spoke like a preacher, though. His voice boomed as he bragged about his daughter and sang Jake's praises to anyone who would listen, which was just about everyone they passed. It was embarrassing. William made him sound like a cross between Kit Carson and Florence Nightingale. Alex glowed each time her father told the story, and only her concern for the baby got him moving down the boardwalk to the stage office.

"You know the trails," William said to Jake. "Tell them where that coach went down."

So much for keeping his whereabouts to himself.

"It's about twenty miles up the Glenville trail," Jake said, deliberately not mentioning Flat Rock. The clerk promised to send men out to salvage the mail and the women's trunks, then he looked Jake squarely in the face.

"Do I know you?" he asked.

As if he had nothing to hide, Jake tipped back his hat. "I don't think so."

Had Henry Abbott died? Was there a Wanted poster with his face on it? Gabe had thrown him out of town for being drunk and for fighting, but murder was another matter. If Abbott was dead, Gabe wouldn't hesitate to turn him in.

Jake lowered his chin a notch. If the clerk twitched he'd be on his way to Mexico in two minutes. Forget the hot meal. Forget sleeping in a bed. Or a bath and clean clothes. Or kissing Alex again, which he shouldn't be doing anyway.

The clerk was still eyeing Jake when he snapped his fingers. "I've got it! You look like Robert Higgins, that New York actor. My wife and I saw him in a revue in Denver. You're his spitting image."

"Just a coincidence," Jake said with a bland smile. If anyone recognized him, he'd mention Higgins. As long as no one knew him, he'd be glad to stay for a few days.

He listened as Alex and William gave the clerk the few details they had about Charlotte Smith, then the three of them headed toward his horse and William's buckboard. It was the most natural thing in the world to give Alex a hand up to the high seat, and it felt just as right to haul himself into the saddle and follow the Merritts home.

But what had gotten into him? He should have been camped out in the Wild River Saloon instead of following a swashbuckling farmer and a brown-eyed angel like a docile puppy. He was even more surprised to find himself listening with genuine interest as the old man talked about the fruit business.

"You'll like this place," William said as he shifted the reins. "Katherine and I got it going about five years ago just as the Ute tribes moved west. Growing peaches was risky back then, but with a little bit of rain and God's grace, we've done pretty well."

Jake asked a few questions, and William rambled on about the peach trees he had shipped in from Georgia, the perfect climate, water problems and the August harvest. The Merritts had a productive farm in spite of bad odds, and Jake found himself liking the old man more and more.

Thoughts of the Wild River Saloon faded as the road wound past a mesa and turned south at the boundary of the orchard. Jake hadn't eaten a peach in years, and he wondered what a ripe one would taste like at harvest time.

"The job offer still stands," William said as if reading his mind.

"I'll think on it."

As they rounded a bend, Jake saw a two-story house, freshly whitewashed with a large garden. Alex caught her breath, and a burst of longing filled her eyes as a tall woman with dark hair, like hers except for streaks of gray, dropped a basket of laundry and ran toward the wagon.

A lump the size of a melon rose in his throat.

William stopped the horses. Jake reined in the bay, climbed out of the saddle and touched Alex's shoulder.

"I'll take Charlie. Go see your ma."

Her eyes burned bright, and Jake felt a sting of pleasure as Alex tucked the baby into his arms and jumped out of the wagon. He understood the need to run, only for him it was the need to run from something, not to it. He envied her that happiness as she clung to her mother. Somewhere in the middle of the tears and laughter, William slapped him on the back and Alex's mother hugged him and called him a hero.

Katherine Merritt took Charlie from him, and the two women went inside, arm and arm.

William nodded in the direction of the barn. "We'll take care of your horse, and I'll show you where you can clean up."

The old man puffed like a locomotive as they crossed the yard. His cheeks were too red, and his fingers were swollen, as if the blood could get to the tips but couldn't get back out. He unhitched the team and led both horses through the open door with Jake tagging behind.

The barn was cavernous, full of fresh hay, harvest tools and packing crates. The cool air made a man relax, and Jake liked the feel of the straw on the floor. He wouldn't mind sleeping out here at all.

"You can put your horse in the front stall," William said as he led the workhorses to clean stalls on the opposite side of the barn.

Jake loosened the cinch, heaved the saddle to the floor and tossed his saddlebags next to it. Relief rippled through the bay's flanks. Hell, he could feel relief in his own bones at the thought of a hot meal and a soft place to sleep.

"Where should I stow my gear for the night?" he asked.

"The tack room is over there." William pointed to a closet in the far corner of the barn.

"And the bunk room?"

William shook his head. "You're a guest here. We have plenty of room in the house."

Jake wasn't sure how he felt about sleeping inside. The barn was private, and if he got the urge, he could saddle up and leave in the middle of the night. "I'd rather sleep out here."

"I'll make you a deal," William said. "You sleep in the house tonight, but if I talk you into working for me, you can clean up the bunk room and make it yours. I need someone to tend to the thinning, and the picking when the time comes."

Jake took a brush off the wall and rubbed the bay with sweeping strokes. The animal whickered softly, as if he were enjoying the attention and wanted more.

"When is the harvest?" Jake asked.

"Not until August. I'm going to be straight with you. My heart's giving out. The man who worked for me for years went back to his family in Mexico last week, and I can't do the work I used to. I need help. I'll pay you well and the food's good."

"I don't think so."

"Why the hell not?"

Jake bristled. "Believe me, old man. You don't want me here."

"Are you wanted?"

Maybe, if Henry Abbott had died, but that remained

to be seen. "Not that I know of," he answered truthfully.

William stood in front of Jake's horse and crossed his arms. "I'm not picky about the stuff most people get riled about. I don't care where you've been or what you've done. If you handle yourself like a man, you can stay as long as you want. You act like an animal, I'll kick your butt myself."

"You really think you can?"

"I know so. I'm meaner than sin when it comes to my family."

The message was clear. *Respect Alex or else.*

Jake decided then and there to apologize to her for saying "tits" and talking about whores. There had been no call for it, and his mind flashed back to another time his tongue had gotten the better of his good manners. He'd cussed in front of a neighbor lady, and Gabe had slapped his face and hauled him over to her house to apologize. He'd done it, but then he'd called Gabe a bastard and his brother had pounded him into the ground. Somehow, though, with a single look William Merritt had him wishing he'd minded his manners.

Of course if the old man could have read his thoughts when it came to his daughter, he'd slap him silly. But so far that hadn't happened, and somewhere deep in his gut, Jake felt the need to rest awhile.

William was still pinning him with a hard gaze when Jake nodded. He didn't need the money, but some questions had to be asked. "How much are you paying?"

The old man named a wage that was more than fair. "You get paid once a week, plus a room and my wife's good cooking."

A smile played across Jake's lips. He could count on one hand the number of home-cooked meals he'd eaten in the past year. "In that case I'll take the job."

"I'm glad to hear it." William stuck out his hand, Jake shook it, and they moved on to business.

In addition to wages, William promised him a bonus after the harvest. It was a good offer, too good for a man who wasn't fond of hard work. Jake started shaking his head. He had to get out while he still could. "I appreciate all this, but I really can't—"

"Can't what?"

"Can't stay."

William huffed as if he'd just heard the lie of the century. "The way I see it, son, you can let life push you around, or you can stand your ground and start swinging. You don't seem like a coward to me."

"Far from it," Jake said evenly. He wasn't afraid of anything or anyone. Nothing much mattered to him, certainly not heaven or hell. But he didn't want to give *Reverend* Merritt that tidbit about himself, so he bit off a wry grin. "The only thing that scares the daylights out of me is an angry woman."

"Ha! You're even smarter than I thought."

Jake stroked the bay. "I'll work through August."

"Through September. There's a lot to do after the harvest."

"All right, but don't be surprised if you're ready to boot my ass out of here at lot sooner than that."

"Don't count on it. I need your help."

William headed for the barn door and then pivoted on his heels. "Speaking of angry women, don't be late for dinner. There's a washtub out back. Use it."

He strutted out of the barn, and an hour later Jake

was naked and up to his hips in soapy water warmed by the sun. The tub was large and deep, and next to it he found clean clothes, a new razor and a bottle of bay rum.

The bay rum made him smile. How many times had Gabe told him he smelled like a horse and needed to bathe more? He'd been doing it since Jake was eight, and for the first time, he wondered if perhaps Gabe had a point. The pants were a fine black linen, the bottom half of a stranger's discarded suit. But they looked long enough in the leg, and the white shirt had fresh creases down the sleeves. Jake liked the idea of showing off a little. He was a good-looking man, at least most women seemed to think so.

With a lazy grin, he leaned back in the tub and looked up at the sky. The bathwater sloshed as he shifted his hips. The sun bounced off the metal, blinding him as it warmed his exposed skin. With his eyes squeezed tight against the brightness, he felt his muscles soften as the hard gold light warmed his chest.

Damn, but it felt good to be clean. Even if it only went skin-deep.

Chapter Five

As the men walked to the barn, Alex watched as her mother peeled back the white petticoat from the baby's head, got misty-eyed and cuddled him to her chest.

"Oh Alex, you've brought home a treasure," she said, her face soft with old regrets. She hadn't had just one child by choice. "Let's go inside. This young man needs a bath, and you must be starving."

"I am," Alex replied.

Arm in arm, they walked into the house. Alex bathed Charlie in an enamel basin while her mother fixed her a meal and poured her a bath. Clean and fed, she went upstairs to rest while Katherine tended to the baby.

Three hours later, Alex woke up feeling lazy and safe, and through the bedroom window she saw layers of orange and mauve mixing with the hues of night. The aroma of roast beef and fresh bread wafted up the stairs, and her stomach rumbled. Stretching her aching legs, she climbed out of bed and opened the wardrobe where her mother had left clean underthings and a burgundy day dress. Except for a slight difference in height, the two women were the same size, and the dress fit in all the right places.

Buttoning the bodice, Alex looked in the mirror and went to work on her hair with a silver brush. The sun had burned reddish streaks at the crown, but she wrestled the lengths into a passable knot. Only her eyes seemed untouched by the desert. They were still a rich brown, and she wondered if Jake Malone would notice or care.

She had dreamed about him while she slept. He was kissing her again, slowly, endlessly, and she felt the tug of a string connecting her heart to her womb. At twenty-seven years of age, she had kissed a dozen men. One made her toes curl, but nothing had come it.

Finally there had been Thomas. His wife had been her best friend until she died of influenza more than a year ago, and Alex had known him for years. He was poised, an excellent conversationalist, a warm and friendly man who had joked with her about his wife's matchmaking efforts.

When Rebecca died, Alex became his confidante. She was the family friend he could escort to fundraisers for the Rebecca Hunnicutt Home for Girls, and finally she had become something more. She'd become a necessity, and she liked that.

He had kissed her for the first time last January. It was after a political dinner, just past midnight, and he'd surprised her with a soft brush of his lips. She shivered, and he'd kissed her again, lingering a bit longer than the first time, and she had gone to bed that night wondering about the mysteries of marriage.

As she pushed a comb into her hair to hold the knot in place, Alex felt her cheeks catch fire. Jake's lips had smothered her with need and want. There hadn't been room for curiosity. There hadn't been room for anything but the sensation of souls soaring toward heaven.

Was that what her father meant when he told her not to settle for less than everything God intended marriage to be?

She was compromising in other ways, too. She wanted children, and though Thomas and Rebecca had been married for years, he'd never fathered a child of his own. When she mentioned the possibility of somehow starting a family, he had shaken his head. "I'm sorry, my dear. Does that break your heart?"

"Of course not," she had replied. "Being your wife is more than enough for me."

But in her dreams she imagined him dropping to one knee and holding her hand. "I love you," he would say. "We'll adopt two girls and a boy, and pray for one of our own."

But what kind of foolishness was that? She had brushed away her doubts as if they were flecks of dust on a sturdy table, and they had set the date for a fall wedding.

Except her parents wouldn't come to Philadelphia. Her father's heart was giving him fits, and her mother didn't want to risk the trip. Frightened, Alex told Thomas she had to go to Colorado. He took her to the train station, checked in her trunk and forgot to kiss her goodbye.

As the train pulled away, the dust motes of doubt turned into seeds, and with each mile she traveled those roots thickened until they became a presence in her belly, a constant whisper in her soul. The snakebite should have made her crave Philadelphia and its comforts, but it hadn't. With death tainting her blood, she could only think of what she had missed, not what she had left behind.

Jake had been right. She wanted to taste the sun and

dance and sing at the top of her lungs. And when he
held her in his arms and kissed away the fear, the seed
of doubt turned into a seed of hope, of love, of un-
speakable joy. And yet there would be pain, too, and
maybe even blood and terrible need, but like an im-
pending birth, it couldn't be stopped.

The thought made Alex tremble. She had no business dreaming of a blue-eyed stranger in a black duster,
especially one with silken lips and bruised eyes, a man
who looked hungry for more than food. She would be
a good wife to Thomas. She loved him in the truest,
most unselfish way, and that meant she had to forget
Jake Malone.

She had to forget the width of his shoulders sheltering her from the sun. She had to forget his eyes, their
loneliness and that little-boy hunger for kindness. She
had to forget the sweetness of his mouth on hers.

Forget, forget, forget.

Never mind that he held Charlie in strong, tender
arms. He was a man who sweated whiskey from his
pores and craved its comfort, a man with quick fists
and a mouth from the gutter. He was a stranger with a
Winchester rifle and a Colt .45, a wanderer who would
be gone in a day. She had to keep those facts firmly in
mind.

Sighing in front of the mirror, Alex decided she
looked like her old self and headed down the hall. Her
father's booming voice carried up the stairs. He was
telling a story from his early days as a preacher, when
a saloon was easier to find than a church.

Rounding the corner, she heard Jake laugh and saw
Charlie asleep in a basket near her mother. He was
swaddled in a yellow blanket with his fist at his mouth.

The sun was gone, and her mother had placed can-

dles on the table along with the good china and a white
tablecloth. The men stood as she came into the dining
room. Her father beamed. "You're a sight for sore
eyes, Miss Merri."

He had given her the nickname when she was five
years old. She hadn't heard it in years, and tonight she
liked it.

Her mother glowed at the end of the table, and the
only empty chair put her across from Jake. He was
freshly shaved and bathed, dressed in a white shirt with
pearl buttons, and as tall as her father. His dark hair
was combed, but the ends still brushed his collar. Her
gaze traveled down to his broad shoulders and back to
his face.

The dirt, the scowl, the sour smell of whiskey were
gone, but the bruises couldn't be washed away. A wild
bird fluttered in her chest as he stepped around the table
and held her chair. His fingers brushed her arms as he
slid her close to the table, and she shivered. Her family
wasn't usually this formal, but with the china and candles, the gesture was fitting, and Alex wondered where
he had learned his manners.

As Jake sat down, their gazes met through the glow
of the candles. Alex reached for her water glass.

"Like I was saying," William said. "It was a hot
night in July, and there we were, me and ten miners in
a saloon, singing 'Silent Night' because it was the only
church song we all knew."

Alex smiled, in part because it was her favorite story,
but mostly because she was home. Her father had re-
tired from full-time ministry, but he still preached
every other Sunday, never failing to draw a crowd. He
had a way of touching people with bits of himself, and
no one was ever quite the same.

Her mother cleared her throat. "Alex, would you say grace?"

Thankfulness flooded through her as she swallowed hard, and said the words from memory. "For this bounty we are about to receive, we thank you, Lord. Amen."

Her father blinked twice and cleared his throat. Her mother dabbed at her eyes with a napkin.

"Well, let's eat," Katherine said too loudly. "Jake, start with the roast beef, and take plenty because my husband will work you like a mule."

"I'll be happy to oblige."

"Are you staying?" Alex asked.

William answered for him. "He's working through harvest, and I intend to get my money's worth."

"You always do," Katherine took a dollop of potatoes and passed them to Jake. He took two spoonfuls, ladled on the gravy and waited for Katherine to take the first bite. Only she was busy slicing bread.

"Dig in," she said. "We aren't formal around here."

"Thank you, ma'am."

"Please, call me Katherine."

"Katherine it is," he said as he sliced a bite of beef, raised it to his lips and chewed. His throat twitched as he swallowed. It was a sight Alex would have to get used to. The men her father brought home always ate with the family.

Her mother had a knack for making people feel welcome. Turning to Jake, she said, "Tell us where you're from."

"Here and there."

Curious, Alex pushed. "Where were you born?"

"Virginia."

It was a single brush stroke on a life-size portrait, and reminding herself she had no interest in this man, she took the bowl of green beans from her mother.

"I want to hear everything about your trip," Katherine said.

Alex started at the beginning. By the time she finished the story her mother had tears in her eyes and her father was giving Jake a cigar and promising him the moon in gratitude for saving his daughter.

"I can't thank you enough," William said.

"You already have with this fine meal." Jake looked up at Katherine. "I haven't eaten this well in about twenty-five years."

Her mother laughed as she stood to clear the dinner plates. Alex rose to help her, but Katherine put a hand on her shoulder. "You keep these gentlemen company while I get dessert."

Alex started to protest, but Jake had already picked up the empty bowls and was carrying them into the kitchen. Through the open door, she heard him offer to help with the dishes, but her mother handed him two plates of pie and shooed him back to the dining room.

Walking toward William, he said, "I'll flip you for the biggest."

"No, you won't. You'll give it to me now because if I know my wife, you'll get seconds and I won't."

Jake set the biggest piece in front of her father, then he slid the smaller one to Alex.

"Ladies first," he said, smiling.

The candles turned his face into planes of shadow and orange light. The same hue had lit the desert sky at sunset, and she was back on his horse, pressed against his chest, feeling his thighs against hers. Heat pooled in her belly. Never before had she sat across from a man knowing that his muscles were hard and his hips were narrow.

The warmth spread to her chest, up her throat and across her cheeks just as her mother walked in carrying the rest of the pie. Her gaze settled on Alex, shifted to Jake and returned to her daughter.

She set down the pie, cut a huge wedge and slid it over to their guest. "Alexandra, you haven't told us about Thomas yet."

"He's running for mayor next year."

Jake arched his eyebrows.

"We certainly wish him well," her mother said. "I can't believe my daughter is going to be married to the mayor of Philadelphia."

William pounded the table with his fist. Cups rattled and silverware jumped. "Over my dead body! You're too good for him by half, Alex. I can't believe he didn't make this trip with you. You should never have come by yourself. It's dangerous out here."

"I'm a grown woman, Papa."

"I could spit when I think of what might have happened to you. It was just plain stupid to take a stagecoach. You should have waited for the train."

"The bridge through the Red Rock gorge went out right before I got to Leadville. I couldn't wait."

William growled low in his throat. "You could have died in that goddamned desert."

"But I didn't, did I?"

"No, you didn't, thanks to Jake." William shoved at his empty plate. "It was mercy and luck, Alex. Pure and simple."

"I'm very grateful to Mr. Malone."

Alex glanced at Jake just as he took a bite of pie.

Katherine glared at her husband and set her napkin on the table. "Thomas hasn't written your father lately."

"He's a busy man."

Charlie squawked as if he had an opinion of his own, and Katherine lifted him from the basket. Alex's throat went dry at the sight of his tiny red face. Even if she never had a child of her own, this baby would be enough.

Her mother broke into her thoughts. "We have to look for Charlie's father."

"She told me she was meeting her sister. Frankly, I don't think she was married."

"Blood doesn't count as much as love," her father said. "But we owe it to Charlie to look for his family."

"I want to keep him, Papa."

William didn't even blink. "Of course you do. But you have to be realistic. Thomas may not want to raise him as his own."

She wouldn't even consider it. Charlie was a gift. Surely Thomas would see him in the same light.

William leaned back in his chair and drummed his fingers on the tablecloth. "What do you think, Jake?"

He'd just taken a swallow of coffee, and steam rose from the cup as he lowered it to the table. "I think Charlie needs a mama who loves him more than he needs the fool who fathered him."

"He needs both," William said firmly. "He needs a mother *and* a father. A young fellow who can teach him what he needs to know about being a man."

William gave Jake a meaningful look. Alex could have cut his tongue with scissors, but Jake didn't take the bait.

"I don't think that will be a problem, sir. If Mr. Hunnicutt isn't inclined to fatherhood, I'm sure your daughter will have her pick of men who'd make fine husbands.''

"I don't think you two have any right—"

"Like that doctor, for instance," Jake said, stifling a smile.

"He'd beat all hell out of Hunnicutt." Her father was dead serious. "Anyone would beat all hell out of that old man."

"Papa! Can't you show a little respect?"

"Not for a man who should know better than to marry a woman half his age!"

Jake's eyebrows shot up. "How old is he?"

"As old as the hills," William said. "As old as me."

"Will, that's enough," Katherine ordered. "He's younger than you are and you know it."

"He's got less hair than I do!"

"Papa!"

"Well, it's true. You said so yourself."

Jake looked like a cat with a bowl of cream. The question was begging to be asked. "Just how old is he?"

"As old as dirt!"

Alex gritted her teeth, William arched his eyebrows at her, and Katherine reached for her dignity as easily as she would have reached for a spoonful of sugar at a formal dinner.

"Mr. Hunnicutt just had his fifty-third birthday." She glared at her husband. "*Hair loss* is irrelevant to a man's good sense, as my husband's full white head will tell you. Now, you two go out and smoke those cigars while I finish in the kitchen, and Alex, take Charlie and get him ready for bed."

"I won't apologize, Alex," her father said. "You and I need to talk."

"All right. You speak your mind, and I'll speak mine."

"That's understood." William went out the door and called over his shoulder. "Jake, come out to the porch."

"One moment, sir." He turned to Alex. "Can I talk to you for a minute?"

"Not if it's about what you just heard."

She turned away, but his fingers curled around her arm. "I want to apologize."

"For what?" She saw irritation flash across his face. He didn't want to explain himself, but she was in no mood to be gracious. "What do you have to be sorry for?"

"Plenty, but that's not what I'm talking about. I should have watched my mouth back in town."

She couldn't resist the urge to make him squirm. "Are you referring to your rather personal reference to tits and whores?"

"You're not shy, are you?"

"Not in the least. Some things have to be said. My father must have given you the lecture. It goes something like, 'Respect my family or I'll tear you in half.'"

"Something like that."

"Well, he means it, but don't worry about watching your language. No one can cuss like my father when he's in an uproar. I've heard words you probably don't even know."

"I wouldn't bet on it."

"I don't make bets."

"That's good," he said, "because you'd lose this one."

A hint of battle lit his eyes, reminding her that she knew nothing about this man, where he'd been, what he'd done. She only knew that he'd helped her, and kissed her.

As Jake rested his hand on Charlie's back, the baby arched into his palm. He raised his hand to steady the baby's head just as Alex looked down, and his thumb grazed her throat. She felt the heat of him, but he didn't seem to notice, or care, that he had touched her.

"He looks a lot better," Jake said casually. "Food and clean clothes go a long way for a little boy."

"A man, too."

Jake was grinning as if he knew her secrets, which she supposed he did. He'd kissed her like Thomas never had, and they both knew it. Cuddling the baby, Alex retreated to the safety of good manners. "I want to thank you again for saving us."

"There wasn't much of a choice."

"You could have left us. You could be in New Mexico by now."

He shrugged. "You could have stayed in Leadville until the bridge was rebuilt."

"Maybe I should have." Looking back, she could see leaving the mining town had been a rash decision. "I hate to admit it, but my father was right."

"Maybe he's right about other things, too."

"Like what?"

"Like marrying a man as old as dirt."

Jake's mouth curved into a lazy smile, and tendrils of doubt curled in her belly. "My father lives in a world of his own."

"That doesn't mean he's wrong."

Something strange and sweet filled his voice as he touched her chin and tilted her face up to his. She felt like a child being told to look at the moon and the stars, but instead of the heavens she saw his eyes. He was sharing a secret with her and she took it for what it was, a gift of sorts, the knowledge he found her desirable.

His touch gave her power, as if she were cupping a fluttering bird in her hands. It was a wild and curious thing that wanted to be set free, and yet it was frightened, too.

His gaze traveled to her lips, and the bird flapped its wings in a panic. She felt the beat of it in her chest, in the whisper of his breath on her cheek. His fingers grazed her throat and she swallowed. Ridges of muscle flexed beneath his white shirt as he lowered his hand, stripping away her doubts.

The tiny bird wanted to explore the heavens, and he knew it as well as she did.

Chapter Six

The baby's cry was loud enough to wake the dead, and that's exactly how Jake felt when the shriek yanked him out of a deep sleep. After three days of pruning peach trees, his shoulders ached and his arms felt as if they'd been stretched to his knees. Even his legs throbbed from climbing up and down the stubby ladder.

After Katherine's fried chicken and a cigar with the old man, he'd excused himself and gone to bed. He'd been too tired to think, and it was a welcome relief from the notions that usually kept him awake.

The angel's room was next to his, and for the past three nights he'd listened to her womanly sounds as she undressed for bed and brushed her hair. He shouldn't have taken William's side about Hunnicutt, or brushed his fingers across her chin, but her engagement stank to high heaven, and between the edges of sleep and dawn, he dreamed of opening her eyes to a few basic facts and pleasures.

He didn't have that right, but he had the hunger. The ache in his groin had once been a welcome reason to buy some relief, but with Alex that pain was a nuisance, a reminder that he had no business lusting after an angel.

Jake punched the pillow into a ball and rolled onto his side. The baby's wail hurt his ears, and with that cry came the memory of the dream he'd been having. He'd seen Lettie sprawled on her back, pale and big with his child, moaning as Charlotte had in the desert. He'd been having flashes in his eyes since leaving Flat Rock, and a jagged bolt of light took him back to that last night.

Abbott had come at him through a whiskey-brown haze and swiped at the shot glass on the bar.

"You're going to marry her, Malone. I'll be damned if I get stuck raising your bastard child."

Jake sneered at him. "Who says it's mine?"

"She does!"

He'd turned his back on Abbott and crooked his finger for more whiskey. Crazed and raging, Lettie's brother had yanked him off the stool and landed a blow to his jaw that nearly took his head off. As customers scurried to the walls, the barkeep had bellowed for someone to run for Sheriff Malone.

With his brother's name ringing in his ears, Jake had picked up a stool and swung it hard at Abbott's head. The man ducked, and then he'd made the mistake of laughing. Sober, Jake could have taken him with one punch, but he'd been falling-down drunk that night. Looking back, he could find no other explanation for pulling his gun and firing straight at Abbott's chest.

He could still hear the buzz that filled the saloon as the man crumpled into a heap and started whimpering like a dying dog. Too drunk to care if Abbott lived or died, Jake had spat a mouthful of blood on the floor, wiped his face on his sleeve and turned to leave.

But in the doorway, he'd encountered his brother, huge and daunting, with knotted fists and a shiny badge. Gabe took in Abbott's wailing, the blood on them both, and the gun in Jake's hand. Shaking his head, he'd looked at his little brother as if he'd peed his pants in the middle of church.

Abbott howled in the corner. "Arrest him, Sheriff! He tried to kill me."

Like a fool, Jake had hocked up another mouthful of spit and let it fly. "Your sister's a whore, Abbott."

Gabe had been on him like rancid sweat, pounding his skull, spread-eagling him with his knees and shouting in his face. "You goddamned son of a bitch!"

Jake had been barely conscious when his brother yanked him to his feet and threw him out the door. "Get the hell outta here before I kill you myself!"

Somehow he'd climbed on his horse, rode to the shack of a house they had shared and packed his things. He had been about to slam the front door for the last time when he remembered a loose rock in the fireplace. Gabe had been careful to hide his savings, but Jake had a keen eye. He'd staggered back inside, pried out the stone and taken every cent Gabe had squirreled away. Even bleary-eyed, Jake had seen that it was enough to last awhile. His brother had been saving for something big, maybe a wife and a better house.

As he lifted the last greenback out of the crevice, he spotted the ring their mother had worn until the day she died. The tarnished setting held a tiny blue stone, nothing more than a chip. It wasn't worth much, but it was pretty and Jake wanted to keep it.

He had ridden south that night, and with his eyes nearly swollen shut, he wondered why his brother had let him go. Why hadn't he locked him up? It wasn't brotherly love.

I wish you'd never been born. I wish I'd never laid eyes on you.

And yet Gabe had raised him. He'd been seventeen years old, and Jake had been eight when Susannah Malone Prescott died of pneumonia, leaving her sons, half brothers and both fatherless, to fend for themselves.

Charlie's tortured cry pierced through Jake's thoughts, and he moaned. It was the most god-awful sound in the world.

Between the baby's wails, he heard Katherine hurry down the hall. Stopping outside the door, she said, "Oh, the poor boy."

"He's feverish. I can tell by holding him," Alex answered with a hitch in her voice.

"I think it's colic. We just have to wait it out."

Bending one knee beneath the sheet, Jake draped his forearm over his eyes. He wanted quiet, but there was none to be had.

In the middle of the upset, William thumped down the hall. "What's the matter with him?"

Hell, if Jake were smart, he'd roll over and wait out the storm.

But he wasn't smart, and the baby's cries were tearing at him. With a deep breath and muscles as tense as dried leather, he swung his legs over the side of the bed, pulled on his pants and walked into Charlie's room.

The Merritts were standing in a half circle. Alex was jiggling the baby and humming a desperate lullaby. Katherine's hair was half out of her cap, and William was standing between them in a red union suit. They looked as helpless as Charlie.

"I'll put on my boots and go for the doc," Jake said.

The three of them stared, and Jake wished he'd put on a shirt. Alex's jaw dropped, which he liked. Katherine put on her dinner party face, and William glared and said, "Let Jake handle things. I'm going back to bed."

"But Papa, what if—"

"He's not dying. If you need Winters, send Jake."

With that, William plodded down the hall, and Jake wished he'd never opened the door. "I'll get my boots."

"Not yet," Katherine said. "Babies have upsets all the time, and Charlie has more reason than most. I think it's colic."

"He sounds like he's gut-shot."

"We'll give him some time. Go back to bed, and we'll get you if we need you."

His gaze traveled to Alex just as Charlie arched his back and screamed. She had tears in her eyes as she pressed him against her breast. Katherine took his arm and steered him down the hall. "It's okay, Jake. You're not used to this."

"That's the truth."

He hated the sounds, the smells, the misery of the night, the closeness of them all. He couldn't stand his room, so he yanked on a shirt without bothering to button it, wandered barefoot down to the porch, and sat in the swing where William always smoked his evening cigar.

Crossing his arms over his chest, he leaned back in the swing. He could still hear the baby through the open windows, but he wasn't paying attention. At least not until the crying came closer, until the screen door swung open and Alex nearly sat on him.

"Oh! I didn't know you were out here."

She turned to leave, but he touched her arm. "Stay."

She hesitated. Either William or Kath had put the rocker back in the house, and dew had dampened the other chair. Wearing only a plain cotton nightgown and a thin wrapper, she shivered as she looked down at his bent knees. The only seat was on the swing, next to him.

If he'd been a gentleman, he would have fetched the rocker. Instead he slid over and patted the space next to him. "I can take him if your arm needs a rest."

"That's all right. He's as light as a feather."

Shifting on her bare feet, she rocked Charlie and crooned to him, swaying in the moonlight like a silver bell. Just when Jake started to feel like a heel for not getting the rocker, she sat next to him. Arching his back, Charlie screamed again.

"My mother thinks it's gas."

Jake smothered a smile. Growing up with Gabe and without a woman's influence, it had been a while before he understood belching and farting weren't considered sports by everyone.

"Could be a problem," he said, biting back a smile. He expected Alex to blush, but the baby's bodily functions didn't bother her one bit. She wasn't timid or prim, though she was careful to keep to her side of the swing.

Jake's legs stretched a mile longer than hers, and he rocked for the three of them. The gentle sway lulled them all, and he fought the urge to wrap his arm around her shoulder, to feel her hair brushing against his hand.

Her feet just barely touched the ground, and the rhythm made it hard for her to sit up straight. Her left shoulder sagged, and her hips slid an inch closer to his.

She shifted the baby to her shoulder, and her elbow grazed his ribs.

His shirt slid sideways, exposing a trace of dark chest hair and tanned skin. Her cheeks flushed. It didn't take a genius to know she'd never seen a bare-chested man until tonight, and Jake rather liked being the first. He sat still as her eyes roamed from his abdomen, down his legs to his bare feet. Her cheeks turned a little pinker, and he was absolutely sure she had never seen a size-twelve foot outside of a boot before.

Stifling a grin, he wiggled his toes.

"Your feet are huge!"

"They're big, that's a fact."

When she stuck out her foot and held it next to his, he knew for sure that Alexandra Merritt was brave in all the ways that mattered, and that she wouldn't run if the moonlight got to him and he kissed her senseless.

It was tempting. She was still staring at his foot, and kissing her would have been as easy as shooting fish in a barrel. Two weeks ago he would have already tasted her lips, maybe even had his hand on her breast, inside her nightgown, massaging her bare flesh.

Where would she draw the line?

The baby in her arms made it impossible for him to find out, but looking at her delicate foot, he realized he didn't want to know. Not once had he drawn a line for himself where women were concerned, mostly because they didn't care and neither did he.

But Alex was different. She cared too easily and too much for lost little boys and bruised men. He didn't want to hurt her or take advantage of her trust, and that meant not kissing her tonight, even if her lips were pink and curious.

Jake put his bare foot back on the porch and set the

swing in motion. Alex took a breath and rested her cheek on the crown of the baby's head. Charlie sucked on his hand, filling the space between them with tiny smacking sounds.

"Is he feeling any better?" Jake asked.

"A little bit. He likes to rock."

The creaking soothed the baby, and Jake, too, though the rhythm was slow, suggestive of the things he wanted from her but wouldn't take. Alex leaned back, tilted her face up to the starry sky and closed her eyes. She had to be exhausted, and he flashed back to storm in the desert and her body pressed safely against his. He wouldn't kiss her, but that didn't mean he couldn't provide a bit of comfort.

Stretching his arm across the back of the swing, he pulled her close and pressed her head against his shoulder. She sighed, and he thought of willow trees brushing the surface of a lake. Snuggling closer, she pulled her legs up on the swing and tucked her toes under the wrapper.

"I pray to God he's okay," she said. "I don't know what I'd do if we lost him now."

Jake didn't have an answer. He rarely thought beyond the moment, but the angel had a broader view of life.

"You'd go on," he said, wanting to encourage her.

"I would, but I wouldn't like it."

Whether out of comfort or exhaustion, Jake didn't know, but Charlie finally fell asleep. As the tension seeped from his tiny body, it left Alex, too, and she sank deeper into his arms. The heat of her skin seeped through his loose shirt. He smelled Charlie's milky scent and felt Alex's hair wisping on his fingers. He didn't move a muscle, and her breathing took on a slow cadence that matched his.

The night went silent except for her breath, low and even and sure, and it became the most natural thing in the world to be sitting in a swing holding a woman and a baby, waiting for dawn.

William woke up with the sun. Katherine was curled at his side, breathing deeply, and he was glad because she needed the rest. The baby had scared them last night, and though he didn't want to admit it, William was fond of the kid even though he brought back memories of that shameful night twenty years ago.

Alex should have had brothers and sisters, and there would have been at least one if he hadn't been such a fool. Rolling on his side and peering out the window, William watched the sun rise over the distant hills. As he did every morning, he took it as proof of God's mercy and the promise of new beginnings.

He needed that assurance as much as any man and more than some. A long time ago he'd forgiven himself for those drowning years, but they'd left bloody gashes on his family, and the scars ran deep. He had to wonder if Alex would have had an easier time finding love, a husband, if she had grown up with the teasing of a brother, or a baby sister whining, "Take me with you."

He hadn't missed the look she gave Jake last night. Her eyes widened as if she'd never seen a healthy bare-chested man in her life, and William supposed she hadn't. It was a crying shame, from his point of view. He wanted her to have all the joys of love, the best of everything, a family of her own.

With a loud harrumph, William pulled on a pair of dungarees and rammed his arms into a fresh shirt. After putting on his socks and boots, he was ready for his morning walk.

The front door squeaked as he stepped onto the porch where the whispery breath of life caught his ear. His gaze traveled to the swing, where Alex and Charlie were asleep in Jake's arms. She looked young and pretty, but it was Jake who made William stop.

The bruises had faded to shadows, and the deep lines around his mouth were gone. He'd gotten younger overnight, and William saw that, like his daughter, Jake's life had been turned upside down. He'd gotten old before he had a chance to be young.

William tiptoed down the steps. There was no point in waking them up, at least not until he'd had his morning walk. As always, he had a lot to say to God.

Chapter Seven

"You can't marry him."

Alex looked at her father across the breakfast table and took another bite of toast. It was her fourth piece, and slathered with her mother's too-sweet jam, it tasted like home. She swallowed and dabbed at a smear of strawberry on her cheek.

"I'm an adult, Papa. Marrying Thomas is the right thing to do."

"Then convince me."

But how could she convince her father that marrying Thomas was the right thing to do when she doubted it herself?

Two days ago she had woken up with her cheek pressed against Jake Malone's hard shoulder, with his masculine scent filling her nose and his fingers stroking her hair. How long had he been awake? She didn't know. He was bleary-eyed and boyish except for the stubble on his chin, and she had wanted to touch his face.

And she might have, except Charlie's diaper had soaked her sleeve and he woke up hungry. What did a woman say to a man at the crack of dawn? She didn't know, but Charlie had broken the mood with a bitter whine.

"I had better go inside," she'd said.

"Yeah, me, too."

And that had been the end of it. She had no business remembering that his toes were long and straight, that his chest rose two inches with every breath he took, that his skin smelled like a hot summer day.

She had been up most of last night thinking about Jake, wondering about his past and why he was headed for California, and then just before dawn the snakebite had turned red and tender. Her bones ached with fever, as if his touch had seeped into her. She had come downstairs intending to make a poultice and take it back to bed, but her father was at the table, waiting for her with two cups of coffee.

With his billowing white hair, he reminded her of Old Man Winter. His words came at her like cold gusts of wind.

"Tell me you love this man more than life itself."

Toast crumbs stuck to her fingers, and she resisted the urge to lick them off. "Thomas is a good man, and I respect him. I want a husband and he needs a wife."

William clapped his hand to his forehead and moaned. "Please don't tell me you're marrying this man because he *needs* you."

"Yes, I am." Alex took a long swallow of coffee, set the cup on the table, and pulled the wrapper tight across her chest. "I'm twenty-seven years old, Papa, and I want a home of my own. Thomas is decent and honorable. I hope you'll like him when you get to know him."

"What *I* think of the man isn't important. I'm not

the one who has to look him in the eye every morning.''

''That's true,'' she said quietly. ''It's my decision, but I'd like your blessing.''

''Would you marry him without it?''

She didn't know. ''I'd rather not find out.''

William rested his hands on the kitchen table, squared his shoulders and frowned. His eyes dimmed from Irish blue to gray, and knowing he was about to dig deeper, she steeled herself for his velvet-hammer voice.

''Can you see spending the rest of your life with this man, Alex? A marriage needs glue to hold it together. It needs passion. Do you have that with Hunnicutt?''

''I *respect* him. That's more than some people ever have, and it's enough for a good marriage.''

''It isn't.'' Her father's gaze pinned her to the chair. ''There's only one thing that stopped your mother from throwing me out twenty years ago, and it sure as hell wasn't respect.''

Alex tensed at the memory. She had been seven years old, but she could still hear him shouting in the slurred voice that meant he'd been drinking. Hiding under her blanket, she heard a gasp and a scream. The smell of whiskey had been everywhere, and her mother had—

Blocking the ugly picture, Alex wiped her fingers on the napkin in her lap. A chain of pink roses lined the worn edges, and she could see her mother's fingers forcing a needle through the linen, mending their lives one stitch at a time.

Her father's eyes glistened, and he cleared his throat. ''The truest kind of love kept us together after that night. God knows, I didn't deserve your mother's forgiveness.''

He hadn't touched a drop of liquor since and never would again. "You changed, too," she said.

"How could I not? I love your mother. I love you too, and that's why I can't let you marry Thomas without saying things that need to be said."

"Go ahead."

"All right. If Thomas were the man you say he is, he wouldn't marry you for convenience."

"He has great affection for me."

"That's not enough."

"But it has to be." It was all she'd ever have. Why couldn't he see that? He was drumming his fingers on the table. Alex heard time passing in that beat, and she knew he wasn't finished, and that he'd saved the deepest truth for last.

"You want children," he said.

"Yes."

"And Thomas has no children of his own."

She knew what was coming. "Yes, that's true. The boys were Rebecca's from her first marriage."

"Do you know what a chance you're taking? He can't give you children. If you really loved him, I could understand, but friendship isn't what God had in mind when he said that 'two shall become one flesh.'"

Her throat swelled with longing. "I'm accepting the facts of the situation. Is that wrong?"

He shook his head. "Not always, but this marriage is wrong for you, Alex. We both know you want children."

"And that's why we're going to adopt Charlie."

William leaned back in the chair and crossed his

arms over his chest. "You don't have to marry Thomas to keep the baby."

"Yes, I do." Her voice stayed steady. "I want to adopt him legally. I don't want to take a chance that a stranger will show up and take him away."

"Judge Brown is a friend of mine. He'd help us make it permanent, without Hunnicutt."

The offer tempted her. Yes, she had obligations in Philadelphia, a purpose, a ten-year history, but she also had roots in Colorado. They were long and deep, growing in her body, stretching in fertile soil as she absorbed the heat and light of her family's love.

Abruptly she walked to the stove where the coffeepot was still warm. She filled her cup and turned back to the table where her father wiped his nose with a wrinkled handkerchief.

"Damn cold," he muttered.

A gray film tinged his skin. He was sick and getting old. The need to throw herself into his arms was sharp, nearly bitter, but instead she said, "Staying here isn't that simple."

"It could be. It might even be your best hope for keeping the baby. Have you written Thomas yet?"

She shook her head. "I don't know what to say."

"He doesn't want children, does he?"

"No, but I think he'll change his mind."

Her father's eyes narrowed to a squint. "If he loves you at all, he'll be here in a month with a wedding band and adoption papers. If not, wash your hands of him, Alex. He's not the man for you."

An exhausted whoosh escaped from his lips, as if time were leaking out of him. He pushed back from the table, stood at the window and crossed his arms over his chest.

Her gaze followed his to the western sky. The air was pure and crystalline, and she saw grass rippling in the pale light. She remembered the openness of the Colorado Plateau and the vastness of the sky, the sudden longing to shout and dance, and the heat of Jake's mouth on hers.

The residue of coffee turned sharp on her tongue. She poured a cup of fresh water from a porcelain pitcher, raised it to her lips and took a long swallow. It was fresh compared to the brackish water she had gulped from Jake's canteen, but it didn't quench her thirst.

William was still at the window when she heard Jake walking up the back steps. The door swung wide and, ambling across the kitchen, he took off his hat and hung it on a peg. His hair was loose and long, as dark as a bird's wing glistening in the sun. Her blood stirred, and warmth radiated through her belly.

"Good morning, Miss Merritt."

Her fingers tensed around the cup of water. "Good morning."

Jake started to pull up a chair, but he stopped in midreach. "Jeez, old man! Are you all right?"

Alex whirled toward her father. He was hunched with his right hand splayed across his chest. Jake grabbed his arm and slid a chair behind his knees. William slumped back and blew out a breath. His face was the color of ash.

"Can you breathe?" Jake asked.

"Just give me a minute."

Jake gave him a pointed stare. "I'll give you two, and then I'm going to ride like hell for the doctor."

Her father nodded, a tiny confession meant for Jake alone, and Alex panicked. "I'll get Mama."

"No!"

"Papa, you've got to lie down."

"He'll be fine, Alex." Jake sat in the chair next to William and glanced at her. "Why don't you pour me a cup of coffee?"

Coffee? How could he even think of it, and yet it gave her something to do. Her whole body shook as she poured. Pale brown drops splashed like tears on the counter and beaded on the varnished wood. She handed the cup to Jake, nearly spilling it on his chest until he steadied it with both hands. His fingers were cool against hers, and strong.

"I've got it," he said gently.

She slid her hand out from under his, and he took a careful swallow. His eyes never left William.

Her father cleared his throat with a sharp cough. The ceiling creaked, and Alex thought of her mother pinning up her hair, as if this were an ordinary day.

Tipping his chin up to the ceiling, William settled back in the chair and closed his eyes. This was not the time for pride or privacy or even protectiveness, and Alex took a step into the hallway.

Her father held up his hand. "Don't upset her yet."

Yet. He was telling her they had time, but Alex couldn't bear the tension. She looked to Jake for help, but he was sipping coffee as casually as he had once told her that rattlesnake tasted like chicken. Propping an ankle on his knee, he leaned back in the chair and eyed William.

"Any better?" he asked.

Her father grunted. "I'm not paying you to baby-sit me. Don't you have something else to do?"

Jake laced his fingers behind his neck and stretched as if he had all the time in the world. "Moses isn't here, but I'll get started. Which quarter do you want thinned today?''

Alex gaped at the two men. "This can wait! I can't believe you're asking about peaches when—"

William silenced her with a look. "Jake's doing the right thing. We're behind as it is."

"But Papa—"

He shook his head. "I've had these pains before, and I'll have them again. I'm counting on you to be strong, Miss Merri."

The nickname was a command and a caress, and she swallowed the cry in her throat. William laid his palm on the table and gave instructions to Jake.

"The thinning has to get done this week. If Moses isn't here, it means he's not coming. I'll give you a hand this afternoon, after I rest a little."

Alex opened her mouth again, but Jake cut her off. "You'll just be in the way."

Her father had finally met his match, and he grunted like an old bear who wasn't quite ready for winter. "We'll see about that."

"Oh no, we won't," Alex said. "I'll help with the thinning."

Her father frowned. "You've never done it before."

"Neither had Jake until two days ago. I'm perfectly capable of following directions. How hard can it be?"

William nodded. "How's your arm healing up?"

"It's better." It was only a partial lie. The wound was red and hot, but the skin had knit together.

"All right then. Go change your clothes. Jake can tell you what to do."

Alex hurried up the stairs to her parents' room, where her mother was making the bed. Touching the older woman's arm, she said, "Papa had pains again, but they stopped."

Katherine dropped the sheet and pressed her palms against her cheeks. "Dear Lord, I wish the doctor could do something."

Both women knew Winters had given William a new medicine called digitalis, but it hadn't helped. The pains came without warning, and nothing but time could make them stop. Needing to put things in place, Alex reached down and smoothed the sheet. "I can't believe it, Mama. He insists on working this afternoon."

"I'd tie him to a chair if I thought it would do any good."

Alex looked into her mother's eyes and saw a world of hurt and worry. Her parents needed help, but tying William to a chair was like trying to stop the Gunnison River, and hired hands weren't the answer, either. Whether he liked it or not, they all had to face a few facts.

"We need to talk, Mama, the three of us. It's time to sell the farm and move to Philadelphia."

Her mother took Alex's hand in both of hers and squeezed. "I'd like to be close to you, and your Aunt Livy, too, but this is home. We won't leave."

"But it's too much work for you."

"We manage. Jake's here now, and Moses helps out."

"He didn't show up this morning, and Jake's just here for the summer. What then?"

"We'll have to wait and see, but Philadelphia is out of the question."

"But—"

"I'm serious, Alex. Your father would hate living back East."

Knowing a lost cause when she saw one, Alex walked to the window, where she saw Jake striding into the barn.

"I'll drop it for now," she said. "But only because there's work to do. I'm helping with the thinning. Do you have an old dress I could wear, or pants, even?"

Katherine opened the wardrobe and took out an old muslin jumper. "This ought to fit you," she said, holding the garment up to the light.

Alex's stomach did a flip. It was shapeless and the color of rotten nuts. "Do you have something a little less...ugly?"

Her mother lowered her arms and the fabric puddled like mud on the floor. Her eyes locked on her daughter's face. "You like him, don't you?"

There was no point in being coy. "Yes, I do."

"He's a drifter, Alex. You don't know where he's been, or what he's done."

"It doesn't matter. I know what he did for the baby and for me, and now for Papa." And she remembered waking up in his arms and seeing his face in her dreams, the taste of his kiss, the smell of his clean skin.

"You don't know anything about this man."

"I know he's good with Charlie. He works hard and he's kind."

"That's not enough." Katherine draped the brown dress over her arm. "He could be running from the law, or a wife, or God knows what."

But Alex didn't believe any of those things. Jake had earned her trust, and her father had given him his respect as well. Shaking her head, she said, "Papa likes him."

Her mother let out a small groan. "Your father has brought home more stray dogs than I can count."

It was true. William collected lost souls like a city dogcatcher. Sometimes he made a friend for life, but most of the people he scavenged didn't leave much of themselves behind. But that wouldn't be true of Jake. Alex had the proof on her arm, a throbbing wound that would turn into a crescent-shaped scar.

"He's different," she said.

Katherine's fingers knotted on the brown cloth, and she sighed. "I like him, too. I just don't want to see you get hurt."

"Maybe it's worth the risk. I can't lie to myself, Mama. Something in me is changing. Papa says I'm settling for Thomas. I told him he didn't understand, but he does."

"Your father has a good heart, but he's not very practical."

"But maybe he's right. Maybe it would be a mistake to marry Thomas. I'm not even sure I want to go back to Philadelphia."

Katherine studied her daughter's face. "God knows I want you to stay, but that's not the kind of decision you should make lightly. Promise me you'll think things through, Alex. Promise me you'll be careful."

"Of Jake."

"Yes."

"He's been a perfect gentleman."

"Yes, he has, but he's still a stranger and he might not play by your rules."

Alex walked to the dresser and ran her finger along the edge of a silver frame holding a photograph of her parents. "You and Papa eloped. You broke the rules. Have you ever been sorry?"

"Not even once." Katherine's gaze moved from her daughter's face to the unsmiling photograph that somehow still held love, then to the brown jumper, coarse and frayed, old before its time. With a sigh, she tossed the dress on the bed. "I'll be right back.

She disappeared around the corner and Alex heard the squeak of the pull-down ladder and the scrape of a trunk being moved. A minute later her mother came into the bedroom with an armload of men's clothing.

"What's that?" Alex asked.

"This is what I wore when we first came here." She handed Alex a pair of pants and a chambray work shirt embroidered with tiny yellow roses. "I helped in the orchard until we had enough money to hire help."

Alex held the shirt up to the light, tucked it under her chin and held out the sleeves as if they were wings.

Don't let the door hit you in the ass.

Jake thought of his brother at the oddest times. William Merritt was sitting in the kitchen looking like a man who'd been kicked by a mule, the angel had flown up the stairs with that white robe fluttering behind her, and Jake was left to wonder how in tarnation he'd ended up running a peach orchard.

It wasn't a bad place to be, except that he didn't belong.

He was three steps away from the house when the back door banged shut. He could almost hear Gabe laughing. *A wolf in sheep's clothing, that's what you are. Sure you talk pretty, but you're not good for squat when things need doing. Why, I remember...*

Jake remembered, too. He remembered being eight years old, struggling with a splitting maul and a round of pine. He remembered cooking for his brother, because it was just the two of them and that was his job. He'd gotten good at it, and he smiled at the memory of last night's beef stew.

As he walked through the back door at supper time, Katherine held up a spoonful for him to taste.

"More salt?" she asked.

He shook his head. "It's perfect. Bay leaf, right?"

She cocked her head like a baffled Rhode Island Red. "You know how to cook."

She was too gracious to ask more questions, and Jake liked that consideration. He took it as kindness and figured William and Alex were the luckiest people on earth.

Except William was dying.

Jake knew about his bad heart, but it wasn't until this morning that he had seen eternity rising like a river in the old man's eyes. It scared the crap out of him, though it wasn't death that made Jake shiver. It was the here-and-now needs of the old man's family. With that tiny nod meant for Jake alone, William had grabbed him by the balls and squeezed.

I'm counting on you.

He hadn't actually spoken the words, but Jake saw the message in his eyes as plainly as he saw the sun in the sky. It blinded him for a moment, but he nodded back, accepting the fact that he'd be the one to ride for help, to look after the women, even dig William's grave if it came to that.

Jake had been relieved beyond measure when William caught his breath, but it didn't change the fact that the old man needed him. It was too late in the growing season to hire regular help. If Jake left now, William would work himself to death, and Alex and her mother

would be left with a thousand peaches rotting in
the sun.

In spite of his best intention to run if things got bad,
Jake couldn't let that happen. He hated the thought of
Alex and her mother struggling.

"Well, I'll be damned," he muttered. William Merritt had nailed Jake's big foot to the floor with a ten-
penny nail.

Shaking his head, Jake unlatched the barn door and
stepped into the gray shadows. He'd been reeled in like
a dead fish, but he wasn't the least bit dead to the things
a man took comfort in. He wouldn't pass up a bottle
of whiskey if one came his way, and keeping his hands
off Alex took more effort than leaving a warm bed on
a cold morning.

But he'd made up his mind. He'd keep his distance.
More than a week had passed since he'd taken the job,
and he was still staying in the guest room because William insisted on buying a new cot before Jake moved
into the barn. Having her that close gave him an endless, low-bellied hunger. More than once, he'd considered riding into Grand Junction for a night of drinking
and paid-for sex, but he didn't want the old man to
smell it on him.

Jake had already milked the cow and fed the horses,
and they were lazily munching hay, even his skittish
bay. William made a habit of patting the horse and
calling him Smiley when he walked by the stall, and
Jake stopped to scratch the animal's ears.

The gelding shoved his head at Jake as if he couldn't
get enough, and thinking of the cigars William shared
with him, Jake obliged the animal with a long scratch.

Every night after supper, the Merritts sat on the
porch for an hour or so, and Jake was part of that habit.

Kath and Alex left first, venturing upstairs to see to the baby, and William would hand him a cigar. Smoking in the dark, the two men talked about peaches, politics and life.

Jake was grateful for those quiet nights, but he still didn't belong here.

You're nothing but dirt, little brother.

Gabe's voice was particularly loud today, and Jake wondered what corners he would have turned if a man like William had ridden shotgun on him. Of course, it was too late now. He was probably wanted for murder, and his bastard child would be born in just over a month.

It was a haunting thought. Foals found their feet and suckled their mothers, but a human baby was the most helpless thing he had ever seen. He could count on one hand the times he'd given anybody something worth having, and Charlie's life was at the top of that short list.

Until now, he had been the kind of man who took what he wanted, maybe because so much had been taken from him. His childhood, schooling, even his own name. He'd been Jackson Jacob Prescott until his mother died. She called him Jackson, but Gabe shortened it to Jake. It was less confusing to go by Malone as well.

Jake gave Smiley a last scratch. He should have been in Arizona by now, maybe even over the Mexican border. He still liked the idea of paid-for sex and tequila, but the appeal wasn't as strong as it had been a few minutes ago. In fact, his fingers were itching to get at the trees.

Jake walked to the wall, where he found the ladder, a pole with a rag-covered tip, a rake and two pairs of leather gloves. He pulled the biggest pair over his fingers and stuffed the smaller ones into his back pocket. Thoughts of the angel's hands getting dirty and torn made him weak inside.

He'd be looking at her all day, wondering if her muscles were aching with the hard work. He'd want to rub her shoulders and sneak a touch now and then. His decision to mind his manners would have been easier to honor if she stayed out of his way, but there was no stopping her. She'd pick buds till her fingers bled if it would help her father, and he had to respect that.

Jake walked down a row of trees with the ladder in one hand and the rake and pole in the other. He and Moses had thinned half of the trees. Working alone, he'd be done in two days. With Alex's help, it would be either one day or four, depending on how much she distracted him.

He liked being close to her when he was dressed for supper in borrowed clothes, but alone in the orchard, he'd have to keep a leash on his bad habits. It was easy to flirt with women, to tempt and tease them, but Alex deserved more. Any woman who could stare down a stranger with two black eyes, kiss him senseless, shove a baby in his arms and make him apologize for bad language was a real prize.

She deserved a man who could hold his own in the world, and that, Jake reminded himself, was the point.

Alexandra Merritt deserved more than he had to give, and that meant he had to keep his hands to himself. It wouldn't be easy, though. She couldn't hide her feelings worth a damn. She liked him a lot more than was safe, a lot more than an almost-married woman should have.

Damn it all, he could still feel her pressed against

him on the swing, asleep in his arms. It brought back memories of kissing her in the desert. His mind ran wild, and he pictured her naked in his bed, curious, wanting, all creamy skin and long hair, with those doe-brown eyes inviting him to teach her things.

Moaning out loud, he whacked at a tree with the pole. Pink blossoms fluttered to the ground like angel wings, and he thought of her skin. He dropped the pole and shoved the ladder against the trunk. Climbing into the lush foliage, he remembered her sweet eyes and clenched his teeth.

There was no choice in the matter. He had to keep the angel at arm's length. He'd be the biggest heel in the world if he did anything else. Worse than low, lower than a skunk, slimier than pond scum, ranker than the mud on the bottom of a well.

You're as horny as an owl, little brother. Don't go doing the ladies any favors.

Gabe was right. Absolutely, positively right.

Jake pulled at a high branch, yanked off a handful of buds and hurled them to the ground. The branch snapped back at the sun, and he grabbed another one, and one after that, until the ground was littered with unwanted fruit.

His mood was foul and black when he saw Alex. She was wearing trousers that showed off her hips and a tailored shirt that gaped at her throat. She had woven her lush hair into a neat braid, but a satiny strand had already worked itself loose, curling around her ear. Just looking at her made him want her.

But worst of all, he saw the look in her eyes. Alexandra Merritt was in the mood to kick death in the teeth.

Jake hated the thought of doing what had to be done.

It was worse than putting that mule out of its misery. He'd be cool and polite to her, but if that didn't do the trick, he'd have to singe her once, or even twice if that's what it took to protect her from his bad habits.

It was like teaching a child not to touch a hot stove. A tiny tap would hurt, but the lesson had be learned.

Chapter Eight

Lacing her hands behind her back, Alex looked at Jake's dusty boots. His big feet were perched on separate rungs of the ladder, and his worn dungarees hugged his backside. Her gaze traveled from his hips to his narrow waist, but the rest of him was lost in the thick canopy of leaves.

"Where should I start?" she asked.

A branch waved at the top of the tree, and a handful of buds fell to the ground. He ducked out of the foliage without climbing down from the ladder and glanced at her. Except for a small crescent-shaped bruise below his right eye, his face had healed.

"I can do this alone," he said evenly.

Disappointment rippled through her. She wanted him to climb down the ladder and stand close to her, to touch her hands as he showed her how to pluck the buds, but instead he buried his head back in the leaves.

It would be a long afternoon if he wouldn't talk to her. Fingering a blossom, she said, "I'll be useful once I get the hang of it."

"You'll be in the way."

"I'm staying. If I go back to the house, my father will come out here and he's got to rest."

"He'd be in the way, too."

"What's your problem this morning?"

He gave the branch a good shake. "I don't need help."

"Well, you're stuck with me." She picked up the pole and held it awkwardly in one hand. "What's this for?"

"I'm done with it. Just leave it be."

What had upset him? Was it seeing her father so ill, or having more work than he bargained for? Neither of those explanations made sense to Alex, but he wasn't about to explain his foul mood, and she wasn't about to leave. "I'm staying here whether you like it or not."

More buds fell at her feet.

"Have it your way, then," he finally said. "You do the lower branches and I'll get the higher ones. You want to break up the clusters of fruit, and leave the buds so that they're six to eight inches apart on the branch. Pull anything that's flawed, and leave the biggest ones."

"I can manage that." She reached into the tree with her bare hands. Leaves tickled her face as she ran her fingers along the branch and reached for a small pink flower.

"You'll need these."

Still scowling, Jake pulled a pair of gloves out of his back pocket and tossed them to her. She caught them against her chest. The leather was warm from his body and as soft as new skin.

"Thank you," she said.

Aware of his gaze on her hands, she wiggled her fingers into the leather and stretched until her nails grazed the rough seams at the tips. Bending down, she ducked under the lowest branch and inspected the flowers and their pea-sized centers. Picking the smallest one, she tugged but it didn't budge.

The branches over her head went still, and she looked through the tiers of leaves. Jake's gaze was on her hands.

"You have to be a little bit ruthless," he said. "Give each bud a good yank, throw it on the ground and grab another one."

William understood people. Telling Jake to be ruthless was like telling a bird to fly, but the same advice didn't work for Alex. She didn't have a mean bone in her body. By the time she had taken off six buds, Jake had torn off more than two dozen. He worked quickly while she dallied, trying to decide which buds to leave and which ones to pluck.

"We'll be here all day if you can't figure out how to be a little less particular," he said irritably.

"I want to leave the best ones. My father says thinning a peach tree is a test of character. Did he tell you that?"

"No."

"You have to find the balance between sweetness and plenty," she explained. "You can't be greedy and leave too much fruit on the tree or it won't be sweet enough to sell, and you can't be shy about doing what has to be done."

Jake let another handful of buds drop to the ground. "Seems to me you're on the shy side when it comes to this."

"No. I'm just careful. I'll get the hang of it."

"Try twisting the stem. It's easier."

The next bud popped off easily. Jake's gaze stayed

on her back, changing from warmth to heat to a pink burn. She looked up and caught him staring. Blinking, he climbed higher and reached for a heavy branch, as if nothing but the fruit mattered.

Out of the blue, he said, "How's your father doing?"

"He's lying down. My mother will keep an eye on him."

"Someone has to."

He tried to sound gruff, but his voice had a catch in it. Her stomach fluttered. He cared about her father, her mother. Maybe even her.

"Do you have any family?" she asked.

He took a full minute to break the silence. "I have a brother."

"That must be nice. I always wanted a sister. You know how it is, someone who knows all the same jokes, has the same memories. Like my mother and my aunt. They're very close."

"It's not all fun and games."

"Of course not, but it's not all bad, either."

His fingers raced across the branch as if he couldn't move fast enough, while hers moved through the leaves as if she were combing a child's hair. Searching for a common ground, she plunged ahead with questions as if they had just met.

"The other night you said you were from Virginia. I've been to Washington a few times. Have you ever been there?"

"Nope."

"Are you from down South? Near Richmond?"

A dozen blossoms sailed past her ear before he said, "I was born near Fredericksburg, but it's none of your business."

"It was just a friendly question," she said gently. "I'm not asking you anything personal."

"Everything's personal with you."

"No, it's not." This was small talk, nothing more than a way to fill the too-silent air. "I'm just being friendly. It'll be a long day if we can't get along."

He climbed down the ladder and swung it to her side of the tree. She didn't hurry to get out of his way. If he wanted space between them, he'd have to put it there. Bending down on one knee, she twisted a blossom until it came loose in her hand. His eyes burned holes in her back as he waited, but she refused to be cowed. She took off a dozen more buds before she stood up and removed the gloves.

Cool air skimmed her hands. Remote and oddly detached, his hard blue gaze softened as he looked at her skin. She sensed an ache behind his eyes, a tremor in his clenched jaw. Flexing her fingers, she decided to take a different approach.

"Can I ask you something?" she said. "Something about Charlie?"

Lifting the ladder with one hand, he carried it past her, leaned it against the tree and climbed up to the third rung. "That depends on what you want to know."

"Do you think anyone is looking for him?"

Jake shook his head. "Probably not. He's worth less than a lost penny."

"That's an awful thing to say. He's a human being."

"The kid's father probably doesn't give a damn."

"But he should know he has a son."

"What for? So he can feel guilty, or send money, or—hell, I don't know. What do you want from him?"

"I want to keep the baby, and I don't want a stranger showing up in a year and taking him away."

"That won't happen."

"But it's not right." Shaking her head, Alex studied Jake's face. Deep lines shaped his mouth, and his eyes resembled a stormy sky, tense and ready to explode.

"If you'll excuse my language," he said with more than a touch of sarcasm, "that kid's father was after a cheap roll in the hay. Charlie was an accident."

"An accident or not, he needs love. He needs a home. He's *entitled* to those things."

Jake tugged at his gloves. "Miss Merritt, you are truly the most naive person I've ever met."

"That's not true. I've seen plenty of misery. I've been to plenty of rough neighborhoods. I know what people are capable of doing to each other, especially to children."

He grunted and grabbed another branch. "Seeing meanness and living with it aren't the same thing. Something tells me all your stories have happy endings."

"Most of them do. That's the idea of the Children's League."

"Just what is this do-gooder league?"

"We run the Rebecca Hunnicutt Home for Girls, and when we can, we place abandoned children in good homes."

"Now, isn't that nice."

"Yes, it *is* nice. It's a lot more than *nice.* Would you like to hear about the twelve-year-old girl who was raped by her stepfather, or about the babies with bottoms so sore from filth they can't sit down?"

"Both."

"Most people don't want to hear any of it."

His gaze held a warning, a piercing light hard

enough to cut glass, and she knew this man understood sin and suffering in his bone marrow.

"Hell, I'm not most people," he said.

He waited, and she thought of two strangers arriving at an open door at the same time. *You first... No, you, please... No, I insist...*

Jake wasn't about to walk through that door, and so instead of arguing, she gave him a simple smile. His mouth softened, an invitation, as if he would be happy to hold the door for her, but not follow.

"I could talk for hours about the children," she said.

"We've got all day."

Dozens of stories poured out of her. She told him about the first hungry child she had seen alone on the street, and how she had taken the little girl to a church where a dozen other children had found help. It had been the beginning of a crusade. She'd gone to the Philadelphia Women's League and asked for money, opened an office and started a foundation that placed orphans in good homes. The Children's League had a seven-year history of success. It was rewarding work, a life of happy endings, except for the limits of what she could do.

From the beginning, Rebecca and Thomas Hunnicutt had been her biggest supporters. When Rebecca died, her husband donated the funds to build a home for orphaned girls to honor her memory. Alex had been thrilled and humbled by the gift.

Jake grunted occasionally and asked a question or two. She told him about Alice, who had been attacked in the household where her mother was a maid. About Hazel, beaten and left for dead. About the way children hid food under their pillows and stole when they were afraid of going hungry. About little boys who fought like demons to protect their sisters.

The torrent of words eased to a stream and finally to a trickle. She heard Jake mutter to himself, something like, "God help us all."

Questions swirled through her mind. What misery had he known? What had he done to end up alone on the Colorado Plateau? Who had given him those clear blue eyes and saddled him with a worthless name like Jacob?

Alex hated that name. It meant "schemer" or "heel grabber." The biblical Jacob had been born minutes after his twin. When his father saw him grab his brother's ankle, as if to steal his birthright, he gave his second son a name that branded him as less than his brother, less than others.

Jake was still standing on the ladder with his arms stretching to the highest branch. Her eyes roamed past his profile and up to his hands as he gripped a blossom. She wanted to take his hands in hers and plead with him to believe in himself, to fight for a better life.

His gaze had been fixed on the trees, but in the sudden silence, he lowered his arms and glared at her. His expression was searching, angry and sad. Narrowing his eyes, he raised his chin a notch. It was a dare, and she took it.

"I like you, Jake."

"You shouldn't."

"But I do."

He put one hand on his hip and glared at her. His eyes were harder than she wanted them to be, his lips a tight smirk.

"In that case, I like you too, Miss Merritt," he said

in a silky voice. "And here I thought you were shy about things."

"I can be very direct when I have to be." Her voice was raspy, almost seductive. She barely recognized it.

He took two steps down the ladder and leaned against the rungs. His eyes turned hard and dark, as if he were staring down an enemy, or prey. "I wouldn't recommend flirting with me."

"I don't flirt."

"Sure you do. You sneak peeks all through supper. You come out here in those cute little trousers. Believe me, a lesser man would get the wrong idea."

"You're not a lesser man."

"Oh, yes I am. Don't forget that I've kissed you. As I recall, you liked it quite a bit." He looked down at her with a gaze she could only describe as predatory, then he climbed the ladder and reached into the tree as if to dismiss her.

He was sending off warning signals like a beacon on a rocky shore, but Alex had no intention of running away. She was tired of feeling helpless today, and so she answered him with the truth that had been clawing at her for days.

"Yes, I did like kissing you. Quite a bit," she said. "Perhaps we'll do it again sometime."

The branches over her head went still. "I don't think you meant that."

"Yes, I did."

He let go of the branch and stepped off the ladder, but she wasn't about to back away. "I think it would be very nice to kiss you again."

"A man can only take so much temptation, *Miss* Merritt."

"Who's asking you to *take* anything?"

His wolflike stare gave way to a heated glimmer as he approached her, peeling off his gloves one at a time. He dropped them on the ground and the pale blossoms stirred.

When he was near enough to touch her, he curled his warm hands over her shoulders. Keeping her an arm's length away, his eyes examined every curve she had, her small feet, her hips, her breasts. Heat flooded through her as he looked at her mouth. Then he ran his finger along the side of her face and down her throat where the shirt gaped wide and loose. With his fingers on her chin, he tilted her face toward the endless blue sky.

Alex was shaking, but she wasn't about to stop him.

She wanted this kiss to happen today, now, in this field with the sun beating between the trees and the smell of summer in the air. She closed her eyes. She felt his breath on her face, inhaled his scent, traces of bay rum and peaches. He was a breath away, and then she felt his lips on hers, moving like ribbons in the wind.

She wrapped her arms around his neck. It was easy to give back to Jake, easy to savor the taste of him, to pour herself into him. When he pulled her even closer and their hips met, she leaned into him.

Until now, she thought a woman gave and a man took, but she had been wrong. She wanted this kiss enough to fight for it, and so she ran her hands through his feather-soft hair, down to the nape of his neck, and then lower to his broad shoulders.

His kiss changed from something he had done a thousand times to a wild exploration. Their mouths opened at the same time. Their tongues joined in a tangled dance. He was leading her to a secret place, opening her eyes to a mysterious heaven.

His lips fit hers perfectly, and he softened in her arms, molding himself to her body. Never in her life had she felt this flood of sensation, the joy of giving and taking at the same time. Her hands slid down his back and then around to the hard planes of his chest. She felt the beat of his heart, the rise of hard muscle as he took a breath. A cry of pure longing squeaked out of her throat.

She nearly wept with the intensity of it, but his lips stilled. Her eyes flew open and he stepped back with a deliberate slowness, as if something inside of him had broken. It was painful to see, and her arms fell to her sides.

''What's wrong?'' she asked.

He rocked back on his boot heels. ''That was a mistake.''

''No, it wasn't.''

''Take my word for it, Alex. For your father's sake, with his poor health and all, I'm going to forget this ever happened.''

''How can you?''

''It's not a big deal.''

''I thought it was.''

''You're making too much of it.''

''I don't think so. I feel things with you. I—''

His teeth clenched as he spun on his heel and shoved the ladder tight against the tree. ''Go on. Get out of here.''

''No.''

Jake laughed out loud. ''Just what the hell do you think is going to happen between us? You think I'm just going to stop with a kiss?''

"Yes."

"Well, you're wrong."

"I know you, Jake."

He shook his head, as if she'd said she could fly. His boots scraped at the ground as if he wanted to run but couldn't. Something wild rose up in Alex. Her deepest instincts told her that this man needed to be touched, gently, deeply, often.

She'd put up with too much today. She'd come too close to losing her father, too close to Jake, too close to touching the sky, and so she walked up to him, stood an inch away and poked him in the chest.

"Listen to me! You're not nearly as bad—"

He snatched her hand and held it tight. "I'm warning you, Alex. Stay away from me."

"No."

His hard blue stare didn't leave her face. "Just what do you want? Will my mouth do it, or are you after something else?"

"I'm not after anything." But she was. She wanted his secrets.

"You're lying."

His gaze narrowed to her mouth, but she didn't back away. Jake raised his hand to her chin and cupped it, squeezing her jaw so that her mouth puckered. His lips pulled at hers, taking without giving anything back, and Alex came close to hating him. Not because of what he was doing to her, but because it was so much less than he was capable of giving. And so much less than she wanted.

His tongue pushed at her clenched teeth, but she wouldn't open to him. He sucked at her lips, but she stood like a wall with her eyes shut tight.

Turn the other cheek...turn the other cheek....

He was daring her to fight, but she refused to strike back. She held her breath, waiting for him to pull back, praying he'd pushed as far as he dared.

But he wasn't finished. Still kissing her, he slid his hand down her throat to the open vee of her shirt and worked the top button. It slid open, and he fingered her camisole, rubbing the cotton between his thumb and forefinger. Breathing hard, Alex held her ground, but Jake advanced, taking the weight of her breast in his warm palm.

His thumb grazed the sensitive tip of her nipple. She gasped, and he yanked his hand away from her.

"Shit, Alex! Get away from me!"

She was close to tears. From pleasure. From pain. From the sheer wrongness of what she had allowed to happen. But she had proved her point. Somewhere beneath all that hardness, Jake understood the difference between giving and taking.

She pressed her hand against her chest. "I know why you stopped."

"You don't know anything!"

"You've got a good heart, Jake. You'd never hurt me. You stopped because—"

His eyes glittered like shattered glass. "Don't push me, Alex. I mean it."

"Or else what?" What could he possibly do to hurt her?

"Or else I'll leave and you can watch your father kill himself trying to harvest these peaches alone."

"You wouldn't do that!"

"Try me."

The dusty air turned to mud in her throat. Her father needed Jake. They all did.

Scowling, he looked at her exposed flesh, then

turned away in disgust. "Button up before you go inside."

Too terrified to argue, she raised her hands to her bare throat. The buttonhole was her mother's work, a masterful bit of embroidery that felt tight beneath her fingers. The button slid into place, and she looked at Jake.

He had been watching her.

Like a rabbit being chased by a wolf, she turned on her heels and ran.

More time…more time…more time.

It was late in the day when William went out to the barn. He needed to sit quietly without Katherine watching him breathe. This dying business was nerve-racking, even for a man with a vested interest in heaven.

He felt like a bug when he woke up with his wife's finger under his nose feeling for his breath. They still slept like puppies, surely she could feel his heart beating, just as surely as he could feel it breaking for Alex.

Breathing like a rusty steam engine, William walked through the barn to the old trunk stored against the back wall. He'd bought it more than thirty years ago, and it had traveled as many miles as he had, from New York to Philadelphia, with Kath to Colorado, and finally to Grand Junction. Years ago it held his clothing, now it held his memories.

Kneeling down, he opened the lid and took out a bundle of envelopes, each one addressed to him in Alex's writing. There were ten bundles from her, and thousands of other letters from the men he'd known over the years.

He'd had a hell of a life.

From the New York docks to running the finest church in Denver, from preaching in saloons to plumbing the depths of his own failings, he had walked a lot of miles, sown a lot of seeds, and wrestled with men and angels alike.

Rummaging through the stacks, William found the first letters his daughter had written after leaving home. It had been Kath's idea to send her to a big eastern city with educated young men, culture and museums. He'd argued with her, but he'd couldn't say no to his wife, and in the end Alex had left.

As he opened the first envelope, William relived the excitement of her first train trip and the pleasure of meeting her cousins. Crouched on the wobbly milk stool, he read the letters in order. Pictures of Alex moved through his mind like a cartoon picture fan. She changed from a seventeen-year-old girl in a new traveling suit, to a young woman going to dances, to a mature woman with a conscience and a heart.

Only that heart was too mature, too accepting, and knowing what he would read, William opened a letter she'd written less than a year ago.

I've made my peace with circumstances. I'm the convenient last-minute dinner guest, the good conversationalist who can sit with an old man or a young one, the single woman who is invited for widowers and elderly bachelors.

It's tiresome, Papa, but it seems to be my place.

She never complained again, and William feared that love had passed her by. Setting aside the last bundle of letters, he took out a folded sheet of paper bearing a sonnet written in his daughter's childish hand.

About a year ago, he'd found the poem tucked in a book, a forgotten marker in *Jane Eyre*. His daughter had been hopelessly in love with Edward Rochester, and William kept the poem because it gave him hope.

Dear God, be with her. Give her peace and joy.

He had a pain then, a short stab in his chest, and leaning against the trunk, he took slow breaths as he slid to the floor. A thousand stars twinkled in his head, and the room whirled in an awkward waltz. He was still seeing stars among the high-pitched rafters when he heard footsteps.

"What the—"

Thank God, it was Jake and not Kath or Alex. The young man knelt at his side. William could feel the anger on him like a cloud, and his own weakness left as quickly as it had come. "If you say a word to anyone, I'll fire you."

Jake gave a bitter laugh. "I'll save you the trouble. I quit."

"Like hell." Grunting, William struggled to his feet. Jake offered him a hand, but he pushed it aside. Standing slowly, he brushed off his pants and glanced at the barn door. "I'm headed back to the house."

Jake slowed his pace as they neared the porch. Thinning was hard work. The young man had been up and down the ladder a thousand times, but he didn't look the least bit tired. William envied that strength.

"How far did you and Alex get today?" he asked.

Jake's face hardened, and he couldn't look William in the eye. "She's in the way. Keep her inside."

It was either love or the truth talking, but Jake was a good actor, and William couldn't tell which it was. The young man changed the subject.

"The irrigation ditches need some work. I'll muck out the south channel when the thinning's done."

He was observant, and William was pleased. "You've got a genuine feel for the trees."

"You've got me until the harvest, and then I'm gone faster than you say jack-rabbit-run. If you had a lick of sense you'd fire me today."

When they reached the front porch, William sat in the swing and Jake marched into the house. A few minutes later he came back with his saddlebags. He hadn't even bothered to buckle them. Balled-up shirts, socks and long johns bulged at the seams, and a wrinkled sleeve hung over the edge.

"I'm skipping supper," Jake said. "Don't look for me tonight."

He was halfway across the yard when the door slammed shut behind him. Five minutes later he led the bay out of the barn and hurled himself into the saddle.

Just as Jake kicked the horse into a gallop, Alex poked her head out the front door. "Where's he going?"

William heard the catch in her voice. He couldn't do a thing to protect her from the misery of loving an angry man, but he had to try. Watching Jake disappear down the road, he said, "He's probably headed to town. He'll be back in the morning."

Her jaw tightened, and she took a deep breath. "Supper's ready."

"I'll just be a minute."

He tilted his head toward the sky and prayed that Jake Malone wouldn't break his daughter's heart.

Chapter Nine

Jake couldn't get to Grand Junction fast enough, and the bay seemed as glad to run as he was. A dust cloud rose behind them, and the rumble of hoofbeats matched his own pounding heart.

There was no excuse for what he'd done, or for the fear he had put in her eyes by threatening to leave. Kissing her like that had been calculated and rude, but touching her breast had been cruel. If Gabe had been around, he would have kicked his sorry butt ten times over and made him apologize, but Jake didn't have that inclination.

He had to keep away from the angel.

It felt good to pick up speed and gallop against the wind, especially with the turquoise sky streaked with apricot clouds and violet shadows falling across the land. The evening air felt hot and cool at the same time, and it matched his mood. A mesa rose from the desert plain like an open door, and Jake knew that soon he'd ride past that rock and not look back. Until then, he'd settle for a night on the town. He'd get drunk and get laid and let tomorrow take care of itself.

The raw buildings that made up Grand Junction

loomed on the horizon, and he slowed the bay to a walk. Colorado Avenue was still bustling with horses and boardwalk traffic, and with a bit of a shock he realized it was Saturday night. Two weeks had passed since he shot Henry Abbott, and as far as Jake was concerned, it was another good reason to get drunk.

Following the noise of men looking for a good time, he found the saloon sandwiched between a feed store and a barbershop. Someone had propped open the barber's door with a speckled rock, and a skinny man in a black bowtie was pushing a broomful of dust into the street.

Running his hand through his shaggy hair, Jake walked through the door.

"Have you got time for one more?" he asked.

"Sure. Have a seat."

It didn't take long for the balding man to whip out his scissors and go to work, and he was just as quick with shaving cream and a razor. With Gabe's money light in his pocket, Jake left the man a big tip and strutted out the door for the Wild River Saloon.

Piano music spilled into the street like jingling coins as he pushed through the swinging doors. He liked everything he saw. Saloon girls in red satin swished their hips as they served drinks. A poker game caught his eye and he considered playing a hand or two, mostly because a shapely redhead bent a little too low as she plunked down a round of drinks.

Murky smoke from a dozen wall lamps tickled his nose, and the rumble of men forgetting themselves traveled from the floor through the soles of his boots. Without a care in the world, he found an empty stool at the bar and straddled it.

Full of laughter, talk and the yeasty smell of beer,

the saloon promised friendly banter, just what he needed to forget Alex, the Merritts, and even Flat Rock. Later the atmosphere would turn smoky and sad, but for now he wanted to settle into the crowd and forget the home-cooked meal he was missing.

Except his stomach was growling.

"What can I get you?" the bartender asked, swiping at a water ring with a clean towel. He was a burly man with a heavy beard and skinned knuckles, and Jake decided to treat himself to the best whiskey his brother's money could buy.

"Texas Gold, and you can leave the bottle."

The barkeep nodded, and Jake propped his boots on the foot rail. Leaning his forearms on the bar, he eyed the liquor bottles lining the narrow shelf mounted on the red velvet wallpaper. The saloon was well stocked with rye, gin and three kinds of whiskey, and above the bottles, he couldn't miss a bigger-than-life painting of a naked woman.

Her pink-tipped breasts were meant to give a man dreams and Jake looked his fill, until he saw her lush dark hair and wide brown eyes. Her lips invited a man to kiss them long and slow, to take what he wanted and leave the rest. But she looked scared to death, and all he could see was Alex running away from him.

You've got a good heart, Jake. You'd never hurt me.

But he'd done exactly that, and he'd done it on purpose. His stomach burned with shame.

The bartender plunked the bottle and a shot glass on the counter, and Jake slapped down his money. His stomach rumbled. "What have you got to eat around here?"

Before the bearded man could answer, a fight broke out at the poker table. A glass shattered against the wall and two chairs scraped against the floor. The redheaded waitress shouted, "Louie! Get over here."

Louie snatched the coins and left without pulling the cork, but Jake didn't care. He ran his fingers down the side of the brown glass and up again, circled the lip of the bottle, and wiggled the cork. He could open it without anyone's help.

But damn, he was hungry for real food.

"You don't look too happy, cowboy. Can I get you something else?" A young blonde with wide blue eyes stood at his side. She was the prettiest girl in the place and the only one wearing a blue cotton dress and an apron. It didn't surprise Jake that she'd come up to him. Things like that happened to him all the time.

"I'd kill for a sandwich or a bowl of chili," he said.

"I can get you chili. I've got a pot on the stove."

"I'd be grateful." He put on his pretty-boy smile and gave her a look that made promises he intended to keep, right after he filled his stomach and got a little drunk.

She came back in two minutes with a bowl of Texas Red and a small plate of jalapeños. "Can you handle those?"

"Most definitely." He bit, chewed and swallowed the hot pepper without breaking a sweat. Chilies didn't bother his stomach at all, it was everything else in life that made his gut cramp.

"What's your name?" he asked.

"Annabelle."

Damn. The name started with an *A* and teased his tongue. His stomach burned, and without giving the reason too much thought, he slid a double-eagle gold piece across the counter and said, "Sit awhile."

She slid the coin back. "I'm just the cook."

Jake's neck flushed. The girl was wearing a worn-out dress and a stained apron. What had gotten into him?

"I owe you an apology," he said sincerely.

"No harm. It's just that I came out to see if Louie wanted his supper and you looked hungry."

A pitiful whine came from the poker table, and Jake saw an acne-faced kid picking a fight. Louie had his hands full.

"It looks like he'll be a while," Jake said to Annabelle. "I appreciate the meal, but I'd like company even more. Can you sit for a bit?"

"I guess a few minutes won't hurt."

"How about a drink?"

"No, thank you. I don't touch the stuff."

Curiosity got the better of him. "Why is that?"

"I've got plans. My sister's on her way, and then we're headed to San Francisco."

"I don't see how one drink is going to stop you from getting there."

She shook her head, softening the refusal with a dry laugh. "That stuff is nothing but trouble."

Man, did that sound familiar. Looking at her more closely, he saw blond hair, a girl's small breasts, and God help him, blue eyes that ached like his own.

Steam rose from the chili and tickled his nose, raising questions that had nothing to do with meat and beans. What made this woman say no to him? What made her think she could start over in San Francisco and not find trouble waiting for her? In Jake's experience, trouble followed a man wherever he went.

Curious about her plans but doubtful her dreams would come true, he said, "So tell me about yourself, Annabelle."

"There's not much to tell. I ran away from Chicago because my life fell apart, except I found out the hard way things out West aren't any easier."

She shrugged, and Jake saw the rest of the story in her eyes. Single women had few options in frontier towns, and Annabelle was pretty enough to make a few dollars on the side. Except she'd turned his money down flat.

"So you're just a cook?"

"I am now. At least until another job opens up, or until my sister gets here and I can get on with my life. I've already made my share of mistakes. I don't intend to repeat any of them."

Nodding at the naked lady on the wall, she said, "Rumor has it that Adeline Webster modeled for that painting. If she could get on with her life, so can I."

Jake recognized the name. Adeline Webster had opened an opera house in Denver, and a year later she married a millionaire and became one of the most respected women west of the Mississippi.

"Is it really that easy? To just get on with things?"

"I've had some help," she said quietly. "I'll never let a man use me again. That's certain. And I don't drink whiskey. That's my choice."

There's always a choice, Jake, and you're making the wrong one.

Bad choices and bad habits…Jake was well acquainted with both sides of that particular coin. He'd made the wrong choice when he seduced Lettie, and he'd been wrong to hurt Alex this afternoon. He should have told her the truth, that he cared about her, and he didn't want to hurt her when he left. It sounded so simple and sane he barely recognized the thought as his own.

With a small smile, Annabelle said, "I'd bet money someone's missing you tonight. If you're smart, you'll eat that chili before it gets cold and go on home."

She knew, and Jake did, too, that getting drunk or burying himself in sex wouldn't take away the misery clawing at his gut. The urge to fight evaporated like steam from a kettle. He had to get home to Alex. He needed to apologize and make things right.

Annabelle sat with him while he wolfed down the rest of the chili. Standing up, he dug the gold piece out of his pocket and again pushed it over to her.

"Take it."

She hesitated. "It's too much."

He pressed it into hand anyway. "You've helped me tonight. Use it to get to San Francisco."

"In that case, I will. Thank you." Dropping the coin into her pocket, she said, "I don't know who chased you in here, but I'd say she's a lucky woman."

Jake shook his head. "She should be cursing the day I was born."

"Then go make it right."

Maybe he could.

The bottle was sitting on the bar when Jake walked out the door and climbed on Smiley. The thirst for speed had gone out of him, and he let the bay set his own pace. The night air cooled his skin, and he relaxed in the saddle.

Go on home....

The words played like music through his mind. Home to Alex. Home to the orchard. Home to William and Katherine, good meals and a warm bed, except he had to laugh about the bed. He'd fixed it so he'd be sleeping on a sagging cot in the barn, and for his own good that's how it had to stay.

Only the orchard wasn't really home, and it couldn't be as long as the mess in Flat Rock was biting at his heels. Acid burned his belly. Even if Henry had lived, and he didn't go to prison for murder, he still had Lettie to face, and his child. *His child.*

He nearly puked at the thought. What did Annabelle say? *That's my choice.*

Tonight he'd made a choice to skip the liquor and apologize to Alex. For now, that was enough.

The miles to the orchard slipped by, and he rode into the yard just as the moon was cresting in the southern sky. A single light burned in Alex's window, and he guessed she was reading or tending to the baby, until he saw her sitting in the rocking chair.

Starlight reached beneath the eaves, touching her face and turning it pale against the shadows. Her dress reminded him of tarnished silver, but a white shawl shimmered as she fluffed it over her shoulders. Her arms were empty, and he understood she was waiting for him.

Riding closer, he heard the steady thump of the rocker. It stilled as he guided the bay closer to the porch.

"Alex?"

"Hello, Jake." There was no censure in her voice, only kindness, maybe regret.

The low ache in his belly hardened with sudden, unrelenting need. He wanted to fly off the horse and pull her close and kiss her gently, to make it right. Only he couldn't do that. To make it right he'd have to be a better man, a different person altogether, the kind of man who stayed in one place and did the right thing. A man without a past, a murder charge and a bastard child.

"I can't fix what happened this afternoon, but I swear on my life I'll never touch you like that again."

"It was my fault."

"No." He couldn't let her think that. She should have been angry with him, not with herself. For once in his life, he'd take responsibility. "I took advantage of you, of the situation."

The rocker thudded to a stop as she walked to the edge of the porch. For one terrifying second he thought she might come near him. He was on the verge of dismounting and reaching for her, tenderly this time, but she stopped at the top step, took a single breath, and said words that cut right through him. "You told me to back off. You gave me fair warning. I am so sorry—"

"Alex, don't."

"I acted like an idiot. I don't know why I thought you—"

"Don't you dare blame yourself. You don't have a damn thing to be sorry for. You should have slapped me stupid. Maybe you still should."

Hell, he'd prefer that to her guilt. "You still can if you want to. I'll climb down from Smiley here, and you can haul back and let me have it right across the chops."

She smiled.

"You can hit me twice if you want. Or you can sock me in the belly if you'd rather. Hit me as hard as you want. I can take it. I'm used to getting beat up."

She whispered, "Oh, Jake," and the pity in her eyes stripped him to bare skin. He wanted to cuss at her, but she wouldn't be offended. He wanted to say something cruel, but she'd forgive him. She would no more condemn him for a moment of meanness than she'd curse a dog for biting a bully.

She was poised at the edge of the steps, a silver angel in the moonlight ready to take flight. She was beautiful, and too damn serious about things that didn't matter. Jake shifted his weight and the saddle creaked.

"It was a joke, Alex."

"It wasn't funny." Her eyes were as steady as the earth. "I don't hit back."

"Maybe you should. You should have hit back this afternoon."

"Never. Not in a million years."

She spoke with the confidence of a thousand armies, and Jake felt sick to his stomach. She'd go to war with him, and as surely as the sun would rise tomorrow, he'd make her cry. It was in his nature, just as it was in hers to see an animal's pain and not its teeth. She didn't have the sense God gave a rabbit to run from a fox.

Being sober was bad. Being noble and sober was more than he could take. Tipping his hat, he turned the bay to the barn. "Good night, Alex."

He'd read her the riot act if she followed him.

He'd tell her to jump in a lake if she got too close.

But then he heard the rustle of her skirt and the pad of her shoes on the dirt, and he realized she wasn't an angel at all, but a woman with burdens and needs of her own.

She was at his side by the time he crossed the yard. He swung his leg over the horse's rump, looped the reins and opened the barn door. A bed of sweet hay glistened in the moonlight and he stopped. This was the last place in the world he wanted to be with her, and the only place.

Except he wouldn't risk hurting her again. He could do things right this time.

She was still standing next to him, her hands clutching the shawl over her chest. She didn't know he had moved his things to the barn, and she expected him to go back to the house with her.

He made his voice matter-of-fact. "I'm going to be out here awhile. You should go inside."

"I have to ask you something first. I have to be sure you'll stay through the harvest. Because if you don't, I've got to find someone else. It's a bad time to find help, but I'm sure I could find someone if I had to."

"You should let William handle it."

"Yes, but…well, if I had to, I could do it."

Jake heard what she didn't say.

If he died, I could do it.

The old man's heart could stop anytime, and the thought of Alex talking to a gadabout farmhand made Jake clench his teeth. She'd offer Billy the Kid a job. Hell, she'd probably find a one-eyed killer in need of a bath and pay him more than William was paying him. She had her father's good intentions but not his muscle, and Jake hated the thought of anyone taking advantage of her.

"You don't need to worry. I'm staying through harvest."

"You can stay longer if you'd like."

He shook his head. "I've got plans that won't change."

"Are you sure?"

"I'm dead sure." He sounded just like Gabe, bossy and a little bit snide. He nearly choked at the misery in her eyes. She wasn't used to giving up hope, and that meant he had to be firm. "It's best that you don't push me."

"All right, but I can still say thank you for what you've done."

"It's been my pleasure. I wish you and your parents well." Before she could say anything else, he led the bay into the barn.

The horse blocked his view of her, but then Smiley bobbed his head and Jake saw her waiting. Her shoulders were hunched beneath the white shawl, and he thought of a dove pulling in its wings for warmth. He couldn't let her go.

"How's the baby doing?" he asked.

"He's sleeping a lot better. No colic tonight."

"That's good." Jake could sympathize with an upset stomach. "I hope things work out for all of you."

A warning bell went off in his head as she followed him into the barn, but she looked so damn sad he didn't have the heart to stop her. He knew how it felt to be at loose ends and he wanted to give her a strong hand to hold, even if it cost him something.

"Thomas is a very lucky man. I'm sure you'll have a good life together."

"I hope so."

"So he's going to be mayor of Philadelphia?"

She shrugged. "Maybe. He has a lot of good ideas."

Jake wanted to spit. Was that all she could say about Hunnicutt? She needed someone strong, a man who knew how to fight and how to love, someone who could give as good as he got. She had no business with a middle-aged milquetoast politician. Except that he could give her a home, more children and Charlie.

He was unsaddling Smiley in the dark when the lantern by the door blazed to life. Alex blew out the match, licked her fingers and squeezed the tip. The routine of it was womanly and cautious, and the ache in his gut turned into white heat.

Blinking in the yellow light, he said, "You'll be a good mother, Alex."

"I hope so."

He hoisted the saddle and set it on a rack. "There's no doubt about it. Ten years from now Charlie will be teasing his little brothers and you'll be having the time of your life."

A strange fondness for Gabe came over him, and he smiled. But Alex wasn't smiling at all. She looked as if someone had sucker punched her. It pained him deep down, and he felt an inexplicable need to cheer her up.

"I know about older brothers. They can be a real pain."

"Having a brother would have been nice."

"You wouldn't want Gabe. He raised me, though. My ma died when I was eight and he took over."

She looked pained again. "He must be a lot older than you."

"Nine years." He ran the soft brush down Smiley's neck and trailed over the spot with his hand.

"It must have been hard to lose your mother, hard for both of you."

The conversation had gotten too personal. Jake pointed at the cabinet where William kept barn tools. "Would you hand me a comb?"

"Sure."

Just as she reached the cabinet, Jake realized his saddlebags were sitting directly under it. He hadn't taken it to the back room, nor had he bothered to fasten the buckle. A red long john sleeve was practically waving at her.

Alex looked at him doubtfully. "You were going to leave tonight."

"No."

"Then why are your things here? That back room is filthy. You'd be much more comfortable at the house."

"I don't think so." No, definitely not. Her woman sounds made him hungry for love and bare skin. She was about to argue with him, and Jake decided Charlie owed him a favor. "The kid's cute, but I'm tired of waking up six times a night."

"It *is* awful sometimes. I don't blame you a bit."

"At least he's stronger."

"Much. I just hope I can keep him."

"Do you really think anyone is looking for him?" he asked.

Alex shook her head. "I don't know, but it's up to me to do what's right. I couldn't live with myself if I didn't try to find his family." Her gaze searched his face. "Could you?"

"Absolutely. I don't think anyone wants him."

"But how do you know?"

"I just do."

Jake wanted to kick himself. He'd just toed a line he didn't want to cross, and Alex was studying him, waiting for more. She was patient but so was he, and he took his time untangling Smiley's mane before he changed the subject.

"The stage company should salvage the trunks pretty soon. Maybe you'll find something when you get them."

"I doubt it. Everything was ruined in the flood."

He'd been burned by circumstances more times than he could count, but for Alex he could hope. "I'd bet money the kid's an orphan."

"But what if he has a grandmother who's worrying herself sick? Or a father who won't see him grow up?"

"Charlotte was running from the past. She didn't want to be found."

"Maybe she was running *to* someone. Maybe there's a man somewhere who would want his son."

"You're letting your imagination run wild. I'd bet money the kid's alone in the world. Any judge in Colorado would sign papers making you his mother."

She shook her head. "My father thought so, too, but it would be a lot simpler if I were married."

Her fiancé might have been a middle-aged weasel, but he could help her in a way Jake couldn't. "I imagine Hunnicutt would come out here if it meant you could keep the baby."

"Maybe. I hope so. I haven't written to him yet."

Jake gave her a sidelong glance. She was chewing on her lower lip, and it occurred to him she had been waiting for this moment. It was up to him to make it clear that this spark between them was just a flicker, nothing more than a match in the darkness, a sulfurous tip that could be extinguished with spit and courage.

"I'm going into town in a few days. If you get the letter written, I'll post it for you."

"Thank you."

"The tracks will be fixed in a few weeks. It would be a quick trip for him."

Her gaze searched his face, and Jake forced himself to relax the muscles in his cheeks, to keep his arms loose and empty.

"Or I could send a wire for you."

"No. A letter is better. There's a lot to explain."

"Just let me know." He stepped out of Smiley's stall and put the brush and comb back in the cabinet. She was just a foot away from him now. She smelled of rose sachet and soap. The lantern light turned pink on her cheeks.

"Alex, I—"

She looked at him with those luminous brown eyes, expectant, hopeful, eager, and he wanted to swallow his tongue. He'd let his good intentions go too far tonight, but he had to speak one more bit of truth. "I want to apologize again for what happened today, for touching you like that."

"Please don't."

"I just want to say you're a very beautiful woman, and Thomas is—" Jake squeezed the cabinet knobs. "He'll be a good father."

Tears brimmed in her eyes. "I've got to go inside."

She hurried away. He knew comforting this woman was going to hurt like hell, but he had to do it.

Striding through the barn, he reached her just as she stepped into the yard. His fingers grasped the sturdy bones in her shoulder and his thumb grazed the smooth nape of her neck. She pressed her hands to her cheeks and took a deep breath, but it didn't stop her from trembling. Turning her slowly, gently but with a purpose, he pulled her into his arms.

"Go ahead and cry, Alex. Let it out."

She buried her face against his chest and the tears came. For William, for Charlie, maybe even for him. He smoothed her back, and she clung to a fistful of his shirt. Her hair brushed his nose, and he raised his head to escape the scent of her. To keep from kissing her, he counted the stars.

A small eternity passed before she wiped her eyes with the end of the shawl. "Thank you."

His arms nearly broke when he let her go. Touching

her chin and faking a smile, he said, "I'll see you in the morning."

Her mouth was both stiff and trembling, and turning her face in the direction of the orchard, she whispered, "Yes, at breakfast. Good night, Jake."

Her skirt pulled up dust as she hurried to the house. He wanted to chase after her, to make promises he couldn't keep, to sleep with her in the swing and watch the sun rise, but that would have been selfish and greedy, even cruel.

The front door clicked shut and a minute later the lamp in her bedroom burned brighter. He thought of her undressing, brushing her hair and leaving it loose, bathing her face, finding comfort in a soft bed with clean sheets.

Jake wouldn't have that comfort tonight. Picking up the lantern, he walked to the back room and took in the bumpy cot and exhausted walls. A few nails had been pounded into a stud for clothes, and someone had put up a rifle rack. A straight-backed chair sat in the corner, though he couldn't imagine anyone actually sitting in it, and a scratched bureau was butted against the wall.

The room smelled of strangers and dust, and Jake rubbed his nose as he sat on the cot. The wood creaked and the mattress crunched, but he couldn't afford to care. He pulled off his boots, undressed and wrapped himself in the blanket that had covered Alex and Charlie in the desert. It smelled like rain, wood smoke and stale whiskey.

All and all, it had been a hell of a day, and with thoughts of the angel crowding the narrow bed, the night looked just as bad.

Alex knew what she had to do.

Tossing her shawl on the bed, she turned up the lantern and rummaged in her desk for paper and ink. She didn't bother to sit down. The light was best on the bureau. She spread the paper on the polished surface, dipped the pen in the black bottle, and started to write.

Dear Thomas,

Please come to Colorado as soon as you can. I wouldn't ask, but the circumstances are somewhat desperate, and amazing, too. Take a breath, because I'm about to share a miracle. His name is Charlie, and he is ours.

The story of his birth is long and tragic, and I'd rather share it with you in person.

God is so good. I'd accepted the fact there would be no children between us, but in his wisdom and kindness the Lord has given us a son. I would like for us to be married here in Colorado so that we can adopt the baby before returning to Philadelphia.

Please say you'll come.

The metal tip of the pen scraped against the bottle, and she shivered. Someday she would forget Jake Malone. She would forget seeing him on Smiley, a dark-haired horseman facing his own apocalypse. She would forget that strange and wild longing to see more, taste more, even be more, that came when he touched her with his hands and his eyes.

A terrible heat burned in her chest, and she shuddered.

I won't think…I won't think…

But she might as well have thrown water on a grease

fire. The memory of Jake's touch spattered her skin. Her body wanted him, and nothing could stop her from remembering his hand cupping her breast, and the buried hunger in tonight's embrace.

She couldn't stop wanting this man, but neither could her heart forget the people she loved. She needed to get married if she wanted to keep Charlie, and her father needed Jake. He had promised to stay through harvest, but she had to respect the line he'd drawn. She wouldn't ask questions, nor would she let herself hope that he'd change his mind about staying.

He didn't want her, and that settled everything.

With no choices to be made, Alex focused on the letter to Thomas. She usually signed her notes "Fondly, A.," but tonight that wasn't enough. She wrote "I love you," and with a slight pause, she signed the letter "Alexandra," her full woman's name, as if that alone could make the words true.

Chapter Ten

William loved Sunday mornings. The sermon was fresh in his mind, and with the golden sun warm on his face, he opened the barn door and smiled. The bay was in his stall. Jake's saddle was on the rack, and the door to the bunk room was ajar. William had never been shy, and he walked in without knocking.

"What the devil are you doing sleeping in on a Sunday?"

"What the hell?" Jake rolled onto his back, clapped his hand over his eyes and pinched the bridge of his nose.

William knew a hangover when he saw one, and he felt a twinge of pity. "We're headed to church. You're welcome to ride along or sleep it off."

"You are out of your mind, old man."

"It might help your headache to listen to the angels sing." William couldn't resist a barb or two. He had a bit of mean streak, and sometimes it got the better of him. "We have a fine organ. Sounds like a cat dying on the high notes, but other than that it's not too bad."

"I'm not hung over, and I don't have a headache. At least I didn't until you started bellowing."

Jake squinted at the sunlight pushing through the small window. His eyes were clear, and the room smelled more like sweat and hard work than whiskey. No, he wasn't hung over. He just didn't wake up gracefully. William knew all about that, and he smiled.

"Kind of a frightening experience. Waking up sober with a mean old man yelling at you."

"It's hell."

"Anyway, the invitation stands. You can make up your own mind, but either way, we don't work today."

"That's fine by me. I've got things to do, like sleep."

Jake was scowling, but his voice held as much malice as a glass of milk. William liked what he saw. "Maybe I'll tell you about that twenty-year-old bottle of whiskey sometime."

Jake rolled on his side, but William knew he'd struck a nerve. He could almost see the younger man's thoughts ricocheting off the walls, but he wasn't about to ask questions for fear of having to answer a few in return.

All men had stories to tell, and Jake wasn't any different.

The front door slapped shut behind Alex as she walked across the porch with Charlie in her arms. The sun was nearing the horizon, and long shadows brushed her face as she sat down in the rocker she remembered from her girlhood. It had been a gift from a Kentucky miner who had stayed with her parents after an accident. The porch swing was newer, and it creaked under her father's weight.

She had been dreading this moment. The letter to Thomas was on her dresser. She had rewritten it three times and ended up with the one she had written the night she had spoken to Jake. The next morning he had offered to make a special trip to town to mail it for her, but she hadn't been ready then.

Now she wished she hadn't wasted the time. Jake had been ignoring her, and her parents were hoping she'd stay. But she had made her decision. Tonight she would tell them she had asked Thomas to come to Colorado for their wedding. Her mother would understand, but her father was another story.

Jake might have been ally, but he wouldn't be back for his nightly cigar until she took Charlie to bed.

She hadn't been feeling well, either. Her mother had removed the stitches from the snakebite, but it was hot to the touch and her bones ached with fever. The poultice she had made this afternoon hadn't helped at all.

Alex leaned back in the rocker, and William reached into his pocket for a cigar. The porch swing creaked as he struck a match on his boot, lit the tip and took a puff. The rich smoke tickled her nose.

"Are you sure it's okay to smoke those things?" she asked.

"Nope. And I don't care."

He smiled like an old rogue, but she saw deep lines around his eyes and his silver hair stood out like a cloud against the purple sky. The front door swung open and Katherine joined them with her sewing basket in hand. William scooted sideways and patted the spot next to him. "Come here, sweetheart. I want you close to me."

"Only if you put out that cigar."

"Come on, Kath. You like the way they smell.

"I do not."

"Sure you do."

Giving him an old-married frown, she sat next to her husband and kissed his cheek. A wisp of smoke disappeared into the shadows. The sun was lower now, a soft orange blurring into a hot pink. Loosening Charlie's blanket, Alex held him up so that he could kick his legs.

Her mother glanced up from the handkerchief she was embroidering and smiled. "I remember holding you like that."

The baby grabbed a strand of her hair and tugged with all his might, as if it were a rope and he were scaling a mountain.

"I'd say that boy knows what he wants," William said.

"Well," she started slowly. "I do, too."

Her father pulled the cigar from his lips. "You're staying."

"No." The word felt like glue in her mouth. "I've asked Thomas to come to Colorado so we can get married sooner."

"Are you sure about this?" William asked.

"I am."

She wanted him to smile at her, to be proud of her choices, but he was strangely silent.

"I thought maybe we could have the wedding here rather than at the church. Just the four of us."

William blew a ring of smoke. "I'll have to think about it."

"What's there to think about?"

"I'm not sure I want to say the words that will tie my daughter to a man she doesn't love."

"But it will be easier to adopt Charlie if I'm married. Thomas is a good, decent man. Why are you making this so hard?" Her voice was shaking.

William squeezed his cigar. "I'm making it hard because it's flat-out wrong."

Alex looked to her mother for support, but all she saw was the flash of the needle piercing white linen. "Mama, you understand."

The needle stopped halfway through a stitch. Pure confusion filled her mother's eyes. "I want what's best for you."

It was worse than no answer at all.

William leaned back in the swing and pinned her to the rocker with his hardest stare. "Does this have anything to do with Jake?"

"No!" *Yes. He kissed me. He made me feel things....*

"Has he done something to hurt you?"

Her eyes misted. "No. It's just that—"

William jumped to his feet. "I'm going to have a word with that son of a bitch right now."

"Papa!"

"Will, sit down." Katherine grabbed his shirt and yanked. "This isn't any of our business."

"It is if he did something to hurt Alex. I warned him."

"Papa, please, drop it."

By pure bad luck, Jake walked out of the barn just as Alex looked across the yard. Their gazes met and she nearly started to cry. With a curt nod, he reached down for the empty bucket sitting just outside the barn door.

"Get over here!" William bellowed.

Jake looked across the yard, dropped the bucket with a clatter, and sauntered over. Each step was meant to frustrate, and it worked. By the time he reached the bottom step, William's eyes were bulging.

"I want to know what the hell happened between you and my daughter."

"Will, you're being—"

"Not now Katherine."

"Papa! It's none of your business. This has nothing to do with Jake."

"It has everything to do with Jake!"

Her father was red-faced and shouting, but she had to explain herself. "I made this decision on my own. If you had a lick of sense you'd see the plain facts."

"And if you had a lick of sense you'd see that you belong here!"

William pointed his finger at Jake. "And if *you* had a lick of sense you'd help her figure that out instead of chasing her away. I'm so damn mad at both of you I can't see straight!"

He was chugging like a tired locomotive, and Alex started to shake. "Papa, please—"

"Not now, Alex." He threw down the cigar, stomped it out and marched into the house.

Katherine squeezed her daughter's hand. "I'll go inside. You know how he gets."

"I shouldn't have upset him. I should have waited or—"

Katherine shook her head. "It couldn't be helped. He'll stop being mad in a little bit, and he might even decide you're right."

"Am I?"

"I don't know." The shadows on Katherine's face deepened as she looked out to the orchard where the peaches were hard and small. Old lines of worry mixed with something new—genuine fear and knowledge of the inevitable. "Somehow it will work out," she said, patting Alex's shoulder. "Try not to worry."

Katherine scooped up her sewing, and Alex jiggled Charlie against her chest. The door closed with a thud, and she remembered Jake standing in the yard.

"What was that all about?" he asked.

"I told him I asked Thomas to come here for the wedding."

"It sounded like more than that."

"It wasn't. My father doesn't like him at all."

"Maybe he'll change his mind."

Alex pressed her cheek against Charlie's warm head. "I doubt it."

"Will it make a difference to you?"

She had never gone against her father's advice, but she wanted to keep Charlie, and she wanted it to be legal—not a frontier adoption that would disintegrate if a blood relative showed up on her doorstep.

"It makes a difference, but I still want to mail the letter. Will you do it for me?"

His throat twitched, and her thoughts swooped like fireflies against a black sky. Wishing on a star that he'd come closer, she waited, but his face went blank and she knew what he was going to say.

"I pick up supplies on Friday. I'll mail it then."

"Thank you."

Dusk fell around them like a warm blanket. A barn swallow fluttered in a tree. The air felt heavier, damp with the cooling earth. The sky had faded from the glow of a fresh-cut orange to deep lavender.

Looking at his feet, Jake kicked at a hard rut with his boot and walked away, stopping once to pick up a rock. Cocking his arm, he hurled it across the yard and into an empty field, far beyond her line of sight.

She pulled the baby closer, and he snuggled against

her neck, clutching her hair in his tiny fist. He wouldn't let go, and Alex knew exactly how he felt.

William snuggled against his wife. As angry as he had been, he calmed down as soon as Katherine touched his back and whispered in his ear that he wasn't God.

"You have to have faith, Will."

She was like a mirror, reflecting back his hope and he cherished her for that.

They hadn't made love in a long time. That intimacy scared the daylights out of her because of his heart. He missed it, but if the truth be told, he was tired and it scared him, too.

But tonight he wanted to hold her. His thoughts were full of wonderful married things because his daughter was downstairs, trying to convince herself she didn't love Jake Malone. When Jake came home sober, William knew he had it bad for Alex. And he knew the young man could be trusted, even if he had made a mistake or two. That trust wasn't something William could explain; it was a gut feeling, and he lived by those.

"Do you think our daughter has met the man of her dreams?" he asked his wife. "And I don't mean Hunnicutt."

"You're an impossible romantic. I think she's going to get hurt and I hate to think about it."

William sighed. "No ''Tis better to have loved and lost' for you, huh, Kath?"

"It's better to hit the jackpot and keep what you win." She sighed and snuggled close. Fifty years old, and she still made him want her.

He kissed her, gently.

She kissed him back, gently.

Then they made love, even more gently. And again William was sure that love was worth the risk. This force, this God-given need to bond with one woman, to protect her, to provide for her, to possess her, was greater than fear, greater than death itself. He would love Kath through eternity. She was part of him, the best part of him.

William prayed for his daughter. And then he prayed for Jake. And with his wife curled against him in the darkness, he prayed for her, too.

More time…more time…more time…

Chapter Eleven

Jake picked up a hard green peach and threw it into next week. He liked working in the orchard. He liked pruning branches and shaping the trees. He didn't mind sweating and going to bed tired. He didn't even mind that William Merritt hadn't made good on that promise of twenty-year-old whiskey.

What he minded was wanting Alex.

He picked up the pruning shears and studied the branches dangling over his head. They were laced together like lovers and he imagined her legs entangled with his, his thighs brushing her hips. He saw her everywhere, but mostly in the rosy light that came with each dawn and in the stars that burned brightest in a moonless sky.

He'd managed to ignore her for the past few days, but it hadn't been easy. The old man would have been doing him a favor if he'd hit him in the head with a hammer, but William had been as sympathetic as a cactus.

Jake, bring this bucket of strawberries to Alex.
Jake, Alex needs a hand with the laundry tub.
Jake, there's bathwater that needs emptying....

Bathwater, for God's sake. The door had been open a crack and he thought the room was empty. He barged in and there she was, naked and dripping wet, with her arms raised high as she loosened her hair from a white ribbon. He saw her for one second too many, just long enough to learn that her breasts were tipped with dark pink circles and her skin was ivory white. He had nearly dropped the bucket. When warm water sloshed down his leg, he'd muttered an oath, set it on the floor and left.

She was a beautiful woman, far too passionate to marry a man she didn't love, and talk of the wedding was more than he could stand. He wanted to believe Hunnicutt would make her happy, but he couldn't see them together any more than he could see himself with Lettie. He regretted sleeping with her beyond words. Leaving her with a child brought no pride, only shame.

He knew the difference now. Saving Charlie topped the list of things he'd done right since leaving Flat Rock. Staying sober ranked second, and the third was keeping his distance from Alex, even though he missed her.

He wasn't disciplined by nature. He'd given in to every bit of lust he'd ever had, but she made him think beyond the moment. She made him want something more, something that would grow like the trees under his care. She took that kind of love for granted, but Jake knew it was rare. If Hunnicutt didn't appreciate her, he'd hunt the man down and knock some sense into him.

Jake was in no mood to be charitable after last night. All through supper, William had glowered at him while the women talked about the wedding. Could they get white silk in time to make the dress, or would pink organdy have to do? Did she want a tulle veil or lace? They chose the tulle, and Alex looked so damn sad that Jake almost came out of his chair in a fury.

How could she marry a man she didn't love?

How could she sacrifice that passionate part of herself, even if it meant keeping the baby? No child in the world could replace Charlie, but there'd be other babies. Did she even know what she was giving up? Probably not, except for what little he'd shown her when they kissed.

Distracted and angry, he hacked off the wrong branch.

"Dammit." He climbed down the ladder just as William came hurrying toward him.

"Get cleaned up," he barked. "You're going into town."

"I just got started. Can't it wait?"

"No."

William never said just one word. Maybe the trunks had arrived. Maybe they had news about the baby. Jake dragged his sleeve across his forehead and put on his hat.

"What happened?"

"Alex needs to see the doctor. Her arm is worse."

A chill ran through him. He felt a pulsing need to hurry, yet he dreaded being close to her for the rest of the day. "I'll get the wagon."

"Use the buggy. It'll just be the two of you."

Jake stared at William. Was her arm really hurting, or was this a scheme to throw them together? Jake decided to take the old bull by the horns.

"Mr. Merritt, I beg your pardon, but—"

"What happened to 'William'?"

Jake ignored him. "This matchmaking has to stop."

"*Matchmaking?* What gave you that fool idea! You aren't half good enough for my daughter, so get those thoughts out of your head."

"Then we understand each other perfectly."

William's eyes turned into flint. "Son, *no one* is good enough for my daughter. Not you, not Thomas Hunnicutt, not the president of the United States, not the king of England, so you can consider yourself to be in pretty good company."

Jake shook his head. "I'll look out for things here. You take her. Take Katherine to lunch at the new hotel."

"I'm not up to the trip." William did look flushed and out of breath, but he had taken to walking the perimeter of the orchard every morning and he'd already made the loop.

"Maybe you should see the doc yourself."

"He's an overeducated fool."

Jake grinned in spite of himself. "Then you watch Charlie and I'll take the ladies. They can go shopping for dresses, or baby things, or—or aprons or something."

"Kath has things to do for the dance on Saturday. The church sponsors it so we'll all be going."

Jake hoped that meant William, Katherine and Alex. He liked taking care of Charlie. He'd be happy to stay home so they could have a good time, but William burst his bubble.

"That includes you. We need help setting up, which leads me to something else. He reached into his back pocket and pulled out a worn leather billfold. "Here's your pay."

There was a time when a wad of greenbacks meant

a night of whiskey and a whore. But today he thought of his promise to Alex.

I'll buy you a hat....

He was back on the Colorado Plateau watching her gulp from his canteen, then he imagined her dressed in red silk, sitting by his side in a fancy restaurant, sipping water, licking the icy beads from her lips. The picture stabbed his conscience. He had no right to think of her that way. She needed a home, children and a future. Jake couldn't give her those things.

He didn't want to give them to Lettie, either, and the thought made his gut burn. Maybe he'd send her some money for the baby. Maybe he'd get drunk after all.

"Thanks," he said, stuffing the bills in his pocket.

"You earned it. Now get going. I'm worried about Alex."

Jake swore under his breath. The old man knew how to yank his chain. Money in his pocket, a pretty woman next to him, a mission of mercy, and enough guilt to shame him into doing what had to be done.

Twenty minutes later he was sitting in the buggy in front of the house, staring at the rump of William's dappled gelding. The horse flicked at a fly with its tail, and Jake scratched his own neck, wishing that all of life's problems were that simple.

Alex was probably feeling the same way. From across the yard, he heard Katherine's worry and the squawk of William bossing his daughter. Between the high and low notes coming from her parents, he heard Alex's soft alto. They sounded like a nest of chirping robins, and it made a harmony Jake had never understood. He and Gabe had just shouted at each other, and whoever made the most noise won.

The front door swung open, and he looked up as William held it for Alex. Her arm was in a sling. Her cheeks were flushed and she moved with an unsteadiness that made him worry. The horse dipped its head, and she looked at the buggy, where Jake was molded to the black leather seat.

"I'm ready when you are," he said casually.

She looked appalled at the thought of riding with him, and he guessed the old man had been badgering her, too.

William hugged her tight, and Jake's jaw tensed. Everything the old man did had an unnatural force to it these days. Staying on the porch, he crossed his arms and glared at Jake, daring him to sit still when they both knew Alex needed a hand into the buggy.

The old man won.

Jake tied off the reins and jumped down from the seat. She avoided his gaze, focusing instead on the ruts in the yard and the hem of her gray skirt. She had one hand on the seat and her foot on the step when he reached her side.

"Here, let me," he said, taking her hand.

Her fingers were hot, and dots of perspiration broke across her brow as she gave him her weight. Her skirt fluffed as she sat down, and the scent of roses and sunshine filled his nose.

"Take your time," William said from the porch. "If Alex is up to it, have supper in town."

He puffed his chest like a wily old rooster. Alex looked as if she wanted to stuff him in a pine box, and Jake felt as sorry for her as he did for himself. Having a two-hundred-pound Cupid on his tail was a new experience, and it seemed new for her, too.

She didn't say a word as they rode through the orchard. The scent of ripening fruit filled the air. Bright sun mixed with the trees, dappling the trail with spots of gray shade. When the house was out of sight, Alex cleared her throat.

"I want to apologize for my father."

She was so serious Jake nearly laughed. There was no point in pretending he didn't understand.

In his most formal voice he said, "He's pretty determined, but don't worry, Miss Merritt. We've already gone around that mountain. Your virtue is safe with me."

And in spite of the ache in his groin and a hunger any man would understand, he had never spoken truer words.

That wasn't the answer Alex wanted to hear.

Maybe he has the right idea, Miss Merritt. May I take you to lunch? His eyes would twinkle shamelessly. His lips would curve into a wicked grin, and the warmth of his skin would reach her nose. He'd lift her hand with his strong fingers and wait for her answer.

I'd enjoy that very much, Mr. Malone.

She would take his arm and feel hard muscle beneath her fingers. She'd be wearing a fancy gown, and he'd be dressed in black. Her hair would be up, and he'd touch the tendrils curling at her nape. They'd be tense and lazy with each other, wanting, anticipating…

Alex choked back a groan as she folded her hands in her lap. She was making a fool of herself. In the past three days, Jake Malone had said fewer than ten words to her, and one of them had been a four-letter expletive.

He should have knocked first, at least that's what she told herself. The bathing room had been full of steam so she had cracked open the door as soon as she stepped out of the water. Jake walked in as she was taking down her hair. He dipped a bucket into the bathtub, and she gasped. He reared back, and for one glorious second, he had studied her body. She hadn't minded at all, except she could barely breathe.

What in the world was she going to do with these feelings? Reaching into her pocket, she fingered the letter to Thomas. With this unexpected trip to town, she didn't need to wait for Jake to mail it for her. She would post it today. If everything went as planned, she would be back in Philadelphia with Thomas and Charlie before summer's end.

It was the best plan for everyone, yet she couldn't stop thinking about a different solution. He was sitting next to her with his thigh brushing hers, his sleeves rolled up to show the dark hair on his forearms, his hat low on his brow even though the leather top blocked the sun.

She looked away, but that picture dangled in her mind like a ripe peach. Her body was heavy with the weight of it, and the scent of sun-ripened fruit filled her with a frightening mix of hope and warning.

She had miserably failed her father's test of courage, of knowing what to leave and what to destroy. She was greedy for the sight of Jake, for the touch of his hands, his smile. Instead of culling back her thoughts, she had nurtured them until they were large and sweet.

But they were sucking away her affection for Thomas. She couldn't let that happen. She had to pluck thoughts of Jake from her mind, so she reached for the biggest one she could find and twisted it loose.

I love you, Jake.

The weight of it filled her hands and belly, and she didn't want to let it go. It was doomed to rot in the summer sun, but she wanted to taste it first.

Reaching down, she touched his knee. "Can we at least be friends?"

He stared at her fingers as if they were snakes. His thigh muscle flexed beneath her palm, and he picked up her hand and put it back in her lap.

"I guess that's my answer," she said with a brittle sigh.

"It's not that simple, Alex."

"It's very simple. You've been ignoring me like I've got some horrible disease. You don't say anything at supper. You wait until I'm gone before you come out to the porch at night. I might as well be invisible."

"You're definitely not invisible."

His gaze stayed glued to the trail, and she wondered what he was seeing in the dust, the distant hills, the acres of blue sky. She saw a vast, dangerous beauty that called for courage. "I miss seeing you at night. I miss knowing you're nearby."

He didn't answer, and it foretold of things to come. One day she would wake up and he'd be gone. He would leave like a passing shadow. Only shadows didn't change the landscape the way this man had changed her life, and Charlie's, too. She exhaled, low and deep.

"Are you all right?" he asked.

Her heart screamed with this new hunger, but she held it in check with a sliver of truth. "I was thinking about the baby."

"He's not much on sleeping, is he?"

"No, but that's normal."

She said Charlie had grown a lot and he agreed. She marveled at his perfect hands, and Jake said he kicked like a mule. Neither of them mentioned Charlotte or the future, but she couldn't stop wondering what she would tell Charlie about his birth and the man who had rescued him. She looked at Jake's profile for clues. He was flesh and blood and bone, but he might as well have been carved from granite. Her father used silence to wear down a man, but Alex wanted answers now.

"What should I tell Charlie about you?" she asked.

"Tell him the truth. I brought you home and then I left."

The fact was so small it bordered on a lie, and she shook her head. "He'd never believe a boring story like that. Maybe I'll tell him he was rescued by a giant gopher with a bad temper."

"A gopher?"

"What would you rather be?"

Jake fought a smile. "Anything but a gopher." Gophers were a nightmare in the orchard.

"Then I'll tell him a big bird carried him through the sky like Aladdin on his magic carpet."

"I think you should stick to the facts."

"That's no fun for a little boy. Children like to imagine things."

His eyes narrowed. "That's a dangerous occupation."

"Not for little boys."

"It is for grown women."

His voice was like tarnished copper, hard and streaked with black. She focused on an embankment where tree roots had been laid bare. The horse's hooves stirred the dust, and a wheel started to squeak like a dying dream.

"You don't have to worry, Jake. Children like made-up stories, but I am very much a realist."

"I am, too. You can tell Charlie anything you want. I won't even think of this place once I'm gone."

"How can you say that?"

"It's the truth," he said.

"But it's not! It's not even close. How can you just forget—"

"It's not hard, and you should do the same thing."

She didn't believe him for a minute. Their lives were forever linked by these past few weeks. He'd left his mark on the orchard and her family; he'd given Charlie life when his real father had failed him; and for the first time she could imagine man-woman love, feel it in her womb, and it was all because of him.

But none of those things mattered. He was going to leave, and she was going to marry Thomas and take Charlie to Philadelphia. Sick and exhausted, Alex leaned against the leather top and closed her eyes.

She nearly jumped out of her skin when Jake clamped his hand on her forehead.

"You're burning up."

Where had he learned to do that? His mother? An aunt? She wanted answers, but Jake wasn't about to give them to her.

Taking the reins in both hands, he said, "We're going to the doctor first. The other stuff can wait."

She didn't protest.

The trail dipped down a hill and the buggy picked up speed. The road followed the curve around a small hill and widened as four square blocks of wood and brick buildings came into view.

As he steered past the bank and the Grand Junction Hotel, she saw Waltham's Emporium where they had met her father. A minute later, they reached the doctor's office.

Jake tied the horse and offered Alex his hand. She reached for it, but instead he took her by the waist and lifted her, swinging her to the boardwalk.

A bell jingled as Jake opened the door, and Dr. Winters came out of the back room. His sandy hair was slicked back, and his skin was as smooth as a polished apple. He finished wiping his hands on a towel and tossed it aside as he greeted her.

"This is a nice surprise, Miss Merritt. I was going to ride out to see you this afternoon."

"I'm afraid I'm having problems with my arm," she said.

"Come on back then."

As doctor put his hand on her waist and guided her to the exam room, she felt Jake's eyes burning a hole in the back of her head. The small room held only built-in shelves, a high table, and a chair with a special armrest. He motioned for her to sit down and closed the door to a crack.

Alex didn't like the cramped privacy, but she didn't want to acknowledge it, either, so she said nothing as he straddled a low stool, pushed her sleeve over her elbow and unrolled the bandage.

"What have you been doing for it?" the doctor asked.

She told him about her mother's poultices and the herbs they made into a paste. "Nothing seems to help. Do you have to lance it?"

"No, but it's too bad no one thought to heat the knife when this happened."

Alex drew back in the chair. Blaming Jake was pointless, unfair and snobbish, and she disliked snobs even more than she disliked people who were mean to dogs and children.

Winters stood up and took a bottle of carbolic from a shelf. They chatted about the weather as he pulled the cork and dabbed at the wound. He bandaged her arm and handed her a paper of sulfa pills.

"These should help, but mostly you need to rest so your body can fight the infection."

As he put away the carbolic, Alex rose from the chair and opened the door. "How much do I owe you?"

"Nothing more than a dance or two next Saturday." She must have looked confused because he felt compelled to explain. "The Harvest Dance is coming up. Your arm should be fine by then. I was hoping to escort you."

"I appreciate the invitation, but I'm engaged to a man in Philadelphia."

He said, "I see," but his tone suggested he didn't see at all. "Perhaps you'll still save a dance for me?"

"Of course."

She smiled stiffly, hoping to dismiss him with a look, but he wasn't taking the hint. She felt like a piece of pie on a plate as she stepped into the waiting room where Jake was leaning back in a chair with his arms laced over his chest. His eyes shot bullets at them both.

Alex glanced at the doctor, who was looking down his nose. "Those black eyes of yours seem to be healing, Malone. Are you seeing spots? Any flashes of light?"

"Nope." Jake stared at the man as if he were a stink bug.

"Anything like a curtain coming over your eye? Any decreased vision?"

"I see just fine, Doc. I don't miss a goddamned thing."

Ignoring Jake, Winters touched her elbow. "Come see me if the infection gets worse. Otherwise I'll see you at the dance. I like waltzes the best."

Jake had the front door open wide and she marched through it. She had no interest in Dr. Winters. He was attractive, well-to-do and single, but she didn't like him. The door swung shut, and she was about to thank Jake for helping her when he started muttering to himself.

"Who the hell does he think he is!"

"He's just—"

"He has no business asking you to a dance."

"He was just being nice." She had been about to agree with Jake that the doctor had overstepped, but for some reason she was defending the man. It made no sense, but neither did Jake's rage.

"He's got no business flirting with you like that. He should have kept his hands to himself, and what's this about liking waltzes?"

"What's wrong with dancing? I'm sure other men will ask me, too."

"They better keep their eyes in their heads. Just because he's got a medical degree from some fancy Eastern school doesn't mean he's got the right to ogle you."

"He wasn't ogling me."

"Oh yes, he was! He gave your backside the once-over at least three times. Your father would have slugged him. He looked like he wanted to eat you up."

"Maybe he did." Something wild and daring took flight in her chest. "Maybe I *want* to dance with him."

Jake stopped in his tracks and stared at her. "Miss

Merritt, it is extremely unwise to mess with a man's attraction."

Tall and angry, with his boots spread wide and his arms loose at his sides, Jake was close to exploding. He was wearing a chambray shirt, but she saw him in his black duster silhouetted against the sky, a rebel with a bad temper and perfect manners.

He was still talking to her, but she had lost her train of thought. "I'm sorry," she said. "What did you say?"

His jaw was so tight it could have been wired shut. "I said you don't know what you're doing."

"I know *exactly* what I'm doing."

"Then you led him on."

"I did not! Maybe I'm looking forward to a few casual dances with a man who—"

"A man who what?" he demanded.

"A man who can manage a polite conversation!"

Jake shook his head. "You are out of your mind if you think he wants to talk about the weather."

"I can take care of myself, thank you."

"Oh no, you can't." His voice dropped to a growl. "You can't tell *me* you've had a lot of experience with men."

Alex forced herself to stay calm. "No, but I've had plenty of experience saying 'no' to people who should mind their own business."

Jake stormed down the street. They left the buggy in front of the doctor's office and walked to the stage office, where the clerk told her no one had asked about Charlotte Smith. The stage company had salvaged the trunks, but they had been sent to Leadville by mistake and wouldn't arrive for a few more days.

At the post office she bought a stamp and handed her letter to the clerk. "When will this go out?"

"You're just in time." Looking into the back room, he said, "Hey, Ed, stick this in the sack you just picked up."

"Sure thing."

"It'll go out right now, miss. The stage is leaving in five minutes.

Alex nodded her thanks. "Do you have anything for Merritt?"

"I believe I do."

Facing a wall of boxes, he reached into a pigeonhole, counted five letters and slid them across the counter. Leafing through them, she saw one from her aunt and three for her father. The fifth letter was from Thomas. She slipped all five in her pocket, but not before Jake saw the envelope that bore her full name in a man's bold script.

He followed her back to the street where the sun had risen a notch and the light was hard and yellow.

"So your beau finally wrote," he said. "It's about time."

"Is this any of your business?"

"You made it my business."

"When?"

"When you started singing in the goddamned desert! When you held that baby tight after his mama bled to death! When you kissed me like you've never been kissed, and then when you—" Jake stopped in mid-sentence. "Shit."

Her chest swelled with a keen and fragile yearning. She was back in the desert tasting his kiss. Wind and rain were scorching her face; the sky was the bluest she'd ever seen. She remembered his arms around her, his lips, every touch, the crazy fear and the wild joy.

Their gazes locked. His eyes were like volcanic lakes—hot, blue, almost steamy. She could see each strand of dark hair brushing his collar, the faint stubble of his beard, the lines around his eyes left by the sun.

A sudden joy pulsed from her head to her toes because this man had feelings for her. He was red-in-the-face jealous of Thomas and the doctor, angry to his boiling point and beyond, and pure longing consumed her. The answer was so simple. She loved Jake. She wanted to stay in Colorado and raise peaches and babies with him.

Except Jake Malone would never stay. Except he claimed he didn't want her. Except she had just begged Thomas to marry her so they could adopt a child.

She was on the verge of running back to the post office when she heard a "yaa, yaa" and the stagecoach stirred the dust around her. It was too late. The letter was gone.

Perhaps it was meant to be that way after all.

Perhaps she was just a foolish spinster spinning tales about an outlaw with drawing-room manners. Doubt grew into a tangled vine that wrapped around her legs. She raised her eyes to Jake's face and a terrifying heat passed between them. It was like a rod of pure light hurled down from heaven. The force of it shocked her, but what could she do?

Suddenly sick and exhausted from the fight, Alex wilted. Sweat poured down her back, across her cheeks. Her arm throbbed with each beat of her heart, and her knees threatened to buckle.

Jake wrapped his arm around her waist, and she pressed against his shoulder. It wasn't enough for either of them, and he pulled her into his arms, tilting her chin to the cloudless sky, groaning as he closed his eyes and kissed her, long and deep and slow. Wanting and needing, giving and taking, they all burned together in a red-orange glow.

She didn't care that they were making a spectacle of themselves. She heard a wolf whistle from the saloon and giggles from a passing wagon, but none of that mattered.

What mattered was the moment, the kiss, and what it promised, except she wasn't sure it promised anything, and so she pulled back, needing to hear the words, needing to know what he would do next.

Her fever burned as Jake smoothed her hair. "You need something cold to drink."

Her father was going to have his way about lunch after all, and she laughed because she wanted it, too. The new restaurant was a block away, and they hurried down the boardwalk. The waitress led them to a table by the front window, took their order and brought glasses and a pitcher of water. Jake poured for them both and cleared his throat.

"We have to get something straight."

Her heart pounded. "I suppose we do."

"I'm not sorry I kissed you just now. I'm not sorry for anything, but I'm *not* staying. I have to leave the minute the last peach is picked."

"You don't have to."

"Yes, I do." Jake reached for her hand. "Your father has ideas, and I like you. I like you a lot more than I should. You're a beautiful woman, Alex. Kind, thoughtful, brave as sin and just as bold when push comes to shove. But there can't be anything between us."

"There could be." She wasn't about to give up now.

"No."

"Is it because I'm engaged?"

Under his breath, he said, "Hell, that wouldn't stop me." Then he found the rest of his voice. "No, it's not that. I'll make it through the harvest for William, but then I've got to be on my way."

"Why?"

"Don't push me, Alex. I'm not worth the effort."

How could he talk about himself that way? "But you've helped us. You're a good man."

He shook his head. "Believe me, I'm not someone you want to know."

"You're in trouble, aren't you?"

"That's not your concern, and I mean to keep it that way."

"My father knows important people, Jake. Nothing shocks him. I know he can help us."

His jaw slackened as he took her hand and laid it in his palm, closing his fingers over hers in a loose tent of skin and bone. "I've already stayed too long, and that's just because William needs help. There's no way I'd ever hurt him, and that means I won't hurt you, either."

She believed him, but she wasn't about to let Jake leave without a fight. Her brown eyes stared into his blue ones. Solid earth stood its ground against a stormy sky.

He sensed the challenge, and his fingers tightened against hers. "I wish it could be different, Alex, but you deserve more than I can give you."

"It's not up to you to decide that for me. You're sitting here telling me this and that, and it's just an excuse to run."

He tried to pull away, but she wouldn't let go. Turning his hand so their palms were touching, he said, "You've got to understand. I'll hurt you if I stay."

"I'll take that chance."

"I won't let you."

He scanned the restaurant for anyone who might be listening. When he was sure they were alone, he caressed her wrists with his thumbs.

"I want you," he whispered. "I want to share your bed and take care of you in all the ways a man can. I like working with the trees, going to bed early and getting up with the sun, but none of that matters. Wanting what you can't have is a waste of time."

"Then fight for it, Jake. Face up to what's chasing you. We can do it together."

He dropped her hand as if it had caught fire. "I can't fix the messes I've made, but there are two things I'm not going to do. Ruining your life is one of them."

"What's the second?"

"Get drunk tonight."

She knew better than to acknowledge what he had said, but it told her everything she needed to know.

"Please don't hope for me," he said. "I can't give you what you want."

"And what do you think that is?"

"You want to adopt Charlie, and for that you need a husband. I'm not that man, and if the truth be told, neither is Thomas Hunnicutt."

His gunmetal gaze dared her to argue, and Alex fired a shot of her own. "A woman makes her own happiness, Jake, and I'll do it with you or without you."

"I believe you will."

Before she could argue further, the waitress brought their meal. Jake put his napkin in his lap, waited for her to take a bite and cut into his fried chicken with a knife and fork. His good manners baffled her, and she wondered if she would ever find out who had taught him to be so careful.

Taking a sip of water, she watched as he chewed the meat and swallowed. Their gazes met over the rim of her glass. She dabbed at her lips with the napkin, and he gave her a crooked grin.

"This tastes a lot like rattlesnake. If I remember right, I promised to buy you a hat."

"Yes, you did." She smiled to put him at ease, but a hat would never be enough. She wanted everything he had to give, and more. She just didn't know how to get it.

Chapter Twelve

Confined to the house as the snakebite healed, Alex spent the next three days deciding what to do. The events of the past month had piled on top of each other like cars in a train wreck. She loved Jake, but he didn't love her, at least not enough to stay. She wanted to adopt Charlie, but she didn't have a husband. And worst of all, she had made a promise she couldn't keep.

She couldn't possibly marry Thomas now, and she was even more sure of the decision after reading his letter. He'd asked about her parents, said his back was acting up again, and told her to stay in Colorado as long as she was needed.

Plagued by the shadows in her dark bedroom, Alex tossed back the covers and gave up trying to sleep. Perching on the edge of the mattress, she ran her fingers over the red welt on her arm. The infection was gone but the guilt wasn't. She had to face facts, and that meant writing to Thomas tonight.

Moving to the desk, she lit the lamp, took a sheet of paper from the drawer and dipped her pen in the ink. She explained the circumstances and asked him to for-

give her, and then taking another sheet, she considered
what to say in the wire she would send today. In the
end, she kept it simple.

Circumstances have changed. Please wait for second letter. Fondly, A.

As the ink dried, she worried that the telegraph wires
would be down or a clerk would lose the message. Or
that the first letter would arrive in a week, and the
second would take a month, and Thomas would come
to Colorado expecting to marry her. He was a good
man, but he needed a wife, not a bride. Those years
had already gone to Rebecca.

A vague loneliness settled over Alex as she turned
down the lamp. She wasn't used to sitting in the dark,
to endings that came before new beginnings. She
wanted Jake at her side, loving her through the night
in that bold way of his. She wanted him enough to
fight, but how? She needed to talk to her father, so at
dawn, she got dressed, tied her hair with a ribbon, took
a peek at Charlie and ventured down the stairs.

The morning light paled in the front room, but there
was no mistaking the bolt of white satin sitting on the
divan like an honored guest. Her mother's sketch pad
was next to it, along with a tape measure and a pair of
shears.

Later Alex would tell her everything. She would understand, she always did. It was her father who chal-
lenged her, and knowing he'd find her, she went
through the front door, sat on the swing and waited.

As he lumbered to the porch, William heard Alex
humming to herself. She looked much better today. No

one had to tell him about the vagaries of illness, and he was relieved her fever had broken.

"Mind if I walk with you?" she asked.

"I'd enjoy the company. Let's walk by the water." He indicated a narrow trail that ran between the orchard and the irrigation channel. The easy path wouldn't take them far from the house if she got tired, and side by side, they walked past a speckled rock and around a hedge of live oak. Her skirt caught on a branch, snapping it back with a swish.

"I'll ask Jake to trim these back," William said.

"If he's still here."

"I think he'll make it through summer."

She pushed a strand of hair out of her eyes and crossed her arms at her waist. "What do you do, Papa, when you want things you can't have?"

"You fight, or you walk away and never look back."

"But what if people get hurt? How do you make it right?" Running her tongue over her dry lips, she looked out to the arid plains.

God, please help her.

"Sometimes you can't," he said. "We all have regrets, and we've all survived skinned knees and broken hearts. It's just life."

Angling her head, she said, "I've made a terrible mistake."

William thought of all the things that statement could mean, and one thing in particular that involved a shotgun and Jake Malone. Touching her shoulder, he said, "Whatever it is, we'll manage."

"I'm going to hurt a man who doesn't deserve to be hurt."

He hoped. He prayed. Then he watched as she kicked at a rock like a little girl. "You see," she said, "I'm not going back to Philadelphia."

He pulled her into his arms. "That's the best news I've had in a hundred years, Miss Merri."

Pushing away from him, she walked further down the trail. "I wish it were that simple. I wrote Thomas a few days ago and asked him to come because of the baby. I told him I loved him."

William knew all about ill-timed words. "It's not a crime to make a mistake like that. You're not perfect, Miss Merri. Now *I* think you are, and your mother's about convinced of it, but you're just as human as the rest of us."

"But I lied to Thomas and to myself. Papa, I *pride* myself on being honest, and look at the mess I made."

William shook his head. "You're being too hard on yourself. There's a difference between a mistake and a lie."

"I'm not so sure."

"I am. You're not the first person to do a little wishful thinking, and you've been lucky. It's not too late to write to Thomas and tell him the truth."

She gave him a wry smile. "Actually, I've already written the letter, plus a wire I want to send today."

"I'm proud of you, Alex. You're doing what's right."

"I hope so." She shook her head. "No, that's not right. I'm positive I can't marry him. It's just that I hate to hurt him."

"I think he'll understand, and deep down, he might be relieved. There's a lot to be said for the comforts of middle age, and a baby under the roof isn't one of them.''

"Charlie *is* loud, isn't he?" Her eyes sparkled and she managed a smile. "Can you take me to town this morning? I want to send the wire as soon as I can."

"We'll go right after breakfast, but you need to be prepared. Men can do surprising things."

"Not Thomas. He's as predictable as old age."

"Which means you have no idea what he'll do next. If he loves you, he'll come anyway. And if he doesn't, it's all for the best."

She shook her head. "He's too busy and his back is acting up. There's not a chance in the world he'll make the trip."

William wasn't so sure, but he kept that worry to himself. "Then the problem is solved."

"At least one of them," she answered. "I still want to adopt Charlie. Do you think I can do it without being married?"

"I'll write to Judge Brown today. Charlie needs a family and we're it, unless someone else comes along."

Worry clouded her face. "I want to know more about Charlotte Smith, but I'm afraid of what we'll find."

So was William. After all their years of wanting more children, Kath loved being a grandmother.

At the thought of his wife, William took a deep breath and slowed his pace. The sun was warm on his cheeks, and the earth was almost singing beneath his feet. He glanced at his daughter and saw that she felt it, too. Even before she spoke, he knew what she was going to say.

"I love Jake."

Please, God. Please, God.

"Does he feel the same way?"

"I think so, but he won't admit it." Chewing on her bottom lip, she walked toward a boulder that offered a wedge of shade. "He's running from something, and he won't tell me what it is."

"The man has burdens, Alex. I don't know what they are, but we talk every night and I see the scars. Some are old and deep, and others are pretty fresh."

"I don't care about any of that."

"Then you're being naive."

She cocked her head in surprise. "Are you saying his past matters? I know you don't believe that. If it were true, Mama should have left after that night."

That night.

It was a signpost in their lives, but did Alex really understand what had happened? She was standing ramrod straight in the shadow of a rock, and he realized she saw *that night* through a child's eyes. She didn't understand the trampling of his soul. He had wrestled with angels and wept like a woman, begged God for death, and found mercy instead.

"I thank God every day for giving me a second chance, but it wasn't easy."

"I remember, but what I remember most is that you and Mama loved each other."

She looked right at him, and he saw a depth that both frightened and pleased him.

"I had a good life, Papa. I grew up with laughter and love. No one has ever laid a hand on me in anger. Until those days in the desert, I'd never been lost or hungry or cold for more than five minutes. I haven't known a single day of real hurt or worry. I've never taken a real chance.''

He knew where she was headed, and though he understood it as a man of God, he hated to see his own daughter facing a basic spiritual truth. He'd preached it just last Sunday.

We are changed by time and circumstance, by daring to surrender our comfort. We are changed by faith.

Alex was leaning against the rock, focusing on a cloud being torn in two by an invisible wind. ''What should I do?''

Following her gaze to the sky, he said, ''What are you willing to risk?''

''Everything.''

The cloud was in shreds now, and knowing that someday she would ache with grief, either in a day or a month or, God willing, in fifty years, he told her the truth. ''You should shoot for the moon, if that's what's in your heart.''

''It is. That's exactly what I want.''

''Then hang on to what you know to be true.'' Leaning against the same rock, William cocked one eyebrow. ''Just between you and me, I don't think Jake's as eager to leave as he says.''

''Really?''

''You can tell a lot about a man by the way he smokes a cigar. I've smoked a thousand of them with a hundred different men, and I know what I'm talking about. Jake smokes it slow, and he gets it down low enough to burn his fingers. That tells you he's not in a hurry to leave, and he knows how to make a good thing last.''

''Maybe it's because you buy good cigars.''

"I do, but don't sell yourself short. He's a smart young man."

"So what should I do?"

"Do you remember those little birds we used to feed in Denver? We started off with three, and a month later there were two dozen. How did you get them to stay in our yard?"

"Bread crumbs and kindness."

"Well then, that's your answer."

For as long as he could remember, Jake had kept his saddlebags packed and ready to go. He lived out of them most of the time, but he'd been with the Merritts for a month now, and he'd finally put his clothes in the rickety drawers of the highboy. William had made good on his promise of a new cot, and Kath had added ten pounds of feathers to the pallet. It was the softest bed he had ever slept in.

That sweet comfort made getting up particularly difficult this morning. Scratching his bare chest, he stretched and tried not to think of kissing Alex in a bed big enough for two. It would have been easy to roll over and give in to his dreams, but he had an errand to run and it couldn't wait. The trunks were waiting at the stage office.

Jake dressed and checked his billfold. He needed to buy a few things, and not knowing how much he'd need, he opened the bureau drawer where he'd hidden Gabe's money as well as his own earnings. It would be plenty when he left, but he needed to spend some of it today.

As he loosened the pouch strings and reached inside, his fingers brushed against his mother's ring. The smooth gold gave him an odd comfort, and he thought of her hand resting on his forehead, checking for fever during a bad case of chicken pox.

He'd been remembering her a lot lately, along with other small kindnesses in his life, perhaps because the angel had been at work. Not a day went by that she didn't do something nice for him. She brought sweet tea to the orchard on hot afternoons, washed his clothes, laughed at his jokes, and told stories of her own that wove her childhood into a warm blanket that covered them both.

And yet she had kept her distance. Instead of talking to him at night, she offered him adventure books from William's library and wished him sweet dreams. Seen and unseen, the angel was everywhere, like heat on a summer day, but so far he'd kept his distance.

Yet he hadn't steered clear of her father. It struck Jake as odd, the way William said so little and found out so much. He knew about Gabe, the fighting and drinking, even the afternoon he'd lost his virginity to an Indian girl. He knew about everything except what mattered most. Jake figured a man was entitled to his secrets, especially if he wasn't going to repeat his mistakes.

Skipping breakfast, he hitched the team to the wagon and rattled out of the yard. The miles slipped by, and he was at the stage office when it opened. A burly man with red hair picked up one trunk and motioned for Jake to take the other.

"Bad accident," he said, hoisting the mud-spattered baggage onto the tailgate.

"Any news about Charlotte Smith?" Jake asked.

"Not a word."

Thanking the man, he drove to Waltham's Emporium, where a young girl was sweeping the steps with a new broom.

It took less than five minutes to pick up two work shirts, dungarees, long johns and socks for himself, then he added a dress shirt with pearl buttons and a pair of black trousers to wear to the dance tonight. The festivities marked the beginning of the summer fruit harvest, an event that started in mid-July and could run through August, depending on the weather and the fruit. He didn't want to go, but William had given him a direct order.

"Buy yourself something decent and make sure no one gets fresh with my daughter, especially that know-it-all doctor."

Jake had been about to refuse, but the memory of Winters's hand on Alex's back made him see red. Making up his mind not to dance with her, promising himself he wouldn't notice the color of her dress or the way it fit her curves, he said, "I'll look out for her, but don't expect anything to change."

William shrugged. "Of course nothing's going to change. You're leaving at the end of August."

"That's exactly right. I've got business elsewhere."

"Sure you do." The old man didn't believe him, but he didn't push, either.

Tucking the package of clothing under his arm, Jake put thoughts of the dance out of his mind and walked to the post office. "I'm picking up for Merritt," he said to the clerk.

"These are for the family, but this one is addressed to Charlotte Smith. I seem to recall she's the lady who died birthing that baby you all have out there."

Jake's blood chilled as he took the letter. It had been forwarded from Leadville to Grand Junction, marked for General Delivery. Who had sent the letter? The writing was precise, but the envelope lacked a return address.

All the way home, Jake thought about the letter and what it could mean. No one would ever know if he opened it and sent word that Charlotte and the baby had died, except Alex would have his hide if she ever found out.

As much as she loved Charlie, she wouldn't keep him at someone else's expense. She'd do the right thing, no matter the cost. She was the bravest woman he'd ever met, and yet fragile, too, because she saw only the best in people, including himself.

With the farmhouse in sight, Jake inhaled the scent of ripening fruit. The sun warmed his shoulders, and looking at the porch, he saw Alex shelling peas into a wooden bowl.

"Good morning," she called as he pulled the wagon closer to the front steps. "You missed breakfast."

She sounded worried and it irked him. "I won't run out on you."

She tilted her head. "Of course you wouldn't, but you're not exactly known for skipping meals."

That was a fact. Kath said he ate enough for two men. He couldn't seem to get enough of anything these days. Alex had washed her hair this morning and left it loose to dry. Smiling at him, she hooked a curl behind her ear and he imagined kissing that exact spot.

"I know you're hungry. Can I get you something to eat? Biscuits and gravy? Or—my God, are those the trunks?"

Jake carried the brown one up the steps and set it at Alex's feet. He expected her to open it, but her eyes were on the trunk still sitting in the wagon. Setting down the bowl, she said, "The green one belongs to Charlotte."

The sun and water had done considerable damage, but Jake could see the trunk had been expensive. Hoisting it against his chest, he carried it to the porch. Alex had her fingers on the lock even before he set it down. It landed with a thud, and she dropped to her knees, struggling to pry the rusted metal with her fingernails.

"I can't get the darn thing open," she said.

"Here, let me."

Using his pocketknife, he pried the metal and lifted the lid. The stench nearly flattened him. Mildew streaked the lining, and the few clothes left inside reeked of decay. He took a step back, but the stink didn't stop Alex. Tossing the slimy mess on the porch, she reached inside and opened the drawers.

"You would think she'd keep important papers in here. A picture…letters, something."

"Maybe." He tried to sound hopeful, but he had his doubts.

"Jake?" She held up a leather pouch and took out a four-inch stack of letters. They came out in one piece, sealed together like layers of yellowed candle wax. "Help me with these."

Together they sat in the swing with the ruined paper in her lap. Working like a woman keeping an apple peel in a single strand, she hunted for clues.

It was the most frustrating hour of Jake's life.

They managed to read just enough to confirm what they already knew. Charlotte Smith had intended to meet her sister, and the two of them were headed further west. All the letters had been signed at the bottom where the damage was the worst, and not one included more than a few clear words.

Alex pointed to a smear of ink. "Do you think that says San Francisco?"

The memory of that Annabelle woman serving him chili at the saloon struck like a cold drop of rain. *I've got plans. My sister's on her way, and then we're headed to San Francisco.*

Maybe it was a coincidence. Maybe Annabelle's sister was a chubby woman named Gertrude with blond braids and missing teeth. Giving the letter back to Alex, Jake touched her knee and reached into his pocket.

"You should open this one, too," he said. "They gave it to me at the post office this morning."

"Oh dear," she whispered, tearing at the flap.

Jake put his arm around her shoulders and they read together.

Dear Charlotte:

Do not contact me again. I regret your inconvenience, but there's nothing more to be said. My last deposit to your account was generous and final.

You and the child are of no concern to me. I consider this matter closed.

Sincerely,

S. R. B.

Alex folded the letter in half. She looked mad enough to tear the man in two. "How could he write those horrible things? How could he not care, even a little?''

Jake raised his arm from her shoulders and rubbed at the stiffness in his neck. "Maybe she was black-mailing him. Maybe there's a wife involved, or—''

With a sharp light in her eyes, Alex studied his face. "Why are you defending him?''

"I'm not," he lied. "Things aren't always as simple as you make them.''

Except this time they were. The letter was hateful, and Jake had treated Lettie even worse. His stomach burned with shame. He'd send her money as soon as he left Grand Junction, maybe even a letter saying he was sorry.

He wanted to leap out of the swing, but Alex took his hand and laced her fingers through his, making a knot he couldn't untie. At least not yet, not today, not with her eyes brimming with worry, her fingers blood-less and cold.

Sighing, she said, "At least we know Charlie's father doesn't want him, even if we have no idea who the man is.''

Seeing the pain in her eyes, Jake decided to wait to tell her about Annabelle. It seemed cruel to say any-thing until he was sure. Tonight at the dance he'd ask questions and nail down the answers.

In the meantime, what harm could there be in danc-ing with her? In a bit of pleasure for them both? He'd do everything a man could do to please a woman, ex-cept kiss her. That seemed like a safe line to draw.

Leaning back in the swing, he gave a little push with his leg. The rope creaked, and Alex sighed. "Maybe I can ask about Charlotte at the dance.''

"I suppose."

"I'd skip it if my mother didn't need help." Facing him, she asked, "You're going tonight, aren't you?"

"Sure. Someone has to keep an eye on you and the doctor."

"Really, I—" She caught the twinkle in his eye and poked him in the ribs. "You're the one who needs looking after."

"There's no doubt about that." He liked the idea a bit too much, but he wasn't going to change his mind about showing her a good time. "Do I get the first dance?"

"Sure." She looked down at her feet, and a strand of dark hair grazed his shoulder.

Questioning his sanity, he touched her face, forcing her to look at him. Her lips were a breath away. "I want the last one, too."

She shivered. "If you'd like."

"I'd like it a lot."

It was just one night. They would dance away their worries. What harm could there be in making a memory?

But a few hours later, dressed in his new clothes, standing at the wagon with his eyes on the most beautiful woman he'd ever seen, he was kicking himself for a fool.

The angel was dressed in red. Elegant and bold, with a sweetheart neckline that dipped between her breasts, the dress showed every curve she had. He remembered seeing her naked, fresh out of her bath, her tiny toes and bare ankles, and his jaw twitched.

"What the hell are you staring at?" William growled.

"Your beautiful daughter."

He sounded like a love-struck puppy, or worse, like what he was, a healthy man who hadn't been with a woman in months.

"You'll answer to me if you don't ask her to dance."

"You should tan my hide if I do."

But what he really needed was a long swim in a cold pond. Like a match to dry wood, Alex's shy smile lit him on fire. Feeling worldly-wise and more than able to show her a good time, Jake changed his mind about not kissing her. He'd kiss her all right, but just once. What harm could there be in that?

Chapter Thirteen

Where was Jake?

The fiddler was warming up with a scale, and the dance floor was filling with men in denim shirts and women in their Sunday best. Alex wanted to dance, but she hadn't seen Jake since he had carried in the pies for her mother. Had the red dress scared him off? Cut low and tight over her breasts, the silk whispered with each step she took.

Take a chance, take a chance.

She ached to tell Jake how she felt, to hear the story of his life, to know about his parents and Gabe, and last night she'd made a decision. She'd fight for him. Tonight she would find out why he wanted to leave when it was so clear he'd found a home, and then she'd say "I love you," and show him how much.

The first bars of a polka rippled through the air. With his height, he should have stood out like a pine tree among oaks, but she didn't see him anywhere. Her toes tapped to the music.

"Miss Merritt?"

She whirled around and nearly knocked over the

punch bowl. Dr. Winters cocked an eyebrow at her dress. "You're absolutely stunning."

"Thank you." For the doctor she would have worn lime green polka dots. To distract him, she asked, "Would you like something to drink?"

"I'd much rather dance with you."

"I've already promised it to someone else." But a rift of fiddle music made a liar of her, and of Jake. Standing on her toes, straining to see through the crowd, she spotted him on the far side of the room. He was talking to someone, but a pillar blocked Alex's view and she couldn't see who had his attention.

Following her gaze, Winters said, "I think he missed his chance."

"Really, I shouldn't. I'm just here to help tonight." Except her red dress said something else, and if Jake so much as glanced at her, she'd abandon the punch bowl in a heartbeat. Dipping the ladle, she filled a cup and set it on the table. "I'm still looking for information about Charlotte Smith. Have you heard anything?"

"Not a word," he replied. "It seems a shame to waste this music, though."

Alex thought so, too. She looked across the room expecting to see Jake, but he was gone. Had he forgotten her completely? Who had has attention? She'd worn red just for him, and with the doctor eyeing her slender waist, she realized some men could be easily distracted.

Her heartbeat slowed with dread just as an adolescent girl in braids walked up to the table. "My ma says I'm supposed to help you."

The doctor grinned and held out his arm. "It looks like you have an assistant. Shall we dance?"

Miserable and out of excuses, Alex gave up. "All right, thank you."

Winters guided her into the crowd. The music was lively, and she faked a smile until the polka ended with a screech from the accordion. The doctor pressed his hand firmly against her back, and she took a step away from him.

"Thank you," she said. "That was nice, but I really do need to check on the baby."

"Of course."

She wanted to send Winters on his way, but he followed her to the punch bowl, where her father was standing with his arms crossed over his chest. "Good evening, Doc. Nice night for a dance."

"Yes, it is."

"It's hot, though, and all this dancing makes people thirsty. Alex, find Jake and tell him to get more ice."

At the sound of Jake's name, her temper flared. Whether he liked it or not, she had a few things to say about broken promises. "I'll go right now," she said.

The doctor touched her back. "I'll go with—"

"So," William interrupted. "What can an old man do for bone pain? I've got this ache in my knee...."

The old liar. His knees were fine, and so was his nose. He'd smelled trouble and come to her rescue.

Excusing herself from the two men, Alex walked across the room, scanning the crowd for Jake and then veering over to a side room used for storage. Perhaps an old lady had lassoed him into setting up more chairs, or maybe he'd noticed a young mother in need of a seat. Wanting to believe he had a good reason for missing their dance, Alex walked into the small room that held extra chairs, peered through the shadows and found Jake. With a woman.

Her name was Annabelle. She was blond and pretty and she sang in the choir. Alex had met her at church last week. She had once been a prostitute, though no one ever mentioned it.

Jake was studying every nuance of her heart-shaped face, and Alex wasn't at all surprised to see Annabelle sway into him. To steady her, he grasped her arm and said something only Annabelle could hear.

The hot knife of humiliation brought Alex to her senses. Jake was a friend, nothing more. Whom he spoke with, or kissed, or even bedded, was none of her business. Doing an about-face, she raced out of the room.

He reached her in seconds. Clamping his hand on her bare shoulder, he spun her around. An odd glitter hardened his eyes. "Alex, we need to talk."

"No, we don't." Her tongue ran wild. "My father asked me to find you. We need more ice and the blocks are in the shed out back. I was looking for you. Just so he wouldn't do it himself. You know how he is, and—"

"I need to explain."

"No, you don't." The band launched into a waltz, and Alex cut him off. "Excuse me, but I've promised this dance to someone else."

His eyebrows came together in a hard line, and his gaze shifted to the wall where Dr. Winters smiled, tugged on his cuffs and gestured to Alex.

"I believe I promised you a waltz," she said in a ringing voice.

The doctor whirled her onto the dance floor. With her skirts flying and a smile plastered across her face, she turned her back on Jake Malone.

* * *

Goddamn it.

Alex had seen him talking to Annabelle, but she had no idea what it was about. He'd asked the girl if she'd had word from her sister, and she'd burst into tears.

"Charlotte should have been here by now," Annabelle had said. She hasn't written to me, and no one answered the wire I sent. I don't know what to do."

Sick with the realization that he'd found the dead woman's sister, Jake had touched Annabelle's arm to steady her. This wasn't the time to ask probing questions. Showing her the letters would confirm his suspicion, but first he had to speak to Alex.

Only she didn't want anything to do with him right now. Maybe that was for the best. He'd been a fool to think he could kiss her once and leave with a bittersweet memory for comfort. At the sight of the doctor's hand on her waist, Jake tensed like a bobcat ready to pounce. Damn him for a fool, but he wanted to knock Winters upside the head, throw Alex over his shoulder and carry her someplace safe and dark.

But that wasn't going to happen.

Instead he'd walk away after the harvest, wishing her all the best in life, hoping her future would be full of Sunday picnics and Saturday night pleasures. He'd tell William what he knew, then he'd go back to the farm before he did something stupid, like pick a fight with Winters.

The music blared as he walked to the refreshment table where Kath was showing off the baby to a neighbor. Behind her, William cut him with a hard stare.

"Where's the ice?"

The old man looked tired and out of sorts, but Jake didn't hesitate. "I have to talk to you."

"All right. Let's step outside."

The two men angled their way out the door and down the steps to the street. Jake turned the corner, leading William into a narrow alley. The music was quiet here, the night dark and still, and wishing he had a cigarette, he slammed his palm against the wall.

"So what's got you tied in knot?" William asked.

"I found Charlie's aunt."

The old man swore softly. "Who is it?"

"Annabelle. The cook from the Wild River Saloon."

"Are you sure?"

"She's been waiting for her sister for more than a month. The last names don't match, but the first names do. There's not much of a resemblance, but both women were headed for San Francisco."

William nodded. "It's reason enough to ask more questions."

"The only thing that doesn't add up is Charlotte Smith having a baby, but she might have wanted to keep it a secret. It would explain why she was rushing to get here, and it also makes sense she'd use a name like Smith."

"Did you ask Annabelle about it?"

"No. It's not my place."

"It's your place as much as mine. Maybe more so."

"You're wrong."

William shook his head as if he'd heard the fish tale of the century, and Jake ground his boot heel into the dirt. It was true he had a stake in the baby's past, but he had no claim on his future.

A wagon rolled down the street, and a shaft of lantern light fell across William's face. His jaw sagged. The old man looked like he'd just been kicked. "Someone has to tell my daughter."

Jake couldn't stand the thought of being close to her. But he couldn't walk away now. And the hell of it was, he didn't want to.

"I'll tell her," he said. "Then the three of you can decide what to do after the shock's worn off."

"Thank you, son."

William had called him "son" before, but for the first time Jake understood what it meant. The old man was trusting him with his daughter. It was worse than being responsible for the peaches, but he couldn't back out now.

"I'm sure you'll find the right words," William said.

"She's not too pleased with me right now, but I guess that doesn't matter." Except he had hurt her feelings, and that mattered more than his own comfort.

"So what did you do to make her mad?"

"Hell if I know."

The old man laughed. "Don't try that bullshit on me. You know damn well what you did to set her off."

William stared at him, and Jake wondered where he had learned to read minds. "She saw me talking to Annabelle."

"And?"

"And what?" Jake kicked at the dirt. Annabelle had been crying about her sister and he'd offered comfort, but that wasn't what Alex had seen. From a distance, a comforting touch and male interest looked a lot alike.

"I'm a goddamned fool," he muttered.

"I won't argue with you there, but I'm sure you can fix things if you try."

"I'm not sure I should."

"I am," William said. "You're not the first man I've hired, Jake, but you're the only one I'd trust with my family."

"Then you're as big a fool as I am."

"Maybe even bigger, but I know what I've seen. You care about the things that matter. It almost makes up for what's missing."

"And just what might that be?"

"Have you ever wrestled with an angel?"

A nervous rattle shook his bones. Did the old man know he thought of Alex as an angel? Was he asking if he'd bedded his daughter? He'd done it a thousand times in his thoughts, but William couldn't possibly know how he thought of her. Or did he?

"What kind of angel?" he asked.

"The kind you can't see. The kind that gets a grip on a man's balls and squeezes until he wants to die. It's an ugly fight that scars a person for life."

Heat prickled across Jake's neck. The stars got brighter and William's gaze burned hotter.

"There's nothing in this world that love can't forgive," William said. "What you've got hidden is between you and God, but I think there's an angel out there that won't let go until he knocks you flat. Win or lose, you'll never be the same, and I suspect you've been wrestling with some big ones since you've gotten here."

It was true. Every day had been a wrestling match between wanting a drink and not wanting one. Between wanting sex and hungering for something more, needing to run and wanting to stay. Between caring for Alex and hating himself.

"My daughter loves you."

It was the last thing in the world Jake wanted to hear. "She shouldn't."

"But she does."

His fingers itched to touch her face, her hair, the line

of her back. A waltz drifted through the window in perfect time to the beat of his heart, and he imagined dancing with her, her face close to his, her red skirt brushing his thighs. The picture sent a burning arrow through his chest, and he knew what he had to do.

Just for tonight he'd let William's angel pin him to the ground. He'd dance with Alex and kiss her just one sweet time. He'd dream about staying even though he knew he had to leave. He pushed away from the wall. "I'd better get inside."

"You go on ahead. Just tell Kath I'm all right."

Jake bounded up the stairs and hurried through the door. He found Katherine and told her William was outside sneaking a cigar. He knew she'd smile, and she did.

Then, scanning the dance floor, he spotted Alex with Winters. Her dress was as red as the hot blood in his veins, and her silky hair looked ready to tumble down her back. Her eyes glittered as the doctor touched her back. Jake watched as he pulled her close, then closer still.

Her smile faded and she lowered her gaze. Jake held still, trying to read her thoughts, until the doctor's hand drifted lower, to the tiny indentation just above her round bottom. Her mouth gaped in surprise. Winters's grin slid into something lustful, and Jake launched himself into the crowd. He was seeing four shades of red by the time he tapped the doctor on the shoulder.

"I'm cutting in."

The doctor scowled and looked at the ravishing woman in his arms. "Alexandra?"

Jake didn't give her a chance to say no. Whirling her away, he silently thanked Miss Hatfield for teaching the boys in her school how to dance.

Alex looked as if she wanted to kick him in the shins, but he didn't care. They moved like one person, and somehow dancing with her became a strangely defiant act.

He put a wicked in his eye. "You're mad at me, aren't you?"

"Not in the least."

"You could have fooled me."

He was grinning at her, daring her to admit she was furious with him for missing the first dance, for talking to Annabelle, for being just a little bit dangerous and too good-looking.

She was trying to ignore him by looking over his shoulder, but the heat in her cheeks told him it wasn't working. He gave her an insolent smile, and she glowered at him. "Cutting in like that was rude."

"No more rude than where Dr. Debonair was putting his hands."

"There was absolutely nothing wrong with how he was holding me. In fact, Richard is an excellent dancer."

Jake heard the emphasis on the man's first name, but even that didn't phase him. It was a small thing compared to the way she was trembling in his arms.

Maybe he'd kiss her after all. Maybe he'd stay. Maybe he could become the man he wanted to be. Her face was an inch from his, her lips slightly parted.

They swayed to the music, dipping and whirling, the force of it pulling them apart with only his arms holding them together. They were alone in a circle of dancers, protected by a wall of color and motion, and his arms tightened around her. Dipping his head, he brushed her lips with his.

It wasn't enough. He pulled her hard against his

body so her breasts were warm and firm against his chest, and he tucked her head against his shoulder. They danced that way until the fiddle hit the last high note, then he whispered, "Come outside with me. There's something I have to explain. About Annabelle and—"

She pushed away from him. "You don't have to explain anything."

"What? Annabelle is—" He just had to say Charlie's name, but he couldn't get the word out.

Alex rushed away. Why couldn't he spit out what had to be said? He felt like a fool, and that made him angrier than he'd been all night. He marched after her.

"Dammit, Alex! We've got to talk. Now."

She spun around, looking like she was ready to spit in his face. "You have no right to push me, Jake. I'm sick of your *good* manners. A stray dog has more integrity than you do."

Now *that* lit his fuse. He'd been called a lot of things, most of them deserved, but never anything as low-down as a stray dog, and never by someone he cared about. But one thing could be said for stray dogs. They knew how to fight.

"I'll be damned, Miss Merritt. I think I've just been insulted."

"Well, you have been."

"Is that the best you can do? I've been called worse."

"I'm sure it was deserved."

"Yes, it was, but this *isn't* one of those times. Why don't we step outside and settle this little difference of opinion?"

He could see her weighing the options, wondering if it was worth the risk, if he really did have something to say. Now was the time to say Charlie's name. "It's about—"

"Do you need help, Alexandra?"

Jake groaned at the whine of the doctor's voice.

Winters touched her arm and she touched him back. "Everything's fine, Richard, but perhaps you'll take me home after all."

Dr. Debonair was in serious need of a black eye, but Jake stopped himself from picking a fight. He could be the picture of congeniality when it served his purpose, and making Alex angry would serve no purpose whatsoever. He knew how to fight all right, but he also knew how to pick the time and the place, and this wasn't it.

"It's a nice night," Jake said in a honey-drenched voice. "I hope you two enjoy the moonlight."

Alex winced. The look pained him, but she had made a choice and he had to respect that. News about Charlie would have to wait until morning, and maybe it was better this way. Maybe he'd misjudged the circumstances. Maybe it was better if she got to know Dr. Debonair and he kissed her on the cheek and she—

To hell with that.

The thought of Alex with another man made him hotter than a three-alarm fire, and with his hands balled into fists and his eyes shooting bullets, Jake faced the most painful truth of his life.

He'd fallen in love with Alexandra Merritt. And damn him for a fool, he'd wrestle every angel in heaven if that's what it took to make her his.

Chapter Fourteen

Jake's blue eyes were as wild as a summer storm, and her skin prickled as if lightning were about to strike. Hot and magnetic, his gaze pulled at her, but she understood the threat of fire, torrents of rain, a flood of emotion beyond her control. It frightened her. She wanted him to calm the storm, but it was Richard who took her hand.

"Are you ready to leave?"

She nodded, and he hooked his arm around her waist and tugged. She felt like a sheep being dragged away from a wolf, except the wolf had a frantic look in his eyes, as if the storm had broken and he'd been caught in the rain.

"We should find your parents," Richard said. "Excuse us, will you, Malone?"

Distracted and edgy, Jake ignored them and shouldered his way through the crowd. His dark hair stood out like a trail of ink among the couples clad in light-colored shirts and calico dresses. The fiddle player raised his bow and struck a sharp note.

Richard tugged at her waist. His hand was loose against her side, and they were flushed as if they'd been dancing. To a stranger they looked like a couple, but Alex knew otherwise. Appearances could be deceiving. Jake had been trying to tell her something, but she had jumped to conclusions about Annabelle that seemed pale compared to the pain she'd just seen in his eyes. She'd misjudged him, she was sure. She had to find him.

She slipped out of Richard's grasp and searched the crowd, but Jake was gone.

"What's wrong?" Richard asked.

"I remembered something, that's all. It'll have to wait."

"Are you sure?"

What choice did she have? Jake was gone, but she was sure he wouldn't leave without checking with William. Somehow she would escape from the doctor, find Jake, and hear what he had to say.

Nervously surveying the room, she said, "Maybe we should stay a little longer."

"Whatever you'd like. It's a warm night. Would you like something to drink?"

"Yes, please."

They headed for the punch bowl, where William was talking to the president of the Grand Junction Bank. When he saw Alex, he stopped in midsentence and drew his eyebrows tighter in a worried line.

"Is something wrong?" she asked.

"Where's Jake?"

Alex handed the doctor a glass of lemonade and took one for herself. Making her voice light, she said, "I'm sure he's here somewhere."

Dr. Winters shook his head. "Don't count on it. I just saw him leave. Business must be booming at the saloon tonight."

When William dropped into a chair, fear shot through Alex. "You look tired, Papa. Maybe I should find Jake and tell him it's time to leave."

"No, I'm all right. Find your mother, though. She's probably dead on her feet by now, and the Westons are in charge of cleaning up."

Alex put down her glass and tried to sound apologetic. "I'm sorry, Richard, I should be helping my parents."

"Nonsense!" Katherine ploughed through the crowd with Charlie asleep in her arms. "Your father and I can handle things. You two should dance."

Richard gave Katherine a winning smile. "I'd enjoy that as long as Charlie's not too much for you."

"He's no trouble at all."

Richard looked him over with a professional eye, and like Alex, he saw a happy, sleeping baby. "He's putting on weight."

Alex touched the baby's warm head. He was a lightning rod for the things that mattered most, and she made up her mind to find Jake.

Richard made a show of patting the baby's back. "If no one claims this little fellow, you folks may be keeping him."

"We'd all be pleased to raise him," Katherine replied. "Of course we want what's best for Charlie."

"Nonetheless, you make a fine grandmother," Richard said with a wink.

The older woman huffed to disguise her pleasure and then tucked the baby under her chin. "Go on and dance now. We don't want the music to go to waste."

Alex stiffened with reluctance. "I really should be helping you and Papa."

"Don't be silly! Your father and I are leaving soon,

but you can stay for the last dance if Dr. Winters wouldn't mind escorting you home.''

Richard grinned. ''I was already planning on it.''

Katherine looked like a gray-haired schoolgirl. ''It's a perfect night, don't you think?''

Alex didn't think so at all. She had argued with Jake, insulted him and walked off with the doctor without finding out what he wanted to tell her, and she wasn't any closer to finding out if anyone in Grand Junction had known Charlotte Smith.

Richard's hand curled around her waist. ''Thank you, Mrs. Merritt. Your daughter is an excellent dance partner. I'm sure she gets her light feet from you.''

Katherine smiled, but William crossed his arms over his chest. ''She got a few things from me, too, so get her home early.''

''Of course,'' Winters said with a nod.

The dip of his head seemed respectful, but he was drawing circles on her back with his forefinger. Her skin prickled, and she decided he had as much charm as a brass spittoon.

But Katherine didn't see him in that light. She saw a doctor, a man with a career and a future. ''Now don't worry about the baby,'' she said. ''You just have a good time.''

Alex winced. She'd gotten herself into this mess, and somehow she had get out of it.

It pained Jake to see Alex leave with Winters, but he didn't hold it against her. He knew all about events spiraling out of control. It was the story of his life, but the time had come to put an end to all that. He knew exactly where he had to go, and the next five minutes would make or break the rest of his life.

Ignoring the music, Jake walked to the cloakroom and grabbed his hat. Out of habit he pulled it low as he walked through the door and headed for the center of town. The night air had cooled since his talk with William, but it was still warm enough to raise a sweat as he followed a trio of cowboys down the street. The shortest one slapped his wire-thin partner on the back, while the third called in a bet for a bottle of whiskey.

"You owe me the best, Bobby. I want Texas Gold and one glass. I ain't sharin'."

"You can have it. I'll settle for a pretty woman on my lap and another one pouring me a drink."

The older man shook his head, as if he were already too tired to do anything more than sit. "You two are gonna end up puking on your own boots."

Jake lagged behind, but their laughter reached him like a cloud of bad breath. He had no intention of ever taking another drink. His business was elsewhere, and as the men disappeared through the swinging doors, he stepped off the boardwalk and crossed the street.

The piano music followed him as he neared the Sheriff's Office. Just as he hoped, a dozen Wanted posters were nailed to a board next to the door.

His stomach churned as he squinted at the inky drawings. He had it all figured out. If he was wanted for Henry Abbott's murder, he'd keep a low profile until the harvest was in and then he'd head straight to Mexico.

He'd never breathe a word of the trouble to Alex or her family. He'd say goodbye and wish them well. Angels or not, he'd be on his way before he did any more harm to the Merritts.

On the other hand, if he didn't see his name on the wall, he'd have some serious thinking to do.

His blood ran hot as he studied the posters. Some were new; others were as dry and yellow as an old man's skin. He saw fat men, short men, rugged men, angry men. Men with beards, clean-shaven men. Even a woman with a tale that curled his hair.

The posters were in four neat rows. Jake scanned them all, and nowhere did he see the likeness of a twenty-five-year-old man who had made more than his share of mistakes.

"Can I help you, son?"

He nearly jumped out of his skin. The sheriff was standing behind him, his eyes suspicious, his hand loose on his hip and as big as Gabe's.

"I came down from Flat Rock." The sheriff waited, and Jake felt a flat pressure in his chest. He could tell the truth, and be done with it all. "I had some trouble there over a month ago. I got drunk, got in a fight and shot a man who deserved to be shot. I think I killed him."

Lowering his chin, the lawman squinted in the dim light, sized Jake up and grunted. "The sheriff up there's Gabe Malone. He's a hard-ass. Fair but as tough as they come. If you were in trouble, the entire state of Colorado would know about it."

Jake could hardly believe it. "The man who got shot in the fight, his name was Henry Abbott."

"Never heard of him." The sheriff scratched his chin. "What did you say your name was?"

He wasn't going to start hiding now. "Jake Malone. Gabe's my brother."

Rocking back on his heels, the lawman crossed his arms and glared. "Keep your nose clean around here, and we'll get along fine."

"Yes, sir."

The sheriff huffed just like Gabe sometimes did, and Jake watched as he walked away, fading into the darkness.

Alone in the shadows, he nearly hit his knees. He had to find Alex. He'd bide his time if she was still dancing with Winters. But he'd be damned if the doctor would be the one to kiss her good-night.

He had things to tell her, and this was the night.

Alex sagged with defeat when the doctor helped her into his buggy. It was close to midnight, and for the past three hours she'd been scouring the crowd for Jake. Only a few wagons remained outside the hall, and she didn't see his horse at the hitching post.

Had he gone to the saloon? Her stomach knotted as she glanced down the street. She knew as well as anyone that a man made his own choices, but she'd pushed him away tonight and she regretted it.

Alex folded her hands in her lap as the doctor climbed into the seat next to her. "Are you comfortable?" he asked.

"Fine, thank you."

He was reaching for the reins when a boy riding bareback galloped up to them.

"Wait up, Doc!" he shouted. "It's my pa."

"You're the Morris kid, aren't you?"

"Yes, sir. He got drunk and shot himself in the leg. It's bleeding bad. I tied it off, but you've got to come right now."

"I'll come as soon as I take Miss Merritt home," the doctor said.

"He needs your help, sir. I would be much obliged if you could see to him first."

Alex saw Jake in the boy's good manners, the way

his lips twitched as he bit back frustration. He was too skinny for his age. At the very least she could fix the boy a meal and maybe scrub up the kitchen.

She tugged on the doctor's sleeve. "I'll come with you. I might be able to help."

He looked at her as if she were crazy. "The man's drunk and he has a gun. I can't take you there."

"Of course you can."

"Absolutely not. He could be dangerous."

The boy interrupted. "We've gotta hurry, Doc."

"I'll come right after I take care of Miss Merritt."

Alex jumped out of the buggy. "Go. You're wasting time."

He scowled at her. "How will you get home?"

"I'll get a ride with the Westons. Their wagon is still here. I'll be just fine."

With a curt nod and a flick of the reins, the doctor followed the boy down the street. Alex hurried into the hall to look for the Westons. They owned the farm just past her father's place, and Mr. Weston was a deacon in the church, a reliable man with six children and a butterball wife.

Alex scanned the room, but it was empty except for a man extinguishing the lamps, so she went back outside where a ranch hand was climbing into the last wagon. She stared in confusion.

"Can I help you, ma'am?" he said.

"Isn't that the Weston wagon?"

"Yes, it is. I'm Cal."

She had no idea who Cal was.

"I work for them," he explained. "The family's staying in town. Is there something I can do for you?"

Cal seemed like a decent fellow, but she was an

optimist, not a fool. Her parents would worry, but it would be safer to stay at the hotel for the night.

"No, thank you," she said.

The wagon rattled as Cal drove away, and Alex walked across the street to the Grand Junction Hotel, where she explained the situation to the clerk and took a room. It was late, and the hallway was empty. The oil sconces had been turned low, and she fumbled with the key in the shadowy light.

"Here, let me." Jake's strong hand closed over hers. She smelled soap, bay rum and warm skin, and his breath brushed her cheek as he opened the door, guiding her over the threshold.

Her gaze focused on the bed. It was big enough for two, and it took up most of the room. The mattress was high and firm, covered with a spread of quilted ivory lace. It had been pulled tight, revealing a cascade of roses in the delicate weave.

As Jake closed the door, Alex looked down at the mattress and touched the tip of an embroidered leaf. The floor creaked as he walked to the bed, coming up behind her until they were less than a foot apart.

Without looking up, she said, "How did you know I was here?"

He cupped her shoulders and turned her around, forcing her to look at him. His eyes glittered with something hard and sweet, but the dim light softened the line of his mouth. The wolf was no longer shocked or wary. She saw purpose in his eyes, even presumption, and she liked it.

"I've had my eye on you all night," he said. "I'd ridden ahead and was going to wait for you at home, but then I saw Winters race out of town. Some ranch hand told me you'd headed for the hotel."

Trembling, she raised her face to his, expecting him to kiss her, but instead he cradled her head against his chest. "I found Charlie's aunt."

The night shattered into silvery fragments. She saw Jake studying Annabelle's face, heard the strange way he said her name, recalled the ache in his eyes that she'd mistaken for something instinctive and male.

"It's Annabelle, isn't it?"

"I think so."

Her shoulders sagged, and he led her to the window where moonlight puddled on the floor. She perched on the edge of the bed as Jake looked out to the street.

Did he notice the fine layer of dust muting the light? Could he smell the clean sheets? Did he know that his back was shaped like a shield? That she had prayed for help in the desert and he had come? That even now, he gave her hope.

"It's hot in here," he said. "Do you mind if I open the window?"

Not trusting her voice, she nodded. The squeak of wood against wood sent a chill down her spine as he raised the sash. She heard laughter from the saloon, the tap of boots on the boardwalk, breaking glass, then a shout.

"Tell me everything," she said.

He ran his hand through his hair. "Some things add up and some things don't, but most of the story makes sense."

He gave her the stark details, but Alex heard "if" and "maybe." Questions flew through her mind faster than Jake could talk. Where was Annabelle from? What was her last name? Why didn't she say her sister was expecting a baby? Could there be two women named

Charlotte on their way to Grand Junction in the middle of June?

And if Annabelle was really Charlie's aunt, would she want him?

Questions fell around her like the first drops of a coming storm. Slow. Heavy. The size of a dime, and then a nickel and a quarter, they pelted her. Charlie had a family. An aunt, a woman who would want him.

The raindrops turned into rivulets on her cheeks, and she started to shake. What if this woman wasn't fit to be a mother? What if she wouldn't rock him to sleep when he cried in the middle of the night?

Somewhere in the storm, Jake had pulled up a chair and sat down in front of her. He'd taken her hands and was massaging her palms with his thumbs. His touch was like sandpaper on fresh-cut wood, and they looked up at the same time. He wiped away her tears, and she found her voice.

"I wanted to find someone, but not someone close," she said. "Not someone who would want him."

Did being a blood relative, if it was true, give Annabelle more rights than Alex? She had pulled Charlie from his mother's womb. That had to count for something.

"I love him so much," she whispered.

"I hope it works out. I really do, but the answer is in the letters."

"Even if she *is* Charlie's aunt, I can't just give him to her. How will she take care of him?" Biting her lip and trying not to sound jealous, she asked, "How well do you know her?"

"Not well at all, and definitely not in the way you were thinking earlier." His tone was both insulted and forgiving. "Do you remember the night I went to town? After the thinning?"

"Yes."

"She's the person who talked me out of getting drunk and spending the night. She sent me home to you."

"I should be grateful then." Except she didn't want the woman to be kind and decent, someone who'd help a stranger, someone like herself.

"I need to explain what you saw tonight," Jake continued. "Annabelle started crying when I asked about her sister. She's worried because she hasn't heard from her. I was just comforting her. That's why things looked more personal than they were. During our conversation, Annabelle told me she's been saving for a move to San Francisco."

"I see. Maybe she's ambitious. Maybe she won't want a baby."

"Maybe not, but first we have to find out if she has a claim."

Alex sighed. "Do my parents know?"

"I told your father earlier tonight."

A twinge of guilt rippled through her. "They're going to be worried. They think Richard is taking me home."

He shook his head. "I talked to William before they left. He knows I'm looking out for you."

"He trusts you."

Jake ran his fingers over her palms. "I'm honored by that."

"I trust you, too. What should we do?"

"The harvest starts soon, and your father wants to hire Annabelle to cook for the pickers. Maybe you could get to know her a little bit. She's worried about her sister, but a week or two won't change things.''

''That's true. I want to look through the letters again, and Charlie needs time to grow. He's so small.''

An ache spread from her hands to her heart. Her gaze traveled to the window and back to Jake. Shadows cut across his face, and the longing in his eyes matched the need in hers. She wanted to collapse against him and lose herself in his arms. She was tired of settling for less than she wanted, tired of being strong and empty and alone.

Jake looked away first. ''We should go. Can you stand another ride on Smiley?''

She didn't answer.

''If you want to stay here, I'll ride home and leave a note for your parents. I'll come back with the buggy in the morning.''

She squeezed his hand. ''Stay with me.''

His eyes turned smoky with desire. Her cheeks flushed, and a wicked smile spread across his face.

''I'll stay,'' he said softly, touching her hair. ''But you've got to promise to say no if I forget my manners.''

''Maybe I want you to forget them. Maybe I want to forget my own.''

He shook his head. ''That's not a good idea.''

Alex gaped at him. She was an adult. She understood the whims of her body, and this was a line she wanted to cross. Now. Tonight. Except the man she had chosen was saying no, probably for the first time in his life. She didn't know whether to be proud of him, or insulted.

''I can't believe you're saying no to me,'' she said.

''Me, neither.''

He was grinning as if he'd just tamed a bucking bronco, and she toyed with the idea of changing his mind. Pulling her hand from his, she ran her fingers along his muscular arms, up his neck, until her fingers tangled in his dark hair.

Her breasts strained against her red dress. He glanced down at her chest, her taut nipples visible beneath the bodice, and a soft hum came from his throat. She slid her palms down to his beating heart, then, as if he'd gotten a grip on something sure, he covered her hands with his and stilled them against his chest. "There's only one reason I'm asking you to say no."

"What is it?"

"I love you, Alex."

His eyes were bright with hope, but it was too soon to make it her own. She would have taken a night of passion as a gift, but love meant a future. It meant commitment. And most of all, it meant forgiveness. She needed to know the truth about him. Why was he running? What demons had chased him across the Colorado Plateau?

Questions dangled in her mind, but one thing was sure. "I love you, too."

He gave her another wicked smile, and leaning forward, he took her mouth with his. It was a deep kiss, slow and deliberate. She wrapped her arms around his back and pulled him forward, but he didn't budge.

She fell back on the bed, lifting him out of the chair so that he stood with legs spread wide and his hands planted on either side of her head. Looming over her, he said, "You promised to say no."

"No, I didn't."

Arching upward she clung to his shoulders and kissed his throat. He moaned and laughed at the same time. "I hear that waiting makes a wedding night all the sweeter." His deep voice was edgy, as nervous as the sky before a storm. And then it hit her. He'd said "wedding night."

"Oh, Jake."

She wanted to love him forever, but a warning roared in her ears. If she settled for a future that had no ties to the past, their love would be like a tumbleweed in the desert. Living on water from sudden storms, the shallow roots would pull loose in the wind. She'd seen dozens of the bushes blowing in the desert, aimless, dead and lost.

"I don't really know who you are, do I?"

The edginess came back to his eyes. "No, you don't, but that's about to change."

Chapter Fifteen

And so the tale began.

Jake sat down in the chair, rested his elbows on his knees and spoke in a cadence that held a hint of Virginia and the childhood he had tried to forget. The words were brackish in his mouth, like water that had been sitting in his canteen for the past six weeks, and he was glad to spit them out.

"It's true I was born near Fredericksburg," he said. "But I never knew my father except that his name was Lawrence Prescott."

"But your last name is Malone."

"It is now, but Gabe and I had different fathers. His old man got kicked in the head by a mule and died. Three months later, our ma married the man she'd hired to help out. Lawrence Prescott got killed at Manassas about a year after I came along, and she went back to using Malone."

"So you and Gabe are half brothers."

"And full-blown enemies," Jake said. "The farm would have been his if we'd stayed, but Ma couldn't handle it even with his help. She packed up, and we took a train west."

"I can see why he's bitter."

"It got worse when we settled in Denver. She found a job clerking in a store and Gabe mucked out the livery stable for a few bits a day, but he hated every minute of it. He never stopped talking about getting his land back. He might have done it except our mother died from pneumonia. She made him promise to look out for me, and he's hated me ever since."

Jake couldn't blame him, either. "I was a bitter pill to swallow."

"You were just a child. Gabe must have cared about you. He could have left, but he raised you."

"Only because Ma made him promise to look out for me, and I've got to say this for Gabe. He keeps his word."

"How did you both live?"

"Eventually he became a deputy in Denver, but he didn't like the city and so we moved around. We hit the mining towns first, Leadville, Silverton. I rode shotgun on silver shipments while the mines were running hot, and worked a few ranches, but mostly I just stayed drunk."

He forced himself to look at her. "The truth is, after a while no one would hire me for anything."

"The drinking?"

"That, and I stole money a time or two. Gabe found out and threatened to throw me in jail if I didn't pay it back."

"What did you do?"

"The only thing I could with Gabe breathing down my neck. I got an honest job on a ranch and paid back every penny."

Jake rubbed his neck. "Anyway, I was fed up with working ranches when Gabe moved up to Flat Rock.

It seemed as good a place as any to stay drunk, so I tagged along.''

"And he let you stay with him?"

"He takes his promises seriously. Besides I was supposed to hold up my end of expenses. He gave up on Virginia a long time ago, but he was saving to buy land. He had about three hundred dollars tucked away, and I know that for a fact because I stole it when I left."

Alex didn't even blink. "You'll have to give it back."

"I want to. I will," he said. "But there's more. I shot a man the night I left Flat Rock."

"Are you wanted?" Her eyes turned a deeper brown, and her fingers caressed his. "Even if you are, we can work things out. I'm sure of it. There are people who'd help."

He ran his hand over her cheek. "I'm in the clear."

"But we have to be sure."

"I'm sure. I went to the Sheriff's Office after you shooed me away at the dance, and—"

"I'm so sorry about that."

"Don't be," he said, shaking his head. "I looked at the Wanted posters and I'm not on them. I even talked to the sheriff. I'm a free man, Alex. And I can tell you, I wouldn't be here unless I knew it for a fact. I don't ever want to hurt you."

"The only thing that hurts is a lie, or silence."

"There's not much more to tell." He told her about being drunk and shooting Henry Abbott, the fight with Gabe, and dashing into the desert. "And that's when I found you and Charlie."

Frowning slightly, she shook her head. "You left out the most important part."

Somehow he'd forgotten to mention Lettie. "You want to know why Abbott came after me."

"Yes."

Jake forced himself to look directly into her trusting eyes. "I slept with his sister, and like a fool, I called her a whore."

"I thought it was something like that."

There was more. *I got her with child.* But he couldn't get the words out. He knew Alex would forgive him for Lettie, but she wouldn't let him walk away from a baby. Holding her hand in the dark, he made a decision. That guilt was his alone. She didn't need to know.

"I didn't love her, Alex. It was just—"

"Nature."

"Yeah, but it sounds worthless when you say it that way."

"Without love, maybe it is."

She smoothed his hair and raised her lips to kiss his forehead, but he stopped her. There was one more thing he had to make clear.

"I'm a nobody, Alex. I've stolen, whored, stayed drunk for days at a time. I'm not some famous gunslinger with a rep a mile long. I'm just—"

"—a man."

Her whisper set him free and he kissed her lips. Her sweet mouth opened to him, and he inhaled her breath, tasted her goodness and made it his own. He teased her neck with his lips and worked his way back to her ear. He wanted her more than ever, but he wasn't about to fall off his high horse now.

Running his finger along the neckline of her red dress, he said, "I'm holding you to that promise you didn't make, but there aren't any rules against sleeping close."

Sure, they could toe the line. He could give her pleasure with his hands and his mouth and not risk getting her pregnant, but he wasn't about to compromise now. Kissing her ear, he whispered, "When it's time, I don't want either of us holding back."

She shivered in his arms. "Are you sure you want to wait?"

"I'm sure."

"Absolutely?"

"Positively, and since it's driving you crazy, I'm getting more sure by the minute."

She laughed, and so did he.

He was duty-bound and hell-bent to make her first time perfect, and it wouldn't be perfect unless she had a ring on her finger. He wanted forever, she needed forever. It was the difference between pleasure and joy; the difference between a moment in time and mating for life. He ran his hands over her back, down the sides of her breasts, and back up to her face. Her breath was rapid and light.

"I think maybe we should sleep a few hours and go home," he said.

"All right."

He wanted to peel off that red dress, tumble her backward, and give her his weight. He wanted her naked and wanting and ready for him, but for tonight lying together like spoons would have to be enough. Climbing over her so that his chest brushed hers, he curled against her backside and tucked her head against his shoulder. Moonlight spilled through the window, cutting them off from the rest of the world, at least for now.

"You should take your boots off," she said.

"No, they're staying on."

"I've seen your bare feet."

"And I've seen yours." The thought of her toes sent his mind back to that night on the porch, Charlie, and Thomas Hunnicutt. He pulled her closer. "We need to send a wire to that old man you used to be engaged to."

"It's already sent."

The angel nestled against him and he closed his eyes, breathing in her scent. Turning in his arms, she raised up on one elbow and studied his face. "Have you ever been in love? Before now?"

The question surprised him but it was easy to answer. "Once, about six years ago. She was ten years older, a widow with a farm to run."

"Was she pretty?"

So the angel was a flesh-and-blood woman with doubts of her own. Jake put his hand over her flat stomach, spread his fingers against the warm silk, and pressed. "She wasn't nearly as beautiful as you are," he answered, grazing her cheek with his lips.

Snuggling against him, she breathed a contented sigh. Her backside fit perfectly against his hips, and he got even harder. He slid back an inch, and so did she. Her temperature rose, and so did his. He moaned out loud, and she laughed. Tangling his fingers in her hair, he said, "You're driving me crazy."

"Good."

He trailed his hand up her arm and down her neck to the exposed curve of her breasts. He loved the rose scent of her skin, the silkiness of her hair, and he tugged it loose. The knot fell apart in his hands, and he buried his face in the strands.

He kissed the top of her head, and she bent her chin to her chest, exposing her neck. While he trailed kisses down her back, he told her in vivid detail, just how much he loved her.

She sighed, but she didn't turn around.

He grinned and kept his boots on.

"I can hardly wait," she whispered.

"Same here." But he would.

They fell asleep side by side, with his left arm wrapped around her waist and the other cradling her head. He dreamed of ripe fruit, of the coming harvest, and her naked skin.

But then he saw men on horseback riding across the night sky, a dozen of them on silver horses, dressed in denim and leather vests, but transparent as if they weren't quite human. They were armed with rifles and ready to fight. Jake was trapped on the Colorado Plateau, wearing his black duster with his eyes still bruised from Gabe's fists.

He looked at the angels and they lowered their rifles, except for one. He was bigger than the others, a man with coal-black hair and the kindest eyes Jake had ever seen. He didn't move a muscle as he stared down the barrel.

Pure terror yanked Jake from his sleep.

He should have told Alex the whole truth about Lettie.

He knew in his gut she deserved to know everything, that he had to tell her about Lettie's baby, but with her body pressing against his, he didn't want to do it.

He closed his eyes to the dark room, but he couldn't sleep. Rising up on one elbow, he angled her face upward and woke her with a kiss. Turning and arching against the bed, she kissed him back.

A man could only wrestle so many angels at a time. "We need to go," he said.

She sighed, a sexy sound that made him forget his promises, then she stood up and stretched. He was on one side of the bed, she was on the other. They both knew what awaited them, and Alex turned wistful.

"It's like leaving a little piece of heaven, isn't it?"

"Yes, it is." Only Jake wasn't so sure. The angel in his dream was like a hot mist in the room. "Let's go home."

He took her hand, and they walked down the stairs and through the lobby. He helped her mount Smiley and then climbed up behind her.

"William's going to have my hide for keeping you out so late," he said.

"He's going to be thrilled, and my mother, too."

She turned as if to kiss his cheek, but he looked up and her lips grazed his throat. Heat coursed through him, as if she had branded him with her love. He considered it a badge of honor.

Chapter Sixteen

The next two weeks passed in a blur of joy and worry for Alex. As soon as they got home from Grand Junction, Jake confessed everything to William. She'd never seen her father so pleased. He wanted to marry them on the spot, but Katherine mentioned a dress. They settled on a date in September, and Jake spun her around until she felt dizzy.

They didn't want to wait, but it was easy to be generous with the future as bright and sure as a new day.

The only worry was Charlie. The whole family studied Charlotte's letters for clues, but it was useless. Where her father saw an *A,* she saw an *H.* Like fish in murky water, the letters shifted with the changing light.

The key to the puzzle was Annabelle, and when the first ripe peach fell to the ground, Alex thanked God the waiting was over.

With William in charge and Jake strutting like a new lieutenant, the pickers took the ripest fruit first. The branches grew lighter with every pass through the orchard. Katherine and Alex sorted fruit in the barn, while Annabelle cooked for the small army of workers. Exhausted at night, the women barely talked.

But tonight that would change. The pickers and their families had just finished supper, and William was handing out their pay. The peaches were in, and tonight they would show Annabelle the letters.

With dust heavy in the air, Alex lifted a crate of fruit to a table just as Annabelle walked into the barn.

"It's too hot to be inside," she said. "Do you need any help?"

In her pink calico dress and white apron, Annabelle looked like a porcelain doll with spun-gold hair, friendly eyes and a heart-shaped face.

Alex glanced at the overflowing crates. "We can always use another hand."

"What do I do?"

With a perfect peach balanced in her fingertips, Alex explained how to judge ripeness by the color and feel. In a few minutes they were talking like new neighbors. "How long have you been in Grand Junction?" Alex asked.

"Too long," Annabelle said with a laugh. "It's been almost two years."

"Do you like it out West?"

"It's all right, but I liked Indiana a lot better."

Where are you from, Mrs. Smith?

I'm from Chicago. And you, Miss Merritt?

A band around her heart loosened. "I used to live in Philadelphia. Everything is so much greener back East."

"And flatter, too. We lived on a farm until I was thirteen. After that we moved to Cleveland, and then my stepfather took us all to Chicago."

A coincidence. A thousand women named Charlotte came from Chicago. "I hear you have a sister."

"Just one. She's coming west. We're supposed to

meet here and go on to San Francisco. I hear it's a good place to start a business.''

I plan to meet my sister. We're going to San Francisco.

Alex started to shake. ''Have you heard from her lately?''

''I got her last letter more than a month ago, but she didn't say anything about when she was leaving or when she'd get here. She's like that though. I'm the one who likes to write letters.''

Squeezing a peach until it bruised, Alex said, ''Travel can be unpredictable.''

''I heard about your accident. It must have been terrible for you, and for that woman who died. I'm glad you saved her baby.''

''I am, too.'' Except she felt like a thief. ''How long has it been since you've seen your sister?''

''About three years.'' Annabelle lowered her eyes. ''She's been working for a wealthy family as a governess, but her last letter said they were sending the children off to boarding school and she had to move on. I was surprised she wanted to come west.''

''Why is that?''

''She loved Chicago. It was her home.''

''What does she look like?''

''Dark hair like yours. Hazel eyes. She's taller than I am, and she dresses well. She likes the latest fashions.''

Charlie's mother had dark hair, hazel eyes and eyebrows that arched into crescents. Alex flashed on a coy red hat and Charlotte's silken underthings, and she knew she'd found Charlotte's sister.

What brings you out west, Mrs. Smith?

Family. I'm going to stay with my sister while my husband is in Europe. She loves children.

"Do you like children?"

Annabelle cocked her head. "Of course."

Alex's throat went dry. She had to get out of the barn. "I think I'll see how Jake is doing."

"Sure."

Squinting in the bright sun, she hurried toward the trees. The branches had been stripped nearly bare, and leaves and imperfect peaches littered the ground. The stench of rotting fruit thickened the air. She could barely breathe. She needed Jake.

As if she had called his name, he came around the corner. Tears spilled down her cheeks and she collapsed in his arms. "You were right. She's Charlie's aunt."

"Are you sure?"

The sun burned down on them both. She buried her face against his chest and cried, but she couldn't escape the smells and the heat and the truth of the day. Some things in life couldn't be avoided or changed, and even the most bountiful harvest came at a cost.

"I'm positive," she said.

He supported her weight with his arms, his long legs, his very breath. "We'll get through it. I promise."

"Yes," she said. "Together."

It made all the difference in the world.

The letters covered the dining room table like pages torn from a book. Annabelle was standing with her hands pressed against her cheeks. Katherine was straightening the smudged sheets with her fingertips. William was too quiet, and Alex was telling Annabelle about the day her sister had died.

Jake could barely stand it. Her voice was too calm, and it cut at his heart because he'd been there, too.

It didn't take long to piece together the last few months of Charlotte's life. Annabelle knew about everything except the baby. Her sister had been working for the Brigham family, and she'd fallen in love with Spencer Brigham, the man who had hired her to care for his children while his wife was in Boston nursing her ailing mother.

Any fool could figure out the rest. She'd gotten pregnant, and he'd handed her money and a train ticket.

"I should have known," Annabelle said. "I knew about Brigham, but she never said anything about a baby. She just said there was a problem. That's exactly how she wrote it, I've got 'a very little problem.'"

Jake felt his insides twist. He knew exactly how little this particular problem could be. Alex cleared her throat, and he put his arm around her because he knew what she was about to ask.

"I don't quite know how to say this, but if raising this child is too much for you, Jake and I would be honored to have him as our own." Silence echoed like fading thunder, and Alex took a small breath. "Of course, you're his aunt."

Jake steadied his voice. "We'd be honored, Annabelle. We'll give him a good home."

"You have to think about what's best for Charlie," Katherine added.

Tears slipped from Annabelle's eyes, and William touched her shoulder. "You don't have to decide anything tonight."

Jake hated seeing women cry, and while Annabelle was shattered, Alex was pale and still and that was even worse. He had a sudden urge to smash his fist against the wall, but Annabelle exploded for them both.

"Spencer Brigham ought to be horsewhipped. How dare he use her like that. She loved him. She told me so, and then he—he—" Another sob racked her.

Alex knotted her hands at her waist. "He should be told about the baby."

"He doesn't deserve to know."

"No, but he has an obligation. At the very least, he should provide financial support."

"I don't want his money. I'd like to see him hang."

"I would, too. He doesn't deserve to live."

Jake had never heard Alex wish death on anyone, and tonight she meant it. She'd hate him forever if she knew the truth about Lettie.

Annabelle shook her head. "Spencer Brigham should have shown my sister a little respect."

Heat rose up Jake's neck. He knew Annabelle had hurts of her own, but he couldn't stop himself. "Maybe this Brigham fellow feels bad about it."

Alex stared at him as if he were an idiot. "I don't care how he *feels* about it. The man has an obligation."

"Maybe it isn't that simple."

"Simple or not, they made a baby together."

She sounded just like Gabe. Before he could think, a smirk curled his lips. "I know *exactly* what happened. Nature took its course, and—"

William cut in. "We don't need the particulars."

"Maybe we do," Alex argued.

Jake held up his hands and backed away. "Look, I shouldn't have said anything. It's not my place."

"Of course it's your place. Say what you think," Alex demanded.

He shook his head. "Just forget it."

Alex squared her shoulders. "Don't you dare take the easy way out. How can you shrug Charlie off for him?"

Because he'd done it himself without thinking twice. Close to shouting, he looked Alex straight in the eye, "What the hell was Brigham supposed to do? Accidents happen. People make mistakes."

"That doesn't give him the right to walk away."

"I—he—"

In a gesture of pure disgust, Alex propped her hands on her hips. "A man's no better than a stray dog if he can walk away from his own child."

This time the name fit, and Jake gagged on his own spit. She knew. He saw it in her face. William was eyeing him, and Katherine had aged ten years.

You're not worth dirt, little brother.

Something hard and dark filled the pit of his stomach. He wanted Alex to touch his face and make him soft inside, but she wouldn't look at him. Instead the angel squeezed Annabelle's hand. "I'm so sorry about Charlotte. She was beautiful and kind."

With a low moan, Annabelle gave in to a wrenching sob.

Alex held her while she cried, and William cleared his throat. "We'll talk tomorrow. Annabelle, my wife will get you settled for the night. Alex, you need to get some rest, and Jake, you're coming with me."

William opened the bottom drawer of his desk and took out a stack of bills, enough to cover Jake's bonus and then some, then he took two cigars out of the humidor.

Putting everything in his pocket, he dragged the chair toward a towering bookcase where a bottle of whiskey was collecting dust. For twenty years he'd kept that bottle, far out of reach but never out of mind. Being careful not to smudge the dust, he took the bottle down and carried it out to the porch.

Jake was sitting in the low-slung chair with his hands laced behind his head. He pulled his legs back to make room for William to pass, but everything else about the man was stiff and bitter.

William set the bottle next to Jake's feet and shoved the wad of bills in his face. "Here's your bonus."

The young man narrowed his eyes as he took the money. "Looks like you're getting rid of me."

"That depends on you."

William knew when to take his time. He looked at the stars, the barren trees, and when the air felt thick enough to choke a man, he handed Jake a cigar. "Here."

He shook his head. "I'm not in the mood."

"Take it, or I'll stuff it down your damn throat."

"I'd like to see you try."

"No you wouldn't."

It was a manly game, the wise old buck and the young stag. The cigar dangled between them. When Jake finally took it, William sat down in the swing.

"Now, just what aren't you telling me? And even more important, what aren't you telling my daughter?"

"It's no one's business but mine."

"You're wrong. What concerns you concerns Alex."

"Not this." Jake slid the cigar into his pocket, put his hands on the armrests and pushed to his feet.

"Light the damn thing," William said.

"I'm going to bed."

William shoved the dusty bottle in front of the

younger man. "You're not going anywhere. I've got a
story to tell and you're going to listen. Now, light up
so you've got something to stick in your mouth while
I bare my soul."

Propping back into the chair, Jake clenched the cigar
between his teeth and struck a match. "All right, I'm
listening."

"Do you remember that bottle of whiskey I promised you?"

"The one I never saw?"

"Well, this is it."

"Are you offering?"

"You can take it with you after I tell you about the
night I nearly killed my wife."

"Jeez. I don't want to hear this." Jake rocked forward, but William clamped his hand on his shoulder.

"That's too damn bad, because you *need* to hear it.
Because you're being a fool and someone has to set
you straight. You've got a choice, son. You can get
lost or you can tell me your secrets. And just to make
it a little easier, I'll tell you mine first."

Jake settled back in the chair. "All right," he said,
blowing a fat ring of smoke.

The swing groaned as William began his tale. "I was
drunk off my ass that night. I was the pastor of the
biggest church in Denver, and everyone thought I was
a teetotaler. The truth is, I was drinking every night
and Kath was tired of it. The fights got worse until she
threatened to take Alex and go back to Philadelphia."

William took a drag of smoke and held it until his
throat stopped aching. Some memories hurt more than
others, and tonight his chest was ready to burst.

"On that particular night, I'd had more than usual.
I don't remember much except that I was furious about

something and Kath was trying to get away from me. She was at the top of the stairs when I grabbed her shoulder. Only I missed and knocked her down. She tumbled like rocks in a tin can. Have you ever heard that sound?''

Jake shook his head.

''It's like listening to your own bones break.'' William blew a perfect ring of smoke. ''Hell, I wish they had been my bones. I'd give my life to take back that night.''

''At least she lived.''

''Oh, she lived all right, but the baby she was carrying didn't, and there were never any more after that, though not from a lack of trying.''

William stubbed out the cigar. ''I killed my son that night.''

Jake looked ready to vomit as William sucked in air. ''So what I'm telling you is this. There's nothing a woman can't forgive if a man is willing to face the truth about himself.''

William's gaze traveled from the dust-covered bottle to the gray-gold shadows shifting on the young man's face. His eyes were smoky and full of pain, and he waited for him to make his choice. Stand and fight, tell a lie, or run.

And while he waited, he prayed. For strength, for peace and wisdom, for mercy.

Please God.

The stars glistened in the heavens. Moonlight fell across the yard. The earth itself seemed wide and forgiving. But when Jake stubbed out the cigar and his shoulders rolled forward with the burden of being a man, William heard the crack of breaking bones.

"I blew it, Will. I gave Lettie Abbott a lot more than a good time. I got her pregnant."

Anything but that.

Anything but a baby boy who would need a father to teach him how to hold a hammer, a little girl who would have her father's blue eyes.

Alex pressed her hands to her cheeks and struggled to breathe. She had seen the whiskey bottle and stayed in the shadows, waiting for her father to work his magic.

She had already realized Jake had secrets. She should have been furious with him, but love was kind, enduring, and full of hope, and the line between a lie and a mistake wasn't always clear. She'd crossed it herself with Thomas when she wrote that she loved him. Mistakes could be forgiven, and fixed.

She stepped through the door. "Jake, we can—"

"Shit!"

"We can work this out."

"Hell no! It's no one's business but mine."

"It's mine, too." She grabbed his arm as he shot up from the chair. "There has to be a solution. Maybe she doesn't want the baby. We could raise it. Maybe—"

"Are you out of your mind? I can't go back there."

"We can work it out. It *has* to work out!"

"Like hell it does. Get used to it, Alex. Things *never* go right for me." Jake stormed off the porch.

"Wait!"

Her father rose from the swing and touched her back. "Give him some time."

"But we have to settle this."

William shook his head. "And just what are you going to say to him?"

"I'll go with him to Flat Rock. We'll make sure the baby has a home, or we'll take it with us."

"Do you really think the baby's mother should settle for that? Would you?"

Alex had no idea what to think. She didn't know a thing about Lettie Abbott, except she had Jake's child. Air whooshed from her lungs as she sat in the rocking chair.

"You've had some blows today," William said gently. "You need to think a little bit. It's not as simple as you want it to be."

"I'll fight for him, Papa. I know he loves me. He's not the same man who ran off."

"That's true, but some things can't be changed."

She hated that truth, the strength in her father's voice. "We can put the past behind us. You and Mama did."

"That's true, but all the forgiveness in the world won't change the fact he's got a child. He has an obligation to both the baby and its mother."

"We'll send money."

"Do you think that's enough?"

She couldn't answer. She had spent the past seven years making families for other people. How could she live with a lie?

William sighed. "He's got to do right by her, Alex."

"No!" She stood and crossed her arms over her chest. "He doesn't love her. He told me that. And that's important. *You* said it was important. You said, 'You can't marry a man you don't love.' And now you're saying Jake has to go back? It doesn't make sense."

"There's a difference between not making a mistake, and picking up the pieces after one's already been made.''

''But that doesn't mean he has to marry her.''

William rocked gently in the swing. ''No, that's true. People compromise all the time.''

Compromise. Settling for less, living with less, lukewarm water when she wanted a steaming hot bath; not enough butter on a slice of bread, always wanting more, always wondering. Settling. She hated it.

''I hate to say this, Miss Merri, but in God's eyes and in mine, he's as good as a married man.''

''But they didn't take vows. They didn't say the words.''

''No, they made a baby instead.''

She didn't know what to say.

''Think on it, Alex. But don't go to Jake until you've weighed it all out.''

William pressed his hand against his chest. The twinge had turned into a spreading pain, but he'd be damned before he collapsed in front of Alex. And he'd have a few choice words for the Lord himself if he took him home tonight.

More time…more time…more time.

William took a slow breath, and the pain ebbed. When the ache faded back to a twinge, he opened the front door. ''I'm sure your mother's worrying. I'm headed up to bed.''

''Tell her I love her.''

''I will.''

''Good night, Papa.''

She crossed her arms over her chest, and he knew she didn't want to be touched. The stairs were monstrous, but he managed them one at a time.

When he reached his bed, he let out a long sigh. As he told Kath the story, she wept, and he held her close.

The pain stayed away until she turned out the light. He held still, fighting it with slow breaths. He squeezed his wife's hand and told her he loved her, even though she was asleep.

More time... Please God... More time...

Sweat spilled from his skin. The pain spread to his arm and neck, and the room went blank.

Chapter Seventeen

"Goddamn it to hell!"

Jake slammed his fist into the wall. The wood flayed his knuckles and blood oozed from his torn skin. He grabbed the whiskey flask holding an overblown yellow rose and hurled it against the splintery planks. The pewter hit with a thud and clattered to the floor.

Aching and short of breath, he stared at the dripping water. In the growing puddle he saw the tears and blood of the past two hours. Katherine's body at the base of the stairs. Charlotte's last breath and her sister's grief. Alex's fury and forgiveness. His own selfish lies.

Dropping down on the cot, he buried his face in his hands. He'd spent his whole life being angry and running away. Gabe had been cleaning up after him for years, and right or wrong, Alex would do the same thing if he let her. She'd be the one to mop up the puddle on the floor, and William would patch the wall.

The realization made him feel pathetic, and he didn't like it a bit. What the hell was wrong with him?

He'd given up liquor. He worked hard in the orchard. He'd kept his hands off Alex. He tried his best to be worthy of her, and it all came down to one fact he couldn't change. Lettie Abbott had given birth to his child.

A month ago he didn't give a damn, but sitting in this room with rosewater dripping down the wall, he felt the beat of angel wings. This moment wasn't about giving up whiskey and women. It was about change, a bone-deep, wood-to-ashes transformation that burned a man's body and scarred his soul. It was about facing facts.

Jake reached into his pocket and counted the money William had given him. It was a lot, and he decided to send it all to Lettie with a letter promising to send more. He'd write to Gabe, too. He'd give back the money he had stolen and apologize for everything.

Jake took Gabe's leather pouch out of the drawer and added a few bills to cover what he'd spent, but he wanted to keep his mother's ring. Tonight he'd write the letters to Lettie and Gabe, and tomorrow he'd tell Alex everything. He'd get on his knees, and he'd swear on his life he'd never lie to her again. He'd pull her into his arms and kiss her until she went soft. He'd never let her go.

Jake put the ring in his pocket. He'd do whatever it took to make things right.

He's as good as married.

A ribbon of silver light shot from the moon to the porch, where Alex stood with her arms laced over her chest. Her gaze searched the heavens. She prayed first for wisdom, then a sign that didn't come, and finally for the strength to do what had to be done.

Quietly she climbed the stairs to her bedroom. She had no keepsakes, no jewelry, nothing of lasting value.

Her life had been stripped down to borrowed clothes, a borrowed child and even a borrowed man.

She had nothing to give Jake, so she went to the kitchen to make sandwiches and tea. She put five scoops of sugar in the jug because he liked it sweet, then she chose two perfect peaches and a dozen cookies. Wrapping everything in a dish towel, she slipped it into a burlap sack.

Her father's office was dark, but she didn't need a light to find the humidor on the corner of the desk. He'd just filled it with the best cigars money could buy, and Alex took them all. One by one she laid them in a small wooden box, then she nestled the box in the bottom of the sack and went to the barn.

The building was dark except for a golden V at Jake's door. Straw muffled her steps, but she heard his bed creak as he stood up. His shadow cut a black wedge in the gold light. Touching it with her toes, she walked into his room.

His back was to her, and she watched as he dropped to one knee and mopped up a puddle with a rag. Rose petals littered the floor, and the whiskey flask lay on its side.

"Jake?"

He jumped to his feet. The rag hung limp in his hand as he faced her. "I hope you're here to give me hell, because this time I really do deserve it."

She ached to touch him, but she didn't dare. Twisting the burlap in her hands, she said, "There's something I have to say."

He tossed the rag and a handful of petals into the wastebasket. His eyes traveled from the sack to her face, and her throat went dry.

"I don't know where to start," she said.

"Then let me." He lifted the bag from her hand and set it next to the door. "For starters, you should be furious with me. I flat out lied to get what I wanted without a thought about what it meant, or how you'd feel."

She shrugged. "You made a mistake."

"Don't make excuses, Alex. It shames me worse than the truth already does. I walked away without giving Lettie a thought. Hell, she was a virgin and I didn't even know it."

Alex winced. There were things she didn't want to know. "Are you sorry?"

"More than I can say. And I swear I'll never lie to you again. I've never been sorrier for anything in my life. Can you forgive me?"

"I already have. You know that."

"You're making things too easy for me."

"You haven't heard me out."

His eyes burned into hers as he reached for her hands. His fingers were cold from the damp rag. "I can't change what happened, but I want to make things right."

"How?"

"I'm going to send Lettie every cent I've got and I'll ask Gabe to look out for her."

She had to look away. "It's not enough."

"It *has* to be enough. It's all I've got."

"But it's not." Her voice cracked. She pulled her hands free from his. "You've got to give Lettie a choice, and if she has any sense at all, she's going to marry you."

"There's no way in hell I'm going to marry her. I love you, Alex."

"I love you too, but—"

"Look, I'll send money. I'll make sure the kid has everything it needs. That has to be enough."

Alex met his gaze. "Will it be enough when a bully calls your son a bastard? Or when your daughter wonders why her daddy doesn't love her?"

"I wish I could, but I can't change the past."

"No, but children ask questions, and they need answers. You and Lettie have to work this out. She might take the money and tell you to drop dead. I hope so. I really do, but you can't walk away from the child. Like it or not, you made a commitment when you took Lettie to bed."

"I didn't make a commitment. I made a mistake."

"And that mistake has a name. You've got to do your best to make things right for the child."

"I *am* doing my best. I'll send money every month."

Alex took a chance. Raising her chin, she said, "If you think money is all it takes to raise a child, you're not the man I thought you were."

Jake stepped back with a bitter laugh. "Well, what do you know? You finally opened your eyes and I really am a low-down son of a bitch."

"That's just a lame excuse for being selfish and you know it!"

"Maybe it's true."

"Maybe it was, but not anymore."

The truth hissed like water dousing a flame. He'd proved himself, with William, the harvest, loving her enough to leave, then enough to stay. Only instead of seeing who he had become, he saw her. "I love you, Alex."

"I love you, too." That little-boy hunger for kindness came back to his eyes, and she said, "I think you'd crawl naked through the desert to make things right.''

''I would.''

''Then I'm asking you to give Lettie the choice. You've got to see her.''

He shook his head. ''You're asking too much.''

If he touched her, she'd crumble. She'd beg him to stay. She'd tell him to send the money and be done with it. She'd—

He touched her cheek—a brush that made her look into his eyes. His voice cracked. ''Are you telling me to leave?''

''Yes, I am. I want your word, Jake. Promise me you'll talk to Lettie.''

''Why are you doing this?''

''Because this time I can't fool myself. I can't settle for less than everything.''

''Alex—''

''Wait.'' She held up her hands. ''I've compromised my whole life, and I'm done with it. I won't marry a man who belongs with someone else.''

''I don't love her. I don't even *like* her.''

''You liked her well enough to take her to bed, and at the very least, you'll love that child.'' Tears welled again. ''She's a lucky woman, and—''

''Alex, don't—''

''I just wish I had met you first.''

The tears came in a burst, and she tumbled into his arms. She could smell his skin, his clean shirt, the sweat rising on his neck. She raised her face to tell him she had to go inside, but his mouth found hers in a desperate kiss.

Fierce and possessive, he brought her down to the cot. She was beneath him, tasting her own tears, wanting him. His weight was crushing her. She could hardly breathe until he rose up and air rushed into her lungs. She wanted to feel his hands on her breasts, and she put them there.

"This isn't smart," he rasped.

Raking her fingers through his dark hair, she whispered, "Please. I want this to happen."

"Alex, we shouldn't—"

But she wasn't asking; she was taking. With the gold light of the lantern chasing away the darkness, she unbuttoned his shirt and massaged his throat and bare chest. She explored the planes of flesh, the whorls of silken hair that trailed down his belly in a V.

He groaned, but she smothered his protest with her lips. Kissing her, he unbuttoned the front of her dress, moving his mouth to the pulse in her throat, to the bare skin above her camisole, to the lace covering her nipples. He flexed upward and she slid beneath him. Her knees parted inside her skirt and his hips slipped between her thighs.

He whispered, "Oh, Lord," and turned to stone.

The hard heat of him pressed against her most private place. His hands went still on her breasts. He closed his eyes, and except for his breath, he was as silent as the night. Her nerves stretched like piano wire, until one by one they snapped with pinging echoes.

"I guess you're saying no," she whispered.

His breath singed her neck and she thought about the desert, the empty miles of earth, flash floods, and the passing beauty of a sudden storm.

His mouth hovered over hers. "God damn me for a fool, but I just can't risk it."

He swung his legs off the bed and buried his face in

his hands. She sat next to him and wrapped her arm around his waist, resting her head on his shoulder.

He blew out a breath and dug into his pocket. A bit of gold caught the light, and he pressed a ring into her palm. "It was my mother's. I stole it from Gabe, but I don't think he'd mind if I gave it to you."

She slipped it on her finger. "It's lovely."

"You know I don't want to leave."

His jaw clenched, and she worried he'd been pushed from the nest too soon, that he'd head for California and be done with the whole mess. She couldn't let that happen.

Squeezing his hand, she said, "I want your word, Jake. Promise me you'll go to Flat Rock."

"I'd rather eat a mountain of horse manure."

He'd cleaned up his language, and it gave her hope. She touched his knee. "You need to do this. There's still a chance she'll say no. There's a chance for us."

"I'd like to believe that, but it's just not true. It's up to you, Alex." His lips brushed her forehead and he whispered, "Come with me."

She could gather her things and leave a note. They'd make love under the stars, and the sun would rise with a fiery light. Everything would be wild and perfect and new, except the vision was a lie, a mirage in the desert.

"I can't."

He blew out the breath he'd been holding, and she thought of everything she had lost and would never have.

Jake took her hand and squeezed. "Promise me you'll take that ring off when it's right."

She shook her head. "I'll never take it off."

"I'll make you a deal. I'll see Lettie, if you promise to get on with your life."

He squeezed her hand and she sighed, leaving the promises hanging like the ends of an untied knot. Letting go of her hand, he stood up. "I'd better saddle up."

He picked up his gear and the burlap sack. She held the lantern while he saddled Smiley. With the scent of peaches filling the night, he led the bay into the yard, climbed into the saddle and rode off without looking back.

Alex was staring down the road when the front door opened. She expected her father, but instead Annabelle came to stand behind her.

"Are you okay?" the girl asked timidly.

"More or less."

"I saw Jake leave. I'm sorry if you had a fight because of me."

Alex shook her head. "It had nothing to do with you."

"Men get mad, but he'll be back. I know he loves you."

Hope slammed into her chest, but she couldn't hang on to it. She couldn't hang on to anything or anyone. Still gazing down the road, she said, "You should keep the baby. He belongs with you."

Annabelle's eyes widened. "But you two would be such good parents. I've got so little to give him."

"You have as much as I do." Alex bit her lip. "Jake's gone for good."

"Are you sure?"

"I'm positive."

"I don't know what to say. I don't know if I can take care of a baby."

Frayed beyond endurance, Alex snapped at her. "Don't you want him?"

"Yes, but he'll need things. I'll need a better job."

"My father will help you. That new restaurant might need another cook." She forced a smile. "It's late. I really need to go inside."

She turned around just as her mother came racing down the steps. "Alex! It's your father. Get Jake. We need the doctor."

Dear God, not this. She couldn't speak, and her feet refused to budge. She was back in the desert, helpless and alone, on Smiley but without Jake holding her steady.

Annabelle touched her arm. "I can ride. I'll go."

"Hurry," Katherine pleaded. "I can't wake him up."

Jake reached Grand Junction in less than an hour, but he had to wait for Waltham's Emporium to open. He needed supplies if he was going to strike back to Flat Rock.

If.

The choice was his, but either way his future looked as bleak as the dark buildings on Colorado Avenue. Tying Smiley to a post, he eyed the empty store and sat on the steps to wait for morning. The only sign of life was the rattle of a buggy near the doctor's office. A baby being born, a man dying. At the moment, he was beyond caring.

He'd just walked away from the woman he loved, and the ache in his groin was far from noble. He'd been a second away from making love to her, and now he wished he'd done it. Just one time and she might have changed her mind, but he'd been scared spitless that she'd conceive.

He never wanted to think about babies or women again.

Closing his eyes and leaning against a post, he dozed until the shopkeeper poked him with a broom. It was like old times except he was sober. He bought a month's worth of supplies for the two-day ride to Flat Rock, climbed on Smiley, and rode to the edge of town where a locomotive had just chuffed into the station.

Only a few passengers got off the train, and near the baggage pile Jake saw a middle-aged man with a balding head. Patting his face with a handkerchief, the man grimaced as he rubbed his lower back and hobbled to the baggage clerk. Riding closer, Jake listened to the man's clipped Eastern speech.

"Excuse me, sir," he said to the clerk. "I'm looking for my fiancée, Miss Alexandra Merritt. Her family runs an orchard on the outskirts of town."

"Everyone knows William Merritt. His place is about an hour's ride from here."

The older man shook his head. "I can't go another mile today. My back went out on the train. Perhaps you can point me to the hotel, and would you be so kind as to deliver my bags?"

"Yes, sir."

Refusing to take a second look at Thomas Hunnicutt and his bald head, Jake rode into the empty desert.

The miles passed slowly. The Colorado Plateau hadn't changed except the day was hotter, the sky a little emptier. Maybe he'd go to California and see the ocean, or down to Mexico where he could forget he'd ever been born. Except he was headed down the same trail he'd taken two months ago, only east, into the sun.

Around noon he rode past the spot where Alex had

been bitten by the snake. Rain had washed away the fire and the blood, but his vivid memories rose like ghosts and he had to look away.

It was nearly dusk when he arrived at Charlotte's grave. With the sun casting an orange glow across the land, that day came back to him. He remembered being hurt and hung over, the stench rising from the dead mules, and the terror and sweetness of an angel singing in the desert.

Oh, come, let us worship and bow down
Let us kneel before the Lord, our God, our maker.

Guiding Smiley into the gorge, he saw the spot where Alex had pulled the gun on him. His gaze roamed to the rock where Charlie had been born, then to the spit of sand where the stagecoach had crumbled and the mules were dry bones.

Tying Smiley to the only wheel left on the wreck, Jake climbed the steep bank of the gorge and hunted for Charlotte's grave. The sagebrush had thickened in the summer sun, but between the weeds he saw the pile of stones.

Memories assaulted him. Of Alex singing ''Down in the Valley.'' Of Alex praying for a woman she didn't know, trusting they'd be safe, that he'd take care of her and the baby, too.

A hot wind stirred and Jake squinted against the dust. Dry storms were common in the summer, and the wind built to a gale, pelting his face with grit. Clamping a hand on his hat, he looked north into the wind and saw a brown wall of dirt rolling in his direction.

He hustled to the gorge and hunkered down in a jagged crevice near Smiley. The wind roared like a lion, and the sun dimmed as the raging sand found him. Grit worked its way into his clothes, his hair, even his

ears, and his mouth tasted bitter and dry. He was caked
with dirt from head to foot, as if he'd been buried alive.
The wind still shrieked, but it no longer stung his
cheeks.

His heart pounded. A boulder tumbled past his
shoulder and smashed into the stagecoach. A terror-
filled whinny screeched through the gorge, and Jake
staggered forward, trying to reach his horse. Smiley
was ready to bolt, a gray ghost tap-dancing in the
storm. The reins flapped in the wind, just barely cling-
ing to the rotten wheel.

Just as Jake reached for them, a brutal gust knocked
him on his face. He landed on a stone the size of a
man's fist. Pain shot through his side. He tasted dirt
and blood, and it hurt to breathe. He'd broken a rib,
he was sure, but he'd be damned if he'd roll over and
die.

At his very core, he liked a good fight.

He liked expensive cigars and clean beds. Home-
cooked meals and moonlit nights. Even the roaring
beauty of this storm had a place in his heart, and in the
rising tumult, he heard the cry of an angel calling his
name.

Jackson Jacob Malone.

He refused to slither through the dirt, and rising to
his feet, he inched toward his horse. A melon-sized
boulder careened into the gorge and Smiley reared. He
was about to gallop away, but Jake snatched the reins
and led him deeper into the ravine where the wind was
less alive.

The bay wanted to be done with dirt and wind and
turmoil, and so did Jake. Turning his back to the gale,
he knew what he had to do. He didn't want to go back
to Flat Rock, but he would. He'd give Lettie a choice,

and if she said yes, he'd honor their vows to his dying day.

He wasn't the same man who had passed this way two months ago, a man who could have left a woman and a child to die, a man who didn't give a damn about anyone but himself.

For better or worse, Alex had taught him how to love. She'd stripped him down to his shame and shared the bounty of her life—William and Katherine, honest work, an abundance of peaches, a baby's needs, warm milk on his wrist. His big feet next to her tiny toes.

She held nothing back, not even her body though it was a gift he couldn't accept.

Her touch, her smile, her laughter and hope, Jake clung to her until the wind faded and the stars came out. He didn't want this night to end, but he had to say goodbye to things he couldn't have.

Rising to his feet, he brushed himself off and opened the saddlebag holding the food she had packed. He carried the sack to a flat boulder and reached inside. He took out the sandwiches first, then the peaches and a jug of tea. He ate slowly, thinking of her hands slicing the bread, spreading the butter. He bit into a peach and licked the juice from his lips. The tea was thick and sweet, just the way he liked it.

Sorrow stung his eyes, but he held it back by wrapping the last sandwich in the napkin and tucking it away for tomorrow. A weight in the sack surprised him. He reached inside, found a box and opened it.

He smelled the cigars before he saw them. The old man was next to him, telling him he was proud. With shaking hands, Jake slid a cigar between his lips and struck a match. The tip burned through the darkness, and blowing a ring of smoke to the heavens, he found comfort.

Chapter Eighteen

Gabe felt like a well-groomed buffalo, but the new suit fit him well and the haircut wasn't half bad. It was his wedding day, and in less than an hour he'd escort Lettie to the pastor's house, where they would take their vows.

It was the happiest day of his life.

Three particular words were still missing between them, but she had hung curtains and made up the new double bed. And last night she had kissed him, warm and openmouthed, except she'd ruined it by thanking him.

Had she ever thanked Jake for kissing her? Gabe doubted it, but he shook off the thought by making a note in the ledger. The ink was barely dry when the front door swung open and a man with a fresh haircut and new clothes walked in and took off his hat. At the sight of his brother, Gabe nearly pulled his gun.

"I guess this is a surprise," Jake said with a smile.

Gabe wanted to slap it right off his face. "What the hell do you want now?"

Taking his billfold out of his back pocket, Jake counted out three hundred-dollar bills and slapped them on the blotter. "This is the money I stole from you. I took the ring too, but I can't give it back."

Gabe didn't want to know what he'd done with it. Shrugging, he said, "It belonged to Mama. It was as much yours as mine."

"Thank you, then."

"I thought you'd be in Mexico by now."

"I was headed that way, but things changed." He looked Gabe in the eye and said, "I haven't had a drink for two months."

Gabe could smell a lie a mile away, and Jake was telling the truth. He was glad for his brother, but he would have been downright blissful if he had just sent a wire. Steepling his fingers, he dug deeper. "So why are you back?"

"I want to make things right."

Why now? Why not two years from now after Gabe had given Lettie more children, the kind of home she deserved? It was always this way with Jake, the wrong thing at the wrong time, not enough effort and then too much.

Leaning back, Gabe cocked his head, indicating the chair next to his desk. "Have a seat."

It was where drunks and thieves usually sat, but he wasn't about to cut his brother any slack, and frankly, Jake didn't seem to need it. He sat down without even a hint of attitude, and looking Gabe in the eye, he asked, "What happened to Henry Abbott?"

Gabe huffed. He hated Lettie's brother with every ounce of spit he had. "He raised a ruckus that night but it was just a flesh wound. He's fine."

"That's good. I acted like a fool."

In the past two months, his brother had put on ten pounds and wised up by ten years. Gabe saw granite in him where there used to be sand, a clean-shaven jaw instead of week's worth of stubble. Drumming his fingers on the desk, he waited for the question he didn't want to hear.

Jake rested his elbows on his knees. "How's Lettie? Did she have the baby?"

"A little girl. Her name's Emily."

Jake seemed pleased. "It's a pretty name. I like it."

What are you going to call her, Lettie?

I was thinking of Emily, after my mother.

Gabe recoiled at the injustice of the whole situation. *He'd* been the one to hold Lettie's hand after a difficult birth. *He'd* been the one to offer her respectability and a home of her own, even though he suspected she still loved Jake.

His heart felt torn in two, but what could an honest man do? He loved Lettie too much to chase Jake away without giving her a chance to hear what he had to say. Still drumming his fingers, he asked, "So just what are you going to do?"

"Get married. Get a job. Be a father."

Jake meant it, and foolish or not, Gabe believed him. The clock on his desk struck twelve, and he closed the ledger.

"Lettie's at the store. I'll walk you over there." As he stood and reached for his hat, Jake eyed his new suit.

"Why are you all dressed up?"

"I was on my way to a wedding."

Lettie tapped her toe. Had Gabe changed his mind? He was never late and it was five minutes past noon. She fidgeted with the collar of her dress and picked up Emily. If he didn't hurry, her milk would leak and her dress would be ruined in spite of the extra pads she had put in.

Why was he late?

It wasn't like Gabe at all. He was supposed to walk with her to Pastor Heywood's house where they'd be married in the presence of her brother and the pastor's wife. She wanted a quiet day, a dignified day, and she wanted to be holding Emily as they took their vows.

Her only indulgence was a lavender dress and a tiny hat trimmed with a satin ribbon. She could wear the dress to church, but today it made her feel special, and she needed that boost for courage.

The thought of being Gabe's wife scared her to death. Yesterday she had made up the big bed he'd ordered from Montgomery Ward. Someone had scrubbed the walls, and the floor had been polished to a shine. It felt like a real home, but how could he forget she'd been with his brother? Emily had dark hair and Malone eyes. Even Lettie couldn't look at her without seeing Jake, and the memories had stopped being good.

The bell over the door jangled, and she nearly jumped out of her skin. Knowing her husband-to-be didn't like to be kept waiting, she scooped up Emily and hurried down the stairs.

"We're late, Gabe," she called. "Where have you been?"

She was on the fourth step when she recognized Jake. He was holding his hat in one hand and raking his dark hair with the other. He was broader across the chest than she remembered, and tanned from working in the sun. His black trousers still had a crease, and a fine linen shirt fit him well. His eyes were as clear as melted snow.

Gabe cleared his throat. "My brother has something to say to you, Letticia. I'll wait outside."

"No. I want you to stay. Please."

"All right." He stepped back, shrugging as if he didn't care. Was she just baggage to him after all, another mess to clean up?

Lettie gaped at Jake. This man had seduced her and left her with a child. He'd called her a whore and disappeared. Without so much as a goodbye. Brimming with indignation, she shifted her gaze from Jake to Gabe.

"I don't care what he has to say," she said angrily.

"Give him a chance," Gabe countered.

Jake cleared his throat. "I want to apologize to you, Lettie, and I want to get married for the baby's sake."

Gabe headed for the door.

"Gabriel, don't you dare leave!"

Tremors ripped through her, and Emily fussed in her arms as if she were trying to talk. Lettie figured the baby had good instincts, and she decided to give Jake a piece of her mind.

"Jake, you are *crazy* if you think I'd marry you after what you did. You're a liar, a cheat, and just plain selfish and disrespectful. I wouldn't give you the time of day. Except for Emily, I'm sorry I ever laid eyes on you. You should be ashamed of yourself."

He shifted his feet like a nervous choirboy. "I am, Lettie, and that's why I came back, to make things right."

"Well, you're wasting your breath."

Emily gave a tiny squeak. Patting her on the back, Lettie whirled toward Gabe. "And you, Sheriff, are a fool if you think I'm going to marry him when I love you."

His face was as smooth as river rock. Solid, cool, unreadable. She stepped up to that mountain, and holding on to her daughter, she said, "We had a date for twelve noon. Is it still on?"

"Is that what you want?"

"More than I can say. I love you, Gabe."

He cupped her chin and stared into her eyes until she thought she might cry, then he put his hand on Emily's head, and gave them each a tender brush with his lips. Lettie kissed him back, longer and deeper, and when he smiled, she nuzzled his ear and whispered, "Take me to bed, Sheriff."

Gabe turned as red as an apple. She worried she'd shocked him, but he made a suggestion of his own and she laughed.

The bell over the front door chimed, and they looked up just as Jake stepped onto the broadwalk. After a glance at Lettie to be sure, Gabe called after him.

"Hey, Jake, how would you like to go a wedding?"

With his hand lingering on the knob, he gave them a shining smile. "Nothing would make me happier."

The three of them walked to the pastor's house, where Henry was cooling his heels. Jake figured he owed him amends, too, but he changed his mind when Gabe leaned over and muttered, "I wish you'd shot him in the balls."

The pastor opened his Bible, and Jake stood by his brother's side as he and Lettie took their vows.

For richer or poorer, in sickness and in health...

Jake could barely keep still. He wanted to jump on Smiley and race back to Alex. He didn't give a damn about his sore ribs. There wasn't a moment to spare.

Thomas Hunnicutt was in Grand Junction for a reason, and Jake knew what it was. The man wanted Alex.

I now pronounce you, husband and wife.

Jake tapped his toe on the carpet. He'd send her a wire before he left town, but first he had to talk to Gabe and Lettie. They were smooching like kids behind a barn. The pastor's wife was holding the baby, and there wasn't a dry eye in the room, and that included his.

Someone served him a slice of cake, then the pastor handed him coffee and tried to save his soul. Jake smiled and told the man he knew all about wrestling with angels.

Heywood perked up. "Do you know Will Merritt?"

"As a matter of fact I do."

"Ask him about the night the Silver City Saloon burned down, and tell him Louis Heywood said hello."

"I'll do that."

The pastor grinned and shook his hand as Gabe came over carrying Emily. "Would you like to meet your niece?"

The two men locked eyes, and Jake put aside the speech he had planned about helping with the baby's needs. He intended to put money in the bank for Emily's future, but giving it to Gabe and Lettie as a wedding present was a better idea.

He had no place in this family except as an uncle who might remember her birthday, or send a toy at Christmas. His throat swelled as he touched her cheek. She woke up peering into his face.

"She's got our mama's eyes," Gabe said.

They were Jake's eyes, too, as blue as the summer sky, but she was Gabe's daughter in all the ways that mattered. He had one more thing to say to his brother.

"Can you tear yourself away for a minute?"

"Sure." He slipped Emily into his bride's arms. "Take her, Lettie. I need to have a word with Jake."

They ambled out to the porch where a pot of geraniums baked in the sun. Taking two cigars out of his pocket, Jake handed one to Gabe and leaned against the railing. They lit up in silence, each man striking his own match.

"So what's on your mind?" Gabe asked.

"I want to thank you for all you did for me growing up. I didn't realize what it meant until now."

His brother just grunted, but it was enough to lay the past to rest, and Jake set the cigar on the railing and took out his billfold.

Gabe glared at the leather. "You don't owe us a thing."

Jake stuffed a wad of cash into his brother's hand. "I'm giving you a wedding present." Gabe hesitated, and Jake pressed the money into his hand. "Please. You'll be doing me a favor."

"All right." He folded the money, put it in his pocket and shook Jake's hand, twice. The two men talked about the town and Gabe's job and about where Jake had been. Aware of the sun sinking on the horizon, he told his brother about William and Kath and their daughter.

Gabe puffed on the cigar and stared up at the sky, watching as the smoke ring hovered and broke apart. Jake felt as fidgety as an old lady with hives, but he held himself in check until Gabe broke the silence.

"So are you going to tell me what happened to Mama's ring, or do I have to guess?"

"Actually, I was hoping you'd do me a favor."

"Oh, yeah?"

"I'm riding out in about five minutes. Would you send a wire for me?"

"Sure."

"Send it to Alexandra Merritt in Grand Junction. Mark it urgent, and just say I'm coming home."

Alex sat in the rocking chair and waited for her father to die. Two nights ago, Dr. Winters had said it was a matter of hours, but he'd underestimated William Merritt. He wasn't ready to leave, and in between bouts of unconsciousness, he muttered that he had things to do.

Kath refused to leave their bedroom except for matters of personal necessity, and Annabelle had stayed to care for Charlie. Word of her father's heart attack went out to the neighbors, and Jim Weston had seen to shipping the crop. Except for the late peaches Jake would have picked, the harvest was done and Alex had nothing to do but wait.

The rocker creaked as she pushed with her toes and stared at the trees. The sky glowed with the morning sun, and she saw the black silhouette of a bird swooping into the canopy of leaves. Jake should have been gleaning the last of the fruit, and in a month they would have been married. Next summer a child would have come.

She felt like a pair of shoes with worn-out soles and missing buttons, and she started to cry. Her father *had* to live, at least a little longer. Charlie, Jake, it was too much to lose all at once.

She was bleeding inside, close to dying herself, when she heard the clop of a horse trotting down the road. It was probably the doctor, but she imagined riding Smiley with Jake's arm secure around her waist. The horse whickered, and she looked up.

"Thomas!" Her throat closed with shock. In his black suit and bowler, he looked like a penguin who'd missed the ship to Antarctica.

"Are you surprised?" he said with a smile.

"More than I can say."

He climbed gingerly out of the buggy, pausing to rub the small of his back. She'd forgotten how stiff he got after sitting for a long time. Rising from the rocker, she held out her hands in greeting.

Running his fingers over her knuckles, he said, "I came as soon as I got your letter. I would have been here yesterday, but my back went out on the train. I spent the day in bed at the hotel."

The hotel where Jake had proposed, said he loved her, had wanted to take her to bed but didn't.

"Oh, Thomas, I'm so sorry."

"Not to worry, my dear. I'm much better now."

But she hadn't been talking about his back. "Did you get my wire? Or the second letter?"

He shook his head. "Is it your father?"

"Yes." And so much more. "He had a heart attack. The doctor says it's bad."

"You've had a hard time. Let's sit down, shall we?"

Still holding her hand, he shuffled toward the swing. His fingers were soft and plump, and Alex remembered when her own life had been that untouched.

"Maybe we should start at the beginning," he said.

Charlie, the desert, Jake. Boundless skies and the fullness of desire, love discovered and lost. Alex shook her head. "It's such a long story."

"In that case, I'll start at the end." Being careful to

keep his back straight, Thomas turned in the swing. "I should have given you this before you left."

He took a tiny box out of his pocket and opened the lid. A square-cut diamond caught the rays and sent a rainbow of broken light skittering across her face.

"I love you," he said. "I'd be thrilled to adopt the baby."

Good, kind Thomas. She peered at his round face, the fringe of gray hair, eyes that were blue like Jake's but faded with age, and she wondered if she had it in her soul to find happiness with this man.

The ring sparkled in his palm. She heard Charlie fussing in the house and she wondered if Annabelle wanted the baby. She was a child herself, and the past three days had been hard for her.

The right word to Thomas, and her old life and Charlie would be hers. He was a reasonable man. She could say she had lost her head over a drifter but had come to her senses and sent him away. Thomas would understand, and it was almost true.

The only tie to Colorado was her father, and if the doctor was to be believed, his time was short. Katherine would come with her to Philadelphia and they would be a family. The ring glittered in the sun. Thomas smiled, and Alex closed her eyes. She'd lost them all, Jake, Charlie, perhaps her father.

Papa, Papa, what should I do?

An aching silence filled her ears, but she didn't need to hear her father's voice to know what he would say, how she felt, and what was true.

"Things have changed, Thomas. It's more than my father. He's not well, but—"

"We'll make room for everyone." He reached for

her hand, intending to slip the diamond on her finger, but Jake's ring blocked the way.

Their eyes met, and she made a fist, pressing the gold into her flesh.

"There's someone else," she said.

Thomas looked wounded but relieved, at least that's what she wanted to see, and she told him everything. About Charlie's birth and loving Jake, about sending them both away, and William's heart attack.

"I've lost them all," she said. "But I can't go back."

Raising her hand to his lips, Thomas managed a gallant smile. "I'll miss you, Alexandra."

"I'll miss you, too." And it was true, in a very small way.

More time…more time…more time…

William rested his hand on his chest and counted the thudding beats of his heart. The new rhythm made it hard to breathe, but he sensed Kath and Alex in the room. He listened to bits of their womanly talk, but their faces played tricks on him. Kath looked twenty years younger, and Alex seemed twenty years too old.

The only person he could see clearly was Jake. Lost in a storm of swirling dust, he was battling flying rocks and a cruel wind. William tasted the grit in his own dry mouth. As he croaked for water, the vision shifted to a clear sky and a man racing through the desert to get home.

The thunder of it woke him up.

Katherine, dear beautiful Katherine. She jumped out of her chair like a startled deer. "Will?"

"Where's Jake?"

She clutched at his fingers. "We've been so worried."

"Where the *hell* is Jake?"

"It's a long story, but everything's going to be fine."

"It's *not* fine."

Smoothing his hair as if he were a child, and annoying the daylights out of him, his wife said, "You need to rest."

"Like hell I do!" If she told him to rest one more time, he'd pitch a first-class fit. "What the hell happened?"

"Your heart gave us a scare. It was bad, but you're going to be fine, as long as you take it easy."

Struggling to sit up, he shouted, "I don't care about my heart. I saw Jake—"

"He's gone, Will. Alex sent him back to Flat Rock."

Chapter Nineteen

With dusk cresting like a towering wave, Jake rode into the desert at a breakneck speed. Darkness loomed behind him as the sun faded to an orange glow. When night came, a full moon lit the trail, and slowing to a walk, he rode past the dawn and into the next day.

Around noon he found some shade and stopped. Smiley grazed while Jake dozed, but he dreamed of Thomas Hunnicutt getting off the train and woke up with a spike of fear.

He'd asked Gabe to send a wire, but telegraph lines broke all the time, and in spite of Gabe's best intentions, a new bride had a lot more appeal than a trip to the telegraph office.

He had to get to Alex, home to the orchard and the scent of peaches. Thankful that Smiley liked to run, Jake pushed him as hard as he dared. When they passed through Grand Junction in the dark of night, he barely noticed the empty streets. His mind was on Alex and the words he needed to say.

Dawn was in sight when he reached the first row of peach trees. Free of the heavy crop, the branches pointed to the sky like arms raised in victory, but a curl of worry spiraled through his chest. No one had gleaned the last of the fruit. He smelled rot, and the trees had a wild look about them, as if they'd been forgotten.

It bothered him, but he had other things on his mind. Guiding Smiley down the narrow trail to the irrigation ditch, he found an isolated spit of sand between two boulders. Taking out his razor and a change of clothes, he shaved, stripped naked and waded into the stream.

Splashing water across his chest and under his arms, he imagined coming back to this spot with Alex, a blanket, and a jug of sweet tea. He'd kiss her in the hot sun, feel the warmth of her skin, talk her into a swim…

Please, God. Please, God.

Goose bumps pebbled his skin and he scrambled out of the stream. Water ran down his legs, and he got dressed without bothering to dry off. A minute later he was in her yard, staring at the house. It was silent and still, but he heard a roar in the earth calling to his blood.

He tied Smiley to the railing, pushed through the front door and took the stairs two at a time. The hallway was dark, the walls lost in shadow. The floor creaked beneath his weight, until he froze at her bedroom door. It should have been ajar so she could hear the baby, but it was shut tight, maybe locked.

His heart hammered. What if she had married Hunnicutt? What if she had gone back to Philadelphia? If he opened the door and she wasn't alone, he'd leave and she would never know he'd come back. He'd go to California after all, he'd—

He didn't know what he'd do. Holding his breath, he tried the knob.

Loose in his hand, it turned without a sound. He cracked open the door, peered into the dark room and searched the shadows of her bed. The quilt had been tossed aside, and there was Alex, alone.

His gaze roamed from her bare feet to her slender calves, then higher to where her nightgown had ridden up her thighs. The soft rasp of her breath stirred his blood.

Jake shut the door, tossed his hat on a chair, and dropping down to one knee, he kissed her cheek. She smelled like roses and warmth, and touching her face, he slanted his mouth over hers.

Sighing, she kissed him in her sleep. His hand lingered in her hair, and she sprawled on her back, pulling him with her, kissing him more deeply. The moment was perfect, except she was crying in her sleep.

Trailing his fingers down the side of her face, he whispered her name and brushed away a tear. She clutched at his shoulders and slid her hands down his chest. She found the collar of his shirt and a patch of bare skin. Her eyes fluttered open.

"Oh, my God," she whispered.

"Lettie's married to Gabe." Tangling one hand in her hair and caressing her neck with the other, he brought his lips close to hers, "Say yes, Alex. Please say yes."

She answered with a whisper that parted her lips and he took full advantage. His tongue found hers and he savored the taste of her. Her mouth opened wider, and he filled her with his breath.

She reached inside his shirt and caressed his shoulders. Still kissing her lips, he worked the buttons on her nightgown until he found her breasts. Molding his hands to their softness, he lifted the full circles until the weight of them filled his hands. Moaning, she covered his fingers with hers, pressing him closer.

He needed to slow down, but she wouldn't let him. With a scoot of her bottom, she tugged the nightgown over her head and dropped it on the floor. She was naked, tangled in the sheets, wearing a smile that made him soft in some places and hard in others.

Laughter bubbled inside of him, and giving her a wicked grin, he took off his boots, shrugged out of his shirt, stood up, and loosened the first button on his fly, then the next one.

Being a brave woman, she watched, and being a gentleman, he let her look as he skimmed out of his pants and stood in front of her, as naked and ready as a new day.

She didn't miss a thing, and neither did he. She leaned against the pillow, and raising her arms, she combed her fingers through her dark hair. The sight of her full breasts filled him with both reverence and a man's desire. With the bed sheets askew, he caught a glimpse of her knees, angled sideways and not quite touching.

She was the picture of bold innocence, and she was his.

He'd been with more women than he cared to admit at that moment. They'd struck poses and smiled, arranged themselves and given him pleasure, but no one else had given him unquestioning love and trusted him with her heart.

It was an honor, a gift, a responsibility.

It was a joy, pure magic, wild sweaty fun, but a rebel at heart, he decided to take his time. Putting his hands on his hips, he rocked back on his heels. "I just realized we're not married yet. Your father will kill me if I climb into that bed with you.''

Letting her hair tumble down her shoulders, she shrugged. ''We can wake him up if you'd like, or we could have the ceremony in say, a month?''

''That's not exactly what I had in mind.''

''Of course I'll need a dress. Something—''

''A dress is the *last* thing you need, at least right now.'' His gaze roamed from her breasts to her lips, to the depths of her brown eyes. They were the color of rich earth, loamy and wide and eager, and he said, ''I want forever, Alex.''

''I do, too.''

It was a vow of their own, and knowing they'd say the words again before the sun went down, he came naked to her bed.

Putting her on her back, he kissed her mouth and neck and throat. His lips traveled down the hard bone between her breasts, and her hands furrowed through his hair. He intended to take his time, but Alex had other ideas. Cupping her breast, she raised her nipple to his mouth. With a boy's need and a man's skill, he took the gift.

Whispering ''I love you,'' he touched her belly, her hips, the juncture of her thighs, and in a blur of hands and lips, he found her natural rhythm. Freeing her from the pull of the earth, he took her past the sun, beyond the stars, far into the heavens, until she shattered in his arms.

Still trembling she whispered, ''Oh my,'' and slid her hips beneath his. She wanted him to take everything she had to give, and as she opened to him, he understood the difference between bedding a woman and making love. A man could take pleasure wherever he found it, but a woman's love had to be given.

The thought filled him with joy, but what could he give Alex in return? Nothing seemed good enough, until he thought of the one thing she wanted more than anything else.

Rising over her, he whispered, "When did you last have your monthly?"

Horrified, she said, "You're not going to stop, are you?"

"Hell, no. I was just thinking—"

Her eyes flared with understanding. "It was about two weeks ago."

Blood rushed to his groin. "Get ready, honey. We're going to make a baby."

Pushing gently, he joined his body with hers. Slowly, sweetly, he possessed this new and untouched place, until at last she gasped at the pressure of him.

Her flesh stretched to take him, and he held still until her muscles relaxed and tightened on their own, grasping him as if she'd never let him go. He pulled back and thrust forward. Again and again, he journeyed into her, toward home, until at last she cried out.

With a triumphant joy of his own, he planted his seed in her womb, hoping for a daughter with her mother's eyes.

William woke up irritable and tossed off the blanket. He was tired of being sick, and sick of being tired. He was better now, though the thud of his heart told him he'd never be the same. He'd have to hire help right away, but for now he was glad to be alive.

He wanted to start this day on the porch with the morning sun warming his bones. He pulled on his trousers and put on a shirt, slipped into his moccasins and walked out the front door.

He stared at the lathered bay for three seconds, then he laughed with joy.

Thank you. Thank you. Thank you.

It was a great day for a wedding. Grinning and overwhelmed, he plopped in the swing and thought about the words he'd say for his daughter and the man she'd chosen. He knew for a fact that time and heartache would stretch their love and test it, that Jake wasn't a perfect man, and Alex would have her bad days, too.

He'd get to the usual "I do's," but a little creativity wouldn't hurt to smooth along years.

Her father's wild laugh poured through the window, and Alex curled against Jake and smiled. They'd made love twice, and he'd fallen asleep in her arms. She was spooned against his back, his bare buttocks pressed against her hips as she kissed his neck.

Jake rolled to his back. "William's still an early riser."

"How does he know you're here?"

"Smiley's tied out front."

Running her hand over his chest, she traced the curve of his muscles and pressed her palm over his heart. "Tell me what happened."

"Lettie married Gabe. I got there just in time for the wedding."

"She said no to you?"

"She said a lot more than that. She said I was selfish and disrespectful, and except for the baby, she was sorry she ever laid eyes on me. Then she told Gabe she loved him and she'd kick his butt if he backed out just because I'd shown up."

"That's wonderful," she said, stroking his chest.

"You've got a free 'I told you so' if you want it. You were right about going back."

"But you made the choice." She loved the silky hardness of his skin, the scent of him. She wanted to spend the day exploring every crease and ripple of muscle, but first they needed to talk.

"Tell me about the baby," she said.

"Her name is Emily, after Lettie's mother. She has my eyes," he said with a tinge of sadness. The child was a mark he'd bear for life, one they would share.

"Does Gabe seem happy?" she asked.

"About as happy as a man can be. Judging by the look in his eye, he's loved Lettie for a while."

"I'm happy for them."

"I am, too. I handed Gabe every cent I took, plus everything I earned. I'm broke, but it was a heck of a wedding present."

She smiled. "It sounds like you need a job."

"As a matter of fact, I do."

The teasing hung in the air. He didn't know about her father, or Charlie, or Thomas. "We need you, Jake. My father had a heart attack after you left. The doctor came, but it was awful. We almost lost him."

"I wish I'd been here. I heard Winters leave Grand Junction that night but I didn't think twice. I'm so sorry, honey. I wish I—"

Silencing him with a kiss, she said, "I'm just glad you're back." Someday she would count every hair on his chest. She'd know every stretch of muscle, every sigh. Her left hand was resting over his ribs when she noticed a livid bruise.

"What happened?"

"I got knocked flat on my face by a dust storm, but

I'm fine now." She kissed the purple stain, and he sighed as ray of sun fell across the bed. The aqua stone on her finger caught the light, reminding her of the diamond Thomas had brought. "I had a visitor while you were gone."

"I know. I saw him get off the train." A low growl rumbled in his throat, and he pinned her against the bed with his hips and his hands. "There's no way on earth he could love you as much as I do."

"I would have waited for you forever."

"But you might have said yes for Charlie," he said, nuzzling her neck. "I remember that night. You promised to get on with your life."

"I never promised anything."

"Well, I did, and it's a good thing. I hate to think of what we might have lost. Gabe was going to send a wire. Did you get it?"

"No, but it wouldn't have mattered." He rubbed against her and she sighed with pleasure, except not everything could be forgotten, or recovered, and Jake knew it, too.

"Tell me about Charlie," he said, kissing her neck.

"I told Annabelle I couldn't keep him. I'll miss him terribly, but he belongs with her."

"I love the kid, too, but blood runs thick. And speaking of family, I've got to have a word with your father."

"I'll go with you."

"No, I want to talk to him alone."

"Man to man?"

"It's more like his fist to my jaw. He's going to take my head off for leaving like I did, then there's the matter of being flat broke and wanting to marry you. Not to mention the facts of what we just did."

"We made love."

Looking into her eyes, he said, "It was a lot more than that. We made a promise."

Jake got dressed, gave Alex a quick kiss, and went to the porch where William was standing at the railing with his back to the door. With his feet planted wide and his arms crossed over his chest, he looked like a white-haired warrior, battle scarred and weary.

Jake came up next to him and looked at the orchard. The morning sun streaked the earth with yellow light and gray shadows. A fat bird landed on a high branch, causing it to dip as the bird pecked at a peach. Breathing in the scent of ripe fruit, Jake wondered what next year's crop would be like.

"I didn't think I'd ever see this place again," he said. "I swear to you, Will, I wouldn't have come back unless it was right."

"I know that."

"I shouldn't have run off, though. I should have made sure you had help and thanked you for what you did for me."

"I didn't do a thing," William said in a lazy drawl. "You're the one who took a chance. You did what you had to do, both when you decided to stay and when you decided to leave. It took courage, son. I respect that in a man."

"Leaving just about killed me." Jake's thoughts drifted from the misery of that night to this morning in Alex's bed. He'd been through hell and come back to heaven, with a few stops in between. It was the kind of story William would understand.

Keeping his gaze on the orchard, he said, "Do you remember asking if I'd ever wrestled with an angel?"

"Sure I do."

"Well, it was one helluva of a fight, and I've got a busted rib to prove it."

William shook his head in sympathy. "I bet it hurts."

"It does, but it's nothing compared to how I felt the night I left." Reliving the past few days, Jake talked about the desert, the dust storm and the wind that called his name.

"I've never heard anything like that sound."

The old man nodded. "Sounds like the angel won the fight."

But Jake shook his head. "That's the hell of it, Will. *I* won. I'd given up. I'd made my peace with marrying Lettie, and she turned me down flat. Everything I want is right here. I want to marry your daughter and raise peaches and give you and Kath a houseful of grand-children."

William squeezed Jake's shoulder, and with a catch in his throat, he said, "Nothing could make me happier."

"Are you busy this morning?"

"Are you in a particular hurry?"

"Most definitely."

The old man gave him the evil eye, but Jake didn't mind. Someday he'd have daughters of his own, and, as sure as the sun rose, there'd be hell to pay for any man who looked more than twice.

With a bearlike grunt William went to his study to work on the wedding vows while Jake took care of Smiley. When he came back to the house, Kath hugged him, fed him breakfast and went upstairs to Alex.

He was alone at the table, chewing a strip of bacon, when Annabelle came into the kitchen with Charlie.

Lines of exhaustion rimmed her eyes, and Jake hoped for one more miracle. "How's the boy doing?"

"Getting bigger every day. Can you hold him for me?"

"Sure."

She put the infant in his arms, poured milk, and warmed it on the stove while Jake sat back with the baby on his chest. The infant was in the mood to kick, and he winced when Charlie hit his bad rib. It would have hurt like hell, if it hadn't felt so good to be home.

Glancing up, he saw Annabelle give in to a huge yawn. "I'm sorry about your sister," he said. "I don't think I ever told you properly."

She splashed a drop of milk on her wrist and handed him the bottle. "It was a bad night for everyone. I understand, though. Alex told me why you had to leave. For her, Jake, I'm glad you're back."

Testing the water, he said, "Charlie is lucky to have you."

"Maybe, but I want you and Alex to adopt him."

Could a miracle happen that easily? Could a man go from expecting nothing to having everything without a fight? Not believing what he'd heard, he said, "Are you sure?"

"I'm very sure. I want to be his aunt, but I'm not meant to be his mother. Even with Charlotte's money, I'd have trouble taking care of him. You know where I've been, what I've done."

"I know even more about second chances."

"And that's what you and Alex can give Charlie. He would have died along with my sister without both of you."

Jake wanted to crow with gratitude, but their gain

was still Annabelle's loss. "We'd be honored to have him," he said gently.

"He's yours then. I'll sign whatever papers you want." Smiling with relief, she added, "Think of him as a wedding present."

When Charlie finished his milk, Annabelle took him upstairs for a fresh diaper. Jake went to his old room, shaved again, dressed in his best clothes and joined William on the porch.

The old man was dressed in a black suit with his preacher's collar, sitting in the swing with a cigar.

"Want one?" he asked.

Jake shook his head. He hadn't expected to be nervous, but he could barely swallow air, let alone a mouthful of smoke. Standing at the railing, he tapped his toe against the wooden porch. "Just how long does it take to put on a dress?"

William laughed and told him to get used to waiting for the ladies. Jake managed to joke that he'd waited a lot longer for a lot less, but his chest was about to split in two.

Annabelle called from the living room. "We're ready."

Hoisting himself out of the swing, William muttered, "It's about time." Jake went through the door like a shot.

The men took their places by the hearth. Katherine joined her husband, and Annabelle stood next to her, holding Charlie.

Alex didn't need music to make a grand entrance. She came around the corner dressed in ivory lace with the sun cascading over her shoulders. She held a bouquet of red roses at her waist, a promise of things to come, and his gaze traveled from her sweet face to her white shoes. Tonight he'd take them off and kiss each one of her toes. He'd work his way up and up and up, through the heavens and on to forever.

As a boy he'd dreamed of angels. As a man he'd come to believe. Gazing at his bride with the joy of an overflowing heart, he whispered a prayer.

Thank you. Thank you. Thank you.

Alex wanted to skip and run, fly to the stars and land on the moon. She wanted to lift her arms in victory, sing praises to the sky and spin in circles until she couldn't stand up. But most of all, she wanted to get back in bed with her husband.

There was a lot to be said for anticipation.

But even more to be said for the journey, the risks, and the arrival.

Holding a bouquet of red roses and wearing the ivory wedding dress her mother had worn thirty years ago, she took her place next to Jake. As if he couldn't wait, he reached for her with both hands and squeezed with a fierceness that said he'd never let go.

Blinking, she saw her father as a younger man, her mother as a bride, Annabelle as a friend, and Charlie being born. Through the shimmer of tears, she looked into Jake's eyes, where she saw the vastness of the sky.

"Shall we get started?" William said.

After thirty years of preaching, shouting in saloons, and bellowing for the fun of it, he couldn't be subtle if he tried. Alex knew he wasn't about to hold back now. Raising his arms as if to embrace them all, he began.

"Dearly Beloved, we are gathered here today in the presence of God to witness and bless the joining of this man and this woman in holy matrimony. It's a choice that bonds them together for eternity, a choice that demands discipline and yet promises joy, a choice that speaks to the past, as well as the future.

"With that in mind, I'll get to all of the usual things a minister says at a wedding, but this occasion calls for something more. You're making more than a promise today, you're making a family."

William nodded at Annabelle, who looked first at Alex, then down at the baby. "I want you to have Charlie," she said. "He's already yours in the ways that matter most."

Kath reached for the bouquet, Annabelle put the baby in Alex's arms, and for the first time in his tiny life, Charlie smiled.

"I can't thank you enough," Alex said as tears welled in her eyes.

"I should be thanking you," Annabelle replied. "He'll have a good home, and that's all I want." Her eyes shining with tears, Charlie's aunt stepped back to her place next to Katherine.

Alex asked Jake, "Did you know?"

"Annabelle told me this morning," he said, covering the baby's head with his hand.

Joy flooded through Alex as her mother reached for her first grandchild and her father cleared his throat, ready to get down to business.

"Now there's a lot I could say about marriage being holy and ordained by God, that the Lord intends for you to be one in spirit, but that's only half the story. He also intends for you to be one in body, and that means living under the same roof.

"It means putting up with dirty socks and bad smells, cranky mornings, bad harvests, and loss. It's not easy to comfort a man you want to strangle, nor is it easy to honor a woman who's just wounded your pride.

"A long time ago, the greatest letter writer of all time told a bunch of hell-raisers that love bears all things, believes all things, hopes all things, endures all things. As my wife can tell you, enduring is the hard part."

Katherine laid her hand on her husband's arm. Their eyes met for a single second that spanned the years and reached into eternity.

William cleared his throat. "With that in mind, I'm going to ask you both for promises that are practical and wise, starting with the dirty socks."

Pure joy took flight in Alex's chest, and she nearly laughed out loud as her father worked his magic.

"Jake, I want you to promise to pick the damn things up and get them in the hamper. It'll drive your wife nuts if you leave them under the bed."

"Yes, sir."

"And Alex? I want you to promise to ignore them when he forgets."

"I will."

"That means no sighing, no hinting, no accidentally leaving them on his pillow."

"Yes, sir."

The rest of the ceremony was just as inventive. Her father made her promise to scratch Jake's back whenever he asked, to surprise him with a picnic now and then, to believe in him always, and to trust his judgment unless she was dead sure he was headed off a cliff.

With a voice full of reverence and awe, he recited the vows. "Do you Alexandra Merritt, take Jackson Jacob Malone to be your lawfully wedded husband, for richer, for poorer, in sickness and in health…as long as you both shall live?''

''I do.''

''Jake, I want you to promise before God that you'll rub her feet when the babies come, that you'll listen to her even when you're bored with her womanly whatnot, and that you'll tell her you love her at least once a day from now until eternity.''

''I will.''

''And I want you to promise to respect, honor and cherish my daughter through the hours, days and years, no matter what comes your way.''

''I will, sir.''

Jake's voice rolled over her like a hot breeze. She was already wearing his ring. Charlie was safe in his grandmother's arms, peering at the man who was now his father. With the six of them in a circle, William made the final proclamation.

''By the authority of God in heaven, I now pronounce you husband and wife, father and mother to Charlie, and son and daughter to Katherine and me. Jake, you may now kiss—''

''Oh, Papa.''

Standing on her toes, Alex kissed her father's cheek. William pulled Jake into a circle of three, then Kath, and Charlie, and Annabelle, too. Together they made a family, a chain of love stronger than time and place, even stronger than blood.

William blew out a deep breath, and like petals peeling off a rose, Kath and Annabelle stepped back, leaving Alex and Jake standing face-to-face. Where there had once been bruises, she saw a shimmering light. Her husband looked into her brown eyes, and she looked into his blue ones. Like the sky coming down to meet the earth, he kissed her, and with the angels watching from the heavens, they began a new day.

Epilogue

The good Lord gave me exactly seven months, twelve days and fourteen hours from the moment Jake and Alex took their vows. No man could have had an easier passing. Kath was asleep next to me. I took her hand and she woke up as if she knew the time had come. My last vision on earth was of her face bending close to mine.

She cried for a bit, kissed me one last time, then she went to Alex and Jake, and the three of them comforted each other in the way that only family can. Jake's hand covered Alex's belly and the baby kicked. He made tea for Kath and promised to see to everything, told her he'd like to say a few words at the funeral, that he'd dig the grave on the bluff where flowers would grow. I imagine he'll visit once in a while with a cigar in hand, and I expect we'll both have a few things to say.

If the baby's a boy, which it is, they're going to name him after me. More babies will come with the years. They'll have two little girls with my daughter's eyes, and another boy with his daddy's quick temper. Kath will be in her glory with the houseful of children she's always wanted.

And then there's Charlie. With his curly hair and round face, he's a bird of a different feather in this family. But his last name is Malone and that's all that counts.

Every night I hear my daughter's prayers, asking for blessings on her family. Like the sun, her love brings heat and light and direction to them all. She's their anchor, the center that never moves, just as Kath was once mine.

My time on earth is over, but I'm never far from my wife and the young ones. I still love the smell of a good cigar, the scent of warm earth, the sound of my wife's laughter. I'm still listening to Alex and Jake, and I talk to them both in memories and quiet whispers.

I'm with my family every day in the ways that matter most. Our bodies wither and flowers fade, but love never fails. It's the greatest gift of all.

*   *   *   *   *

LOOKIN' FOR RIVETING TALES ABOUT RUGGED MEN AND THE FEISTY LADIES WHO TRY TO TAME THEM?

From Harlequin Historicals

July 2003

TEXAS GOLD by Carolyn Davidson

A fiercely independent farmer's past catches
up with her when the husband she left behind
turns up on her doorstep!

OF MEN AND ANGELS by Victoria Bylin

Can a hard-edged outlaw find redemption—and
true love—in the arms of an angelic young woman?

On sale August 2003

BLACKSTONE'S BRIDE by Bronwyn Williams

Will a beleaguered gold miner's widow and
a wounded half-breed ignite a searing passion
when they form a united front?

HIGH PLAINS WIFE by Jillian Hart

A taciturn rancher proposes a marriage
of convenience to a secretly smitten spinster
who has designs on his heart!

Visit us at www.eHarlequin.com

HARLEQUIN HISTORICALS®

ITCHIN' FOR SOME ROLLICKING ROMANCES SET ON THE AMERICAN FRONTIER? THEN TAKE A GANDER AT THESE TANTALIZING TALES FROM HARLEQUIN HISTORICALS